PRAISE FOR

'The kind of book tha ... -eared ... It makes one lau ... all the ways in which all lives, ... ariably, ...'
Esquire

'A great comic novel'
GQ

'There isn't a funnier author working today . . . The carefully nuanced look at our own world, at our phobias and obsessions and stupidities, forces us to understand them all too clearly'
The Believer

'If you're the sort of person who underlines amusing or thought-provoking lines in books, you'd best gird yourself, as Lipsyte is an inexhaustible fount of eloquent prurience, deftly mingling high- and low-mindedness. *The Ask* can be easily devoured in one sitting'
Village Voice

'Generally, novels make us turn the pages because we want to know what happens next. But with Sam Lipsyte's *The Ask* we turn the pages because we want to know what's going to happen in the next sentence. Here rants become arias, and vulgarity sheer poetry' *Washington Post*

'We search in vain for a novel that will make us laugh. We gaze fondly at the Amises, reread the best passages of *Scoop* and *A Handful of Dust*, salute Joseph Heller, give Vonnegut a friendly page riffle, and end up where we always do . . . Might I suggest a new place to stop? The collected works of Sam Lipsyte' *Slate*

THE ASK

BY SAM LIPSYTE

Old St

First published in the US 2010 by Farrar, Straus and Giroux

First published in Great Britain 2010 by
Old Street Publishing Ltd
40 Bowling Green Lane, London EC1R 0NE
www.oldstreetpublishing.co.uk

ISBN 978-1-906964-40-5

10 9 8 7 6 5 4 3 2 1

A CIP catalogue record for this title is available from the British
Library.

Printed and bound in Great Britain

For Alfred

Acknowledgments

My deep gratitude to the John Simon Guggenheim Memorial Foundation and the MacDowell Colony for their support, and to Ceridwen Morris, for her honesty, insight, and patience.

In memory of James Conlon.

One

America, said Horace, the office temp, was a run-down and demented pimp. Our republic's whoremaster days were through. Whither that frost-nerved, diamond-fanged hustler who'd stormed Normandy, dick-smacked the Soviets, turned out such firm emerging market flesh? Now our nation slumped in the corner of the pool hall, some gummy coot with a pint of Mad Dog and soggy yellow eyes, just another mark for the juvenile wolves.

"We're the bitches of the First World," said Horace, his own eyes braziers of delight.

We all loved Horace, his clownish pronouncements. He was a white kid from Armonk who had learned to speak and feel from a half-dozen VHS tapes in his father's garage. Besides, here at our desks with our turkey wraps, I did not disagree.

But I let him have it. It was my duty. We were in what they call a university setting. A bastion of, et cetera. Little did I know this was my last normal day at said bastion, that my old friend Purdy was about to butt back into my world, mangle it. I just figured this was what my worst teachers used to call a teachable moment.

"Horace," I said. "That's a pretty sexist way to frame a discussion of America's decline, don't you think? Not to mention racist."

"I didn't mention anybody's race," said Horace.

"You didn't have to."

"P.C. robot."

"Fascist dupe."

"Did you get avocado on yours?"

"Fattening," I said.

"Don't worry, baby," said Horace. "I like big women."

"What about hairy ones?" I said, parted my shirt to air my nipple fuzz. Horace let me be a cretin with him. You could call him my infantilism provider, though you'd sound like an idiot. Otherwise, I was ostensibly upstanding, a bald husband, a slab-bellied father.

"Gentlemen," said our supervisor, Vargina, coming out from her command nook. "Did you send off those emails about the Belgian art exchange?"

Horace swiveled back to his monitor with the mock panic of a sitcom serf. Vargina took scant notice of our talk, tolerated foul banter for purposes of morale. But the fact remained, we had forgotten the afternoon's assignment. The gods of task flow did not easily forgive.

Where we worked was in the development office of a mediocre university in New York City. It was an expensive and strangely obscure institution, named for its syphilitic Whig founder, but we often called it, with what we considered a certain panache, the Mediocre University *at* New York City. By we, I mean Horace and I. By often, I mean once.

Our group raised funds and materials for the university's arts programs. People paid vast sums so their spawn could take hard drugs in suitable company, draw from life on their laptops, do radical things with video cameras and caulk. Still, the sums didn't quite do the trick. Not in the cutthroat world of arts education. Our job was to grovel for more money. We could always use more video cameras, more caulk, or a dance studio, or a gala for more groveling. The asks liked galas, openings, recitals, shows. They liked dinner with a famous filmmaker for them to fawn over or else dismiss as frivolous.

An ask could be a person, or what we wanted from that person. If they gave it to us, that was a give. The asks knew little about the student work they funded. Who could blame them? Some of the art these brats produced wouldn't stand up to the dreck my three-year-old demanded we tack to the kitchen wall. But I was biased, and not just because I often loved my son. Thing was, I'd been just like these wretches once. Now they stared through me, as though I were merely some drone in their sight line, a pathetic object momentarily obstructing their fabulous horizon. They were right. That's exactly what I was.

A solitudinous roil, my bitterness. Horace, after all, was their age. He had no health insurance, just hope. Our rainmaker, Llewellyn, seemed born to this job, keen for any chance to tickle the rectal bristles of the rich with his Tidewater tongue. He was almost never in the office, instead sealing the deal on a Gulfstream IV to Bucharest, or lying topside on a Corfu yacht, slathered in bronzer.

Llewellyn delivered endowed chairs, editing suites, sculpture gardens. My record was not so impressive. My last big ask, for example, had failed to yield a few plasma TVs from the father of a recent film graduate.

Mr. Ramadathan had mortgaged his electronics store so his son could craft affecting screenplays about an emotionally distant, workaholic immigrant's quest for the American dream. But the father's giddiness had begun to wear off. The boy was unemployable. Now Mr. Ramadathan was maybe not so eager to relinquish his showroom models.

I'd made the hot, khaki-moistening hike past all the car dealerships and muffler shops on Northern Boulevard in Queens, stood in the sleek, dingy cool of the store. Mr. Ramadathan sat near the register in a wicker chair. The plasmas were not on display. Sold or hidden, I had no idea. Mr. Ramadathan stared at me, at the sweat patches on my crotch. He pointed toward some old video game consoles, a used floor fan, dregs of the dream.

"Please," he said, "take those. So that others may learn."

Unlike the time Llewellyn secured a Foley stage for the film department, there was no celebration on the Mediocre patio. No sour chardonnay got guzzled in my honor, nor did any lithe director of communications flick her tongue in my ear, vow to put me on the splash page of *Excellence*, the university's public relations blog.

If not so ecstatic in her position as Llewellyn, Vargina seemed happy enough, or at least adopted a mode of wise, unruffled decency in the office. She'd been a crack baby, apparently due to her mother being a crackhead, one of the early ones, the baking soda vanguard. Vargina was a miracle, and that's maybe the only time I have used the word sincerely. Her mother had named her the word her name resembled. A sympathetic nurse added the "r."

"Milo," she said now. "How is the Teitelbaum ask going?"

Vargina had enormous breasts I liked to picture flopping out of a sheer burgundy bra. Sometimes they just burst out in slow motion. Sometimes she scooped them out with her slender hands, asked me to join her reading group.

"Making progress," I said. "Chipping away."

"Maybe you need a larger tool," said Vargina, appeared to shudder slightly, perhaps worried her innocent metaphor would be misconstrued as sexual. Her words, however, were not misconstrued at all. I had already begun to picture my cock in high quiver, sliding up the lubed swell of her chest. We were in a library of lacquered wood. Viola tones rose from a carved alcove. Baby oil beaded on rare folios.

"Well," said Vargina, tapped the plastic parapet of my cube wall. "Just stick with it."

"Will do."

Truth was, the Teitelbaum ask was going nowhere. I was barely hanging on here in development. I wasn't developing. I'd done some good work at a non-profit a few years ago, but the

South Bronx Restoration Comedy Project never really took off. The university snapped me up at a bargain rate. I'd become one of those mistakes you sometimes find in an office, a not unpleasant but mostly unproductive presence bobbing along on the energy tides of others, a walking reminder of somebody's error in judgment.

But today some karmic adjustment seemed due. Just as Vargina slipped back behind the particleboard walls of her command nook, a painting major we knew a bit too well around here charged up to my desk, planted her bony fist on my Vorticist mouse pad. McKenzie was one of those girls who didn't eat enough, so that all one really noticed about her were the mole-specked rods of her arms, the lurid jut of her skull. Students had no reason to visit our office, but her father had paid for our crappy observatory upstate. She was in here a lot, to preen, complain. I guess it beat making her putrid art.

"Hello, McKenzie," I said.

"Hi, yeah, sorry, I can't remember your name."

"Milo."

"Sure, okay. Milo. Listen, Milo, we talked last week and you promised I'd be able to take the Impressionism to Regressionism seminar even though it was full."

"Excuse me?"

"Yeah, you know, you promised you'd talk to the painting department and sort it all out. I mean, if I told my father—"

"Hold on."

"Hold on?"

"I made no such promise. We have nothing to do with academic decisions, with curriculum or enrollment."

"Okay, maybe it was that guy," said McKenzie, pointing.

"Horace?" I said.

"Yeah, Whore-Ass," said McKenzie.

Horace wore a pained grin at his terminal.

"Horace hasn't been well," I told McKenzie. "Now, as I mentioned, we have no jurisdiction over any of these issues, but maybe we can all get together with painting and figure this out."

"Meaning what?"

"Meaning we can figure this out."

McKenzie stared. How could she know I myself had once been a fraud, chockablock with self-regard, at an overpriced institution just like this one, still had the debt to prove it? How could she know she stared down at the wispy pate of a man who once believed he was painting's savior, back in a decade that truly needed one?

She spoke quietly now: "Listen, I don't mean to be rude, but you really are here to serve my needs. My father taught me that the consumer is always right. I am the consumer. You are actually the bitch of this particular exchange. But don't think I don't respect that you are just a guy, like, doing your shitty job."

"Thank you," I said.

"But maybe you aren't cut out to work with artists."

I guess what set me off was her effort to be polite. I should have just leaned on the painting department to make room on the roster for her, ruin the semester for some pimple-seared hump who shared his name with no stargazing facility. Nobody cared. I would be doing my shitty job. It was a good shitty job. I'd done it for a few years and it paid pretty well, enough to let Maura go part-time since the baby. There was a quality family plan, plus a quality theft plan, the paints and brushes I smuggled home for those weekends I tried to put something on canvas again, until the old agony would whelm me and I'd stop and briefly weep and then begin to drink and watch Maura cruise up and down the cable dial all night, never alighting on anything for more than a moment, her thumb poised like a hairless and tiny yet impressively predatory animal above the arrow button, Maura herself bent on peeking into every corner of the national hallucination before bedtime.

She liked reality shows the best, and then the shows that purported to be about reality.

So, yes, I should have just surrendered, cinched the entitled scion her little pouch of entitlements, put in my calls to the name shufflers, done my duty.

I thought about that moment later on. Maybe I got extra-tuned to the concept of bitchhood once I became Purdy's, though I must confess I've always found such usage of the term for female dogs distasteful. My mother was a second-wave feminist. I wasn't comfortable saying "cunt" until I was twenty-three, at which point, admittedly, I couldn't hold back for a time.

Or maybe it's just that I've always despised phrases like "that fateful day," but as time went on I found it hard to deny that the afternoon Horace launched his E Pluribus Pimpus oratory and McKenzie tried to reify my servility and I pictured titboning Vargina in a rare books room was pretty damn fateful. Or was it, in fact, just another random day, and it was I who did the fool thing, forced my hand?

What I said to McKenzie, there is no point repeating. It's enough to report my words contained nothing an arrogant, talentless, daddy-damaged waif wants to hear about herself. When I was finished she did not speak. A thickish vein in her pale head fluttered. The blue thing seemed to veer and switch direction. Then she took a few steps back and, still staring at me, phoned her damager. What was done to me was done in hours. My outburst was deemed hate speech, which called for immediate dismissal. I could hardly argue with them. I think it probably was hate speech. I really fucking hated that girl.

Two

You could say I had experienced some technical difficulties. There had been bad times, years trickled off at jobs that purported to yield what superiors called, with true sadism, opportunities. These yielded nothing, unless you considered bong slavery, a few bogus spiritual awakenings, and the unswerving belief I could run a small business from my home, opportune. Still, before my outburst at the bastion, I had made great strides. No more did I pine aloud for that time in the past when I had a future. Yes, I still painted on occasion, or at least stood at the easel and watched my brush hand twitch. It made for an odd, jerky style I hoped would get noticed someday.

I never confessed this last part to Maura. Our intimacy was largely civic. We spoke at length about our shared revulsion for the almost briny-scented, poop-flecked plunger under the bathroom sink, and also of a mutual desire to cut down on paper towels, but we never broached topics like hopes, or dreams. Hopes were stupid. Dreams required quarantine.

Still, Maura was a devoted mother, which, even if that often amounted to being helplessly present for the ongoing thwarting of a child's heart, meant something. Bernie was a beautiful boy. Good thing, too, as he'd become an expensive hobby. Preschool, preclothing for the preschool. Then there were the hidden costs, like food. Funny, isn't it, how much you can detest the very being you'd die for in an instant? I guess that's just families. Or human nature. Or capitalism, or something.

But the price of Bernie wasn't Bernie's fault. It wasn't Maura's, either. I was the fool who let the starveling have it, who couldn't find another job, though I came close at a few places. The interviewers could maybe tell I had the old brain. Jobs weren't about experience anymore, just wiring. Also, my salary demands might have been high. I lost out to kids who lived on hummus and a misapprehension of history, the bright newbies bosses exploit without compunction because these youngsters are, in fact, undercover aristocrats mingling with the peasantry, each stint entered on their résumés another line in the long poem of their riskless youth.

Not that I resented them.

Besides, there really wasn't work for anyone. The whole work thing was over. I'd even called up my last employers, but there were no further plans for powdered wigs and brass-buckle shoes in the Bronx. I'd grown morose, detached, faintly palsied. I stopped reading the job listings, just rode the trains each day, simmering, until dinnertime.

Back in high school, I remembered, a soothing way to fall asleep after picturing tremendous breasts in burgundy bras (yes, the image pre-dated Vargina) had been to conjure the crimson blossom of bullet-ripped concert tees, the hot suck and pour of flamethrower flame over pep rally bleachers. Typical teen shooter fluff, though I worried I'd inherited my grandmother's nutcake gene. I was fairly popular. Why did I slaver for slaughter?

The visions had stopped in college. Some huge and dainty hand peeled them off my skull walls.

I became a painter, at least at parties. I was happy for a time.

But now, riding the trains, or else home sitting with the bills, the old terrible feeling returned. Whenever I checked my bank balance the terrible feeling welled up in me. The goddamn asks,

I'd sweep them with a Maxim gun or some other wipeout device whose history I learned of late at night on the war channels, a glass of Old Overholt rye on my knee. I was not bad off compared to most of the world. Why didn't anybody do anything? We could get a few billion of us together, rush the bastards. Sure, a good many of us would die, but unless the asks popped off some nukes, eventually they'd get overrun.

What was the holdup?

The terrible feeling tended to hover for a day or so, fade. Then I'd fantasize about winning the lottery, or inheriting vast fortunes. Sometimes I was a flamboyant libertine with plush orgy rooms, personal zoos. Sometimes I jetted around the world building hospitals, or making documentaries about the poor.

It all depended on my mood.

Days I didn't ride the trains, I'd take long walks in the neighborhood. We lived in Astoria, Queens, as close to our jobs in Manhattan as we could afford. One afternoon I made a mission for myself: stamps for the latest bills (I'd ask for American flags, stick them on upside down in protest against our nation's foreign and domestic policies), paper towels, and—as a special treat to celebrate the acceleration of my fatal spiral—a small sack of overpriced cashews from the Greek market.

I'd cure my solipsistic hysteria with a noonday jaunt. Sights and smells. Schoolkids in parochial plaids. Grizzled men grilling meat. The deaf woman handing out flyers for the nail salon, or the other deaf woman with swollen hands and a headscarf who hawked medical thrillers in front of the drugstore.

This was a kind and bountiful neighborhood: the Korean grocery, the Mexican taqueria, the Italian butcher shop, the Albanian café, the Arab newsstand, the Czech beer garden, everybody living in provisional harmony, keeping their hateful thoughts to themselves, except maybe a few of the Czechs.

A man who looked a bit like me, same eyeware, same order of sneaker, charged past. They were infiltrating, the freaking me's.

The me's were going to wreck everything, hike rents, demand better salads. The me's were going to drive me away.

The Greeks were out of cashews. I bought pistachios, ate them in line at the post office. Or on line at the post office. I could no longer recall which phrase came naturally. Either way, there was always a line at the post office, people with enormous packages bound, I assumed, for family in distant, historically fucked lands. What were they sending? TVs? TiVos? Hamburgers? Hamburger Helper? The exporting of American culture, did it continue at this level, too? It couldn't for much longer. Not according to Horace's calculations. The line hardly moved. People couldn't fill out the forms. Others did not comprehend the notion of money orders. Come on, people, I thought-beamed. I'm on your side and I'm annoyed. Doesn't that concern you? Don't you worry your behavior will reduce me to generalizations about why your lands are historically fucked? Or does my nation's decline make my myopia moot? They should produce a reality show about how much this line sucks, I thought. Call it *On the Line*. Or *In the Line*. A half hour later I reached the teller. I was about to ask for stamps when I realized I already had a book of them in my wallet. I did not need stamps. I needed a job. I needed to cool it with those pills from Maura's root canal.

Home beckoned, but so did a coconut flake. I was due back an hour ago, felt the admonishing telephonic pulses in my jeans, but instead crossed the avenue to the doughnut shop. There was a high school boy behind the counter, maybe saving up for the video game where you gut and flay everybody in the doughnut shop and gain doughnut life points. He wielded his tongs with affecting delicacy.

I thought again of my brutal visions of yore. My mother had always said I reminded her of her mother, Hilda. Since therapy, my mother had maintained that her issues, which prior to treatment had been known as her demons, stemmed from the fact that Hilda "withheld." I never knew my grandmother well. She had badly dyed hair and a persecution complex exacerbated toward the end of her life when she was fired from the culture beat at her synagogue's newsletter.

"That pig rabbi should have died in the camps," she said.

Most of Hilda's utterances weren't so venomous. Most of her evil she must have withheld.

Now I took a booth near the window, watched the afternoon bridge traffic. Trucks piled up at the off-ramp, trailer sides browned with exhaust.

Not long ago Bernie said "beep-beep" every time he heard a car horn. Later his favorite word was "mine." Now he was fluent in the cant of his tiny world. His leaps in speech had seemed otherworldly. What else was he mastering behind our backs? Little Judas. Maura and I had worked so hard to dig the family ditch for the three of us to rot in and now here came the rope of language to haul the boy out. "Beep-beep" begets "Mine," which begets "I hate you, Dad." Then, if you're lucky, there's a quick "I love you, Dad," followed by "Let go, Dad," these last words whispered under the thrum of ventilators, EKG machines.

My father had been that lucky.

Some natty loon sat alone at the next table. He wore a pilled herringbone blazer, crusty at the cuffs, guarded a shopping bag packed with neatly folded shopping bags. A notebook lay open on his table. It looked full of sketches, apothegms. His pen still had the wire on it from where he'd maybe snipped it at the bank. The loon muttered, picked white scabs on his head.

I could picture my colleagues back at the Mediocre development suite, Horace at his desk, unwrapping the outer, non-edible wrapping of his turkey wrap, Vargina holed up in her command nook, poring over ask dossiers and budget spreads, Llewellyn patched in from Zanzibar with the skinny on a give.

But I was at my new office now, my Formica workstation smeared with jelly and Bavarian cream. This scab-picker was my potential partner. We could make an ace development combo.

And the ask? Maybe the ask was that boy over there at the far booth, the one with fluorescent earbuds, a forehead full of leaky cysts. There was a horrible glitter in his eyes that looked like murder, or maybe just higher math.

The loon caught me staring at the boy, winked.

"What was that for?" I said.

The loon winked again. Teen brooder stood. I felt the glare of the leaky child, decided to meet the boy's gaze, try my best to transmit this thought: *I'm not the enemy, just an earlier iteration of our kind.*

"Goddamn fucking faggots!" the boy shouted, careened out the door.

Poor kid was a wild child, a homophobe. He might as well have been illiterate, guessing at supermarket signage. For all my adolescent rage, I had never included the marginalized or oppressed in my dream carnage. I never said gypped, or Indian giver, or paddy wagon, or accused anyone of welshing on a bet. If there ever evolved a tradition of locutions such as "She tried to tranny me on that real estate deal," you would not hear them out of my mouth. I never even called myself a yid with that tribal swagger I envied in others, though I had a right, or half a right, from my mother's side. I nearly spoke this truth aloud when the loon cackled.

"Don't mind the boy," he said. "I've known him since he was a child. A marvelous little specimen."

The man's voice had odd nasal authority. He sounded like some mandarin of vintage radio, and hearing him I suddenly recalled certain items from my childhood, a particular carton of laundry detergent, the mouthfeel of a discontinued cola.

The man dove back into his notebooks, his boy doodles and prurient runes. Even from here his sketches looked quite accomplished and insane.

Maybe someday he'd be heralded, a folk museum folk hero.

Maybe someday Bernie, still getting over his father's untimely but somehow not surprising death, would take his new girlfriend to see the disturbed but brilliant drawings by the kiddie-diddler who spent most of his adult life guarding a shopping bag full of shopping bags in a doughnut shop not far from where he, Bernie, grew up, but who also, unbeknownst to the world, inhabited a fabulous and secret universe of the mind.

My phone pulsed again. There were two messages, one from a number I recognized: the Mediocre development suite. The other was a text from Maura: *How's the donut, Fat Heart? Find a job yet? Buy milk for Bern. Also p. towels.*

The bile was a good sign.

It's when they stop trying to destroy you, my mother once said, that you should really start to worry.

Three

Home, hidden by the refrigerator, I hovered over the garbage bin, gulped down a bottle of Vitamin Drink. We still dreaded the day that little Bernie, asquat now on the kitchen floor spooning oatmeal into the body cavity of a decapitated superhero, might spot this iridescent liquid, demand a sip. Vitamin Drink may or may not have contained vitamins, but it was too polluted for the tykes. They needed wholesome nectars humped back from the wholesome food empires in Manhattan. This sugary shit was for the dying. I was dying, surely, sugary-ly.

I made to speak before I did.

"A call. A message. From work."

"What?" said Maura. "Work? What work?"

Maura sat on a stool, fresh from the shower and still unclothed, pecked at her laptop.

She had been raised in one of those happy, naked families from Vermont. I looked at her body now, remembered Bernie's weaning, that era of inconsolable sobs and farewell fondles. Maura's breasts, large and milk white when they'd been full of milk, had darkened, pancaked a bit, but they were still beautiful, and I was not just saying that, or thinking of saying that, to be kind.

"Wait," said Maura, "what?"

It was her I'm-downloading-a-crucial-file-from-the-office tone.

"A call from work on my voice mail," I said. "From old work. Vargina and Llewellyn. They want me to come in."

"Why would they want that?"

"I don't know."

"Wasn't firing you enough? Is this a legal thing? Do you need a lawyer?"

"I said I don't know."

I leaned out from my trash niche. Bernie pointed at the bottle in my hand.

"Daddy, what are you drinking?"

"Coffee, Bern. Why, do you think I need a lawyer?"

"Do lawyers have foreskins?" said Bernie.

"I'm talking to Mommy," I said.

"I have a foreskin."

"I know, Bernie."

"You don't."

"True," I said, opened the refrigerator door, sneaked the bottle back into the door rack.

"How come I have a foreskin, Daddy?"

"We've talked about this, don't you remember? Your mother and I decided that—"

"Hey, that's juice. I want some, Daddy! I want some juice!"

"Shit," I said. "Sorry. Bernie, it's not juice. It's for grown-ups. It's like coffee."

"You said it *was* coffee."

"That's right."

"But it's pink!"

"It's pink coffee, Bernie. It's what I drink. It's what grown-ups drink."

"Do superheroes have foreskins? Like my guy?"

He held up his headless hero.

"Yes. No. I don't know. Probably. So, who would I call, Maura? They want me tomorrow."

"Do they, Daddy?"

"I don't know, Bernie. It's possible."

"Do foreskins help you fly?"

"Maybe," I said.

"All I'm saying," said Maura, "is you don't have to play it their way. That's all you've ever done."

"Excuse me?" I said.

"Give me some juice!" Bernie called again. "I want it!"

"Ask nicely."

"Please."

"But it's not for kids, Bernie."

"Don't confuse him like that," said Maura. "Daddy's going to give Bernie some pink coffee juice that's not really coffee. Would Bernie like Daddy to give Bernie some pink coffee juice that's not really coffee? Daddy, would you please give Bernie some pink coffee juice that's not really coffee?"

"Fine!" I said.

"Fine!" said Bernie.

He flicked his guy and a cold gob of oatmeal slapped my cheek. I could see this was the beginning of something. Like sudden sympathy for Goliath. What was the phrase? Tell it not in Gath? How about we start telling it?

"What?" said Maura.

"Was I mumbling again?"

"Who's Goliath?" said Bernie. "A superhero? Is he a bad guy? A masher?"

"He's a masher, for sure," I said. "Whether he's a bad guy depends on your politics."

"What's politics?"

"Well, let me see. It's—"

"Does Goliath have a foreskin?"

"Not for long. Not when David's done with him."

"Who's David?"

"A foreskin collector."

"What are you telling him!" said Maura.

"Nothing," I said. "He should know about the Bible. He lives in a fucking theocracy."

"Jesus, language, Milo."

"Daddy! Juice!"

"Okay, Bern, but first, how about some water?"

I filled a cup from the tap. Bernie batted it away, lunged toward the refrigerator.

"Give me pink coffee juice, Daddy!"

"Okay," I said. "Okay."

I dumped out the tap water, took the Vitamin Drink from the refrigerator. Back turned, I mimed a long pour, added a drop for color, refilled the cup from the tap.

Bernie stared up at me.

"Let go, Dad," the boy seemed to be saying, but his beautiful mouth wasn't moving.

•

Later, in bed, Maura and I cuddled in the way of a couple about to not have sex. It never appeared to bother us much, unless we watched one of those cable dramas about a sexless marriage. Then we'd curse the inanity of the show, its implausibility, switch over to something where the human wreckage was too crass and tan to touch us.

"I still don't understand why they want to meet with you," said Maura.

"I don't, either. Maybe they realized they forgot to take the shirt off my back."

"It's not funny. That girl's father. I don't know."

"What more can they do to me?"

"Oh, I'm sure there are all sorts of things we'd never even think of."

"That's very calming. Thank you."

"I'm just saying. You never learned to protect yourself. You always rail against the evil and exploitation in the world but you still act as though everybody has your best interests at heart.

I never got it. You're like an idiot savant without the savant part."

"I still have faith in the basic goodness of humanity. Shoot me."

"Don't be so sure that's not the plan."

•

Vargina had reserved the conference room. A tray of turkey wraps sat near the edge of the table. They looked like university wraps, from the cafeteria downstairs, not the deli across the street. They had no avocado.

Llewellyn and Vargina sat across the table. We took turns popping the tops of our sodas, listened to the sounds reverberate in the wood-paneled room. The word "reverberate" reverberated in my mind, which I could now picture as a wood-paneled room.

"It's nice to see you again," said Vargina.

"Hear, hear," said Llewellyn. "So, hoss, what have you been doing to yourself?"

"Excuse me?"

"Just shitting you," said Llewellyn. "Seriously, how's it going?"

"I didn't see Horace when I walked in," I said to Vargina.

"He's at a lunch."

"*A* lunch?"

"He's working on an ask."

"Horace? He's a temp."

"No longer," said Llewellyn. "He's looking like a little earner."

"Very exciting possibility, Horace's ask," said Vargina. "Very worthy. The lady is a major admirer of our dance program."

"Where's the money from?"

"Her husband's company. Private security. Military catering."

"Blood sausage, anyone?" I said.

"Oh, please," said Llewellyn. "We can't wash the bad off anybody's money, now, can we? But we can make something good out of all the misery. That's what you never understood."

"I understood it. I'm just not sure I believed it."

"Oh, some kind of martyr now, are you?"

"A martyr has to give a shit."

"Get over yourself, Milo. You're a sad man. A born wanker. You were born into the House of Wanker. You're a berk, and you probably think I'm just saying your last name."

Llewellyn's Cambridge year was the stuff of office legend, thanks to Llewellyn, but I'd always suspected he lifted most of his lingo from the British editions of American men's magazines.

"Wanker," I said. "Don't know that word. Is that a Southern thing? What is that, Richmond? Newport News? Is that like peanuts in your Coke?"

"You have a provincial mind, hucklebuck."

"Pardon?"

"It's a global globe now," said Llewellyn. "We sink or swim together."

"It's a global globe?"

"That's right."

"Moron."

"Gentlemen," said Vargina.

"Why am I here?" I said. "I thought I was fired."

"You were," said Vargina.

"You are," said Llewellyn.

"Then what's going on?"

"We have special circumstances," said Vargina.

"You have special circumstances," I said.

"Yes."

"I have not-so-special circumstances," I said.

"If you help us with our circumstances," said Vargina, "we might be able to assist you with yours."

The door opened and in walked a large man with a moist pompadour and a tight beige mustache. Dean Cooley was not a dean. He was Mediocre's chief development officer. Several groups worked under him, and he spent most of his energy on the more lucrative ones, like business, law, or medicine. His art appreciation did not reach much past the impressionistic prints from the Montreal Olympics he'd mounted on his office wall. He'd been a marine, and then some kind of salesman, had started with cars and ended up in microchips and early internet hustles. Here in the cozy halls of academe, as he had put it during our first team talk, he meant to reassess his priorities. Meanwhile he would train us maggots how to ask asks and get gives. Cooley was a hard-charger who often began his reply to basic office queries by invoking "the lessons of Borodino." He was the kind of man you could picture barking into a field phone, sending thousands to slaughter, or perhaps ordering the mass dozing of homes. People often called him War Crimes. By people, I mean Horace and I. By often, I mean twice.

"Dean," said Vargina. "This is the man we were telling you about. Milo Burke."

"Nice to meet you."

We'd met a dozen times before, at lunches, cocktail receptions. He had stood beside me while his wife explained a project she'd embarked upon in her student days, something to do with Balinese puppets and social allegory.

"I assume you are wondering why, after being terminated for cause two months ago, we've asked you to come in," Cooley began.

"A fair assumption," I said.

"What you need to understand is that the incident with Mr. Rayfield's daughter was very serious. Mr. Rayfield is still angry. You made his daughter doubt herself, artistically. He had to buy her an apartment in Copenhagen so she could heal."

"I'm sorry, sir."

"The whole debacle nearly cost us a new, working telescope for our observatory."

"I do understand that."

"But what you also need to understand is that we are not simply some heartless, money-mad, commercial enterprise. We are partly that, of course, but we are also a compassionate and, yes, money-mad place of learning. And while we're on the topic of learning, we think people can learn from their mistakes. We believe in redemption."

"As long," said Llewellyn, "as it is not tied to a particular ideology or religious tradition and promotes inclusiveness."

"Is that from the handbook, Lew?" said Dean Cooley. "Anyway, the point is, we are a family."

"A family dedicated to furthering science and the humanities in an increasingly meaning-starved culture," said Vargina.

"Well put," said Dean Cooley.

"But may I remind us all," said Llewellyn, "that here in development our task is to raise money for said furthering. We can't hug all day. We've got to get out there and work."

"Also well put. Especially these days. We need every drop of philanthropy we can get. We must fasten our lips to the spigot and suck, so to speak. Which is where you come in, Mr. Burke."

"Pardon?"

"It's an ask," said Vargina.

"A big one," said Llewellyn. "Not quite Rayfield range, but big."

"Why me?" I said.

"Good question," said Vargina.

"Yes," said Cooley. "That is the question, as the Bard might say."

"The Bard?"

"What's so funny?" said Cooley.

"Nothing, sir," I said. "I just didn't know people still used that term."

"Well, I'm a people, Burke. Am I not?"

"Of course."

"If you prick me, do I not bleed, you scat-gobbling, mother-rimming prick?"

Occasionally Dean Cooley reverted to a vocabulary more suited to his marine years, but some maintained it was only when he felt threatened, or stretched for time.

"Yes, sir," I said.

"Trust me, Milo," said Llewellyn. "Nobody wants it to be you. You were nothing but dead weight since the day you arrived. Nobody respects you and your leering got on people's nerves."

"My leering?"

Vargina shrugged, tapped her pen against her legal pad.

"Listen," said Cooley. "I don't give a slutty snow monkey's prolapsed uterus for your office politics. The point is that Burke needs to come back and complete this mission."

"Why?" I said. "Why me?"

"It's the ask," said Vargina. "The ask demands it."

"Excuse me?"

"He says he knows you. His wife is an alumnus of our extension program and they want to be donors, but when he found out you were in our office, he requested your presence. He wants to work with somebody he trusts."

"Who is this person?" I said.

"His name is Stuart. Purdy Stuart. You do know him, don't you?"

"Yes. I know him."

I said nothing more, felt now like the boy in the fairy-tale book I often read to Bernie, the polite farmer's son who stands before the cruel ogre's castle.

Each time Bernie would ask: "Daddy, why does the boy have to knock on the door? Why can't he just turn around and go home?"

Each time I'd chuckle with stagey amusement, say: "Well,

kid, if he didn't open the door, we wouldn't have a story, would we?"

Odds were good I was, in the final analysis, nothing but a scat gobbler from the House of Wanker.

"I mean," I said now, "I used to know him."

"Well, that's just swell," said Cooley, rose, petted his mustache with a kind of cunnidigital ardor.

"I'm late for another meeting," he said. "Tell our contestant what he's won."

The door clicked shut behind him. It did not reverberate.

"What have I won?" I said.

"Your old job back," said Vargina. "If you make this work."

"And if I don't?"

"You'll be finished," said Llewellyn. "Forever. Do we have clarity?"

"Obscene amounts."

Llewellyn stood, stalked off. It would not be the last I saw of him, I knew. The ogres, they just lurk behind those gnarled oak doors so ubiquitous in fairy-tale carpentry, wait for gentle lads to knock. Trolls, on the other hand, they must have a paging device. Either way, the odious is ever ready.

Vargina and I sat there for a while, a new, electric awkwardness in the room.

"Can you make it happen?" said Vargina.

"When have I ever disappointed you?"

"Nearly every day that we have worked together."

"Listen," I said. "I just want to apologize."

"For what?"

"For the leering."

"The leering?"

"You know. That stuff Llewellyn said."

"Don't apologize to me. Apologize to Horace."

"Horace?"

"He's the one who reported you. But don't worry. He wasn't

vindictive. He just said he didn't understand why somebody would need to be in the closet in this day and age. At least around here."

"In the closet," I said.

"But he's a kid. He doesn't know how complicated these things can get."

"No," I said. "I guess he doesn't."

Four

There is art to the ask. There is craft. There is lunch. There is also research, but Purdy did not require much. I had been following my old college friend's career for years.

Purdy had made his own money, or so he told the reporters from those magazines about fellating rich whites, those rags with names like *Wealth*, or *Capital*, or *Fellating Rich Whites*. This was true to a point. Purdy made his own money out of some of his father's money.

Still, he had been ahead of his time with his online music outfit. It might sound ridiculous now, but he had been one of the first to predict that people really only wanted to be alone and scratching themselves and smelling their fingers and staring at screens and firing off sequences of virulent gibberish at other deliquescing life-forms. So for us he provided new music and photographs of fabulous people making and listening to the new music, as well as little comment boxes for the lonely, finger-smelling people to comment on the looks and clothing of the fabulous people who had managed to achieve some sweaty, sparkly proximity to each other and to life as it was lived in more glamorous eras.

Purdy even had a loft packed with stoned designers. He'd offered me a spot in his posse, doing God knows what, maybe just fetching lattes and shooting hoops on the office half-court. But I turned him down. My painting, I believed, was poised on the precipice of genius, though I never would have phrased it like that. "Thanks, but I'm cool" is how I probably put it, sealed myself in my schmucky dome. Purdy sold his company for a few hundred million.

I missed out on a nice little nest egg. A nest latte.

Since then Purdy had become a venture capitalist, a philanthropist, an occasional gossip-site item. He dated models, married one. That was no surprise. I recalled a conversation we had in college, after he'd fallen for the beautiful, plumpish Constance, realized he had to dump her.

"I'm not attracted to her," he told me.

He'd come out of his room in the sagging off-campus Victorian we shared with some others, joined me in the kitchen for a late evening bowl. Through the slit in the door I could see Constance asleep in his bed.

"If the chemistry's not there . . ." I said through smoke, as though I knew anything about sex and love other than the hard-won certainty that if I ignored the sore on my penis, it would probably go away.

"Oh, the chemistry's there," said Purdy. "The fucking is fantastic. I'm just not attracted to her."

"Huh?" I said. "Is it the teeth? I like the teeth."

"It's societal."

He said it had something to do with fashion magazines, cultural conditioning. We were big on this kind of thing.

"But, Purdy," I said, "the point is you subvert the codes, not adhere to them."

"I'm trapped, man," he said.

Purdy stood, wandered out into the garden. I sneaked into his room, slipped my head between Constance's knees. I was big on that kind of thing. Constance and I were together for a while after that. I was crazy about her, her fierce horsey mouth and chipped teeth and black braids and high shelf of an ass, but I don't think she ever got over Purdy.

Many didn't, though he never acquired the cad tag he might have deserved. Maybe his attachments were too diffuse. He lived with us, the faux-bohemian alcoholics, but he also had ins with engineers and future hedge fund managers, or political science types who believed in the American exception, that there was something dirty about a dirty martini.

He'd disappear with the children of the super-rich—his tax bracket, if not exactly his people—make weekend visits to the family compounds of ambassadors or early software titans or progressive oil sheikhs, which he'd later describe to us in rather cryptic and astonished terms, so that we might come to know the features and dimensions of a Saudi squash court but still not understand how petrochemical influence was wielded in Washington, or we might snicker at the gestures a major political family made toward the folkways of ordinary Americans—the cheapest sort of beach equipment, off-brand knockwurst on the grill—but still not comprehend how dynastic service shaped electoral outcomes. We were just glad that he ended his nights with us, the pretentious wastrels. He had insomnia. We stayed up the latest. I think that's mostly what it was.

He had mystery, this boy. He didn't need a persona. I might have been the painter, the way our friend Maurice was the drug dealer, or Constance was the Marxist feminist who fucked, or Charles Goldfarb was the larkish Frankfurtian who desperately wanted to fuck, but Purdy was simply Purdy.

There was nothing striking about him. His clothes weren't spattered with paint. His teeth weren't nicked. He didn't, like Maurice, have a tattoo on his arm of a man inking a tattoo on his arm. He didn't, like Billy Raskov, my rival, the artist who didn't paint because painting was dead, have a possibly affected case of Parkinson's, nor was he, like Sarah Molloy, timber heir and environmental feminist who did not fuck, a hater of his kind.

He was just Purdy, and though he was loaded—ruling class, in the parlance of our insufferable set—his father a knight-errant of a CEO, dashing from one corporate damsel to the next, slaying those dread dragons Health Plan and Pension wherever they preyed upon the margin, Purdy himself lived modestly, much more modestly than his family stipend allowed. He lived then pretty much how Maura and I lived now.

I suppose there was a certain glory in it, this slumming with the middle and upper-middle classes. Maybe not the glory of rushing a Nazi mortar position, or braving municipal billy bats to stop a war in Indochina, but the privileged of our generation did what they could, like the rest of us. We were stuck between meanings. Or we were the last dribbles of something. It was hard to figure. The fall of the Soviet Union, this was, the death of analog. The beginning of aggressively marketed nachos.

True, there was nearly no glory in my paintings of that time. They featured some dribbles themselves, some drips, some glued-on porcelain and politically meaningful popsicle sticks, though I could not now recall what they looked like, not really. I doubted anyone could, even Lena, the professor who anointed me our liberal arts boutique's aesthetic hope, took me to bed. Purdy wouldn't remember, either, but I certainly recalled his kindness to me, and not just the money he'd loan without that whiff of vassalage, of fealty, most rich kids required, but then maybe he feigned belief in all of us, in some ultimate utility to our mannered flailings. Somehow he helped us pretend we were all anointed, could become the icons wearing sunglasses in the dorm hall posters of the future, pioneers of jackass phenomena, ancestor gods of cool.

A sad dream, but it sustained us.

Purdy and I, we'd smoke those late-evening bowls while I bitched about Billy Raskov suddenly getting attention, or a student prize, for shitting on a Rand McNally atlas to interrogate hegemony.

Once Purdy just chuckled his trademark chuckle, which was really just the trace of one.

"He's a charlatan," said Purdy.

"Fucking Raskov," I said.

"A shitterton," said Purdy.

"That's it."

What he might have said to Billy Raskov about me I didn't want to know, though in a sense it hardly mattered.

He was somehow both of us and beyond us. He did not need to be anointed, ordained. He had powers of cajolement, a gentle, quasi-Christ-y authority. Maybe he just knew how we'd all turn out. He would guard our spasms of shame, of ego, from the others, wait with patience, forgiveness, for us to slip free of our charades, embrace our destinies, as bond lawyers, dental surgeons, new media consultants, housewives, househusbands, or unemployed development officers. Then he would stand there in his beautiful truth, the truth of money.

Five

Purdy met me at a steakhouse in Tribeca, a modern joint with futuristic sconces that looked like laser mounts. Here, the waiters sliced your meat because you were the feeb end of the species. The room seemed cozy and cavernous at once, the kind of place I would later describe to Maura as tastefully lit. A few bourbons, and so was I.

Though not particularly hungry, I succumbed to a certain unseemly ferocity with regard to my porterhouse. Sometimes I lost it around food I could not afford. I gnawed bone, tongued gristle, and while my old friend repaired to the men's, I reached for a bite of his almost untouched cut, popped a few of his rosemary-speckled potatoes into my mouth. I was fairly certain that upon his return he would not notice his plate's depletions, unless he'd made an earlier, silent spud count. This was possible. Men of his station were bred for such pettiness.

Though I was also pretty sure I had to work tomorrow, or at least report to the office, I ordered a second Calvados. Purdy, who never had to work again, sipped his wine. He pushed his glass an inch or two across the table, the universal sign that the convivial portion of the evening was over, although maybe it wasn't universal. I hadn't traveled much beyond Europe, and Canada didn't count.

"It's good to see you, Milo, really. You look great."

"No, you actually look great, Purdy."

God knew what diets, unguents, procedures, protocols had preserved him, his taut golden skin and plush honeyed hair, the roped muscle beneath his thin, collared shirt. Then again, maybe he'd won both of life's lotteries, required no protocols.

"I'm so glad to hear about Maura and Bernie," said Purdy.

"Hear what?"

"Everything you've been telling me for the past hour. Damn, a kid. We've been trying, you know. Melinda and I. We've got half the doctors in New York on the case."

"I'm sure it'll happen for you guys."

"I'm sure it will, too. Probably have to fertilize Melinda's eggs on the surface of Mars, but it will happen. Our happiness depends upon it."

"You'll be happy either way, Purdy."

"Happiness is tricky. It sounds like you've figured it out."

"Sure."

"Sure, he says," said Purdy.

"Sure, I say," I said.

"Don't be bitter, Milo. It doesn't become you."

"I'm not bitter," I said.

Purdy leaned back, as though to better assemble an exceptionally nuanced expression on his face, maybe some amalgam of pity and revelation.

"You're pissed because I'm so rich," he said. "You've always been pissed. You think I didn't earn it."

"You didn't."

"Of course I did. The trust fund made me comfortable. My own hard work made me rich. I knew when to cash out during all that interweb crap. Not many did."

Interweb, webnet, interpipe—the joke had begun to grate. If they flubbed it and winked, what? I was tired of the semantic evasions, mine included. I was tired of many things. I had been keeping a list, got tired of the list.

"I guess not," I said.

"Don't be a hater," said Purdy.

"I'm not just any old hater," I said. "I'm a hater's hater."

It was as though Purdy hadn't heard me, or perhaps it was precisely that he had.

"You're doing better than ninety-nine-point-nine percent of the people in this world," he said. "Capitalism might have shit the bed, but it's been very good to you, buddy, whether you know it or not."

"Hooray!" I said. "Let's drink to me. I'm not rich, and I'm not famous, but I am fat and white, or white-ish, and my debt load is at least testament to the fact that over the years various institutions have considered me a worthy mark."

"Good for you," said Purdy.

He sounded sincere and it scared me.

"You want another drink?" I said. "Maybe I'll get another drink."

"I'm fine," said Purdy.

"I'm not fine. I'm not fine at all. Let's have some drinks! Some fucking mojitos or something. Don't they have that fifty-dollar mojito here? With that rum from the island where they make one case a year, and the hydroponic mint they fly in weekly? I want one! It's all on the Whig, okay?"

"The who?" said Purdy.

"The Whig. Our founding daddy."

"Maybe you should slow down, Milo."

"Why the hell would I want to do that?"

"Because I don't think they fly that mint in anymore, for one thing. Look, Milo, I know we're old friends. I've held you over the toilet a few times, back in the day, but come on. The age of the expense account is over. I read it in the paper two years ago. And two months ago. And today."

"Sure," I said. "Yes. Of course."

"Excellent," said Purdy. "Now, do you have any questions for me?"

"Yes, I do. Why give to us? Why not give to the truly needy? The bombed-out, the starved-down, the families running from butchers on horseback. Or folks whose fate depends on whether they can score a fucking shovel and a bag of seeds."

"You mean genocides? Microfinancing?"

"Yeah, or even all the devastated people here."

"We give to those causes. Less and less, of course. We've all gotten murdered."

"How about giving to just a random assortment of middle-class families? Or not so random? How about mine?"

"Funny," said Purdy, in the way of a man who did not find it funny. "Any more questions? Wait, hold on."

Purdy took out a weird phone, the device we'd all be using next year, punched some keys.

"Forgive me," he said. "Forgot about something I needed to send. Where were we? Oh, yeah. Questions?"

"Just the canned ones. Like maybe you can tell me how you first got interested in the Mediocre University at New York's arts program."

"The Mediocre what?"

"Sorry. What I mean is—"

"Melinda had a wonderful experience at your university. Especially in the film and theater classes she took. It was the best investment I ever made, sending her there after we met. Sure, it was the only place she had any chance in hell of getting into, but it enriched her. That sounds stupid, but it's true. It helped her become the woman she wanted to be, and needed to be, to be with me. Actually, Melinda handles a lot of our giving these days. Museums, orchestras, film societies. My area of interest is more narrow. I enjoy finding younger female artists and helping them at that crucial stage when their asses are firm and un-blemished."

"You're joking," I said, clenched my jaw to squeeze the booze from my skull.

"Of course I'm joking. But of course I'm not really joking. Ultimately it's nothing like a joke. You know, now that you're trying to act sober, I can see how drunk you are. How many of my potatoes did you eat, freak? And what about my steak? Did you think I wouldn't notice? Do you always grope other people's meat? It's cute when you're twenty, Milo, but come on. Get a grip."

"I will."

"Will what?"

"Grip it."

"Grip it now, kid."

"Okay. I'll try. Really."

"Good. Now. Let's talk our talk. Your beloved institution seems like it wants to step up to the next level. Be a culture player. Crank out all those smug nullities who can make the stylish, insipid, top-notch crap. Stuff we can jerk off to but that will also make us sorry, but not too sorry. Sexy sorry. Am I right?"

"Sorry about what?"

"I don't know. Imperialist wars, torture, poverty, disease. How we've gotten past slavery except that we will never get past slavery, no matter who's the CEO. How the immigrants are good hardworking people, except for the lazy border-violating ones, except that it was their land to begin with and they work even harder than the hardworking ones. That kind of stuff. And also how we are such third-raters at this point, but what does that really mean? And what happened to being Rome? Seems like we didn't get much of a chance to be Rome. Seems pretty fucking unfair."

"Bitches of the First World," I said.

"Nicely put."

"That's Horace."

"Is it? I don't quite remember that. But I think you know what I'm saying."

"I know that you're saying something," I said.

"And by the way, FYI, I share all of these thoughts with you as somebody descended from both slave-owners and struggling immigrants. In some cases, they were the same people. It might sound cynical but I'm not cynical at all. I believe in the sensitive jerk-off stuff. I get off on the jerk-off stuff. But am I right? About your school? About wanting to ratchet things up, bring on the brand consciousness? Piss with the big art fairies? That's what that slick Southern kid intimated. What's his name?"

"Llewellyn."

"That's the one. He's impressive. What my dad used to call a comer. You must hate his guts."

"He's okay."

"Sure he is. Anyway, that's what he gave me to believe, when I met him at this sort of art happening. An historical re-enactment of the dotcom bubble. Some guy rented a loft and hired actors to pretend to be designing websites. Have to say he nailed the details, the clothes, the snacks, the drugs, the toys. Thought I was in a time machine. But the point is he said you guys wanted to go big. Stop pussyfooting, as he put it. Here's your mojito."

The waiter laid a tumbler at my elbow. I stared into the crushed ice, the muddled mint, and thought, oddly, of Scandinavia, of hissing, mist-sheathed fjords. It must have been the crushed ice.

"Judging by your face, the what-the-fuck nodes in your cerebral cortex must be a real light show."

"You texted the drink order?"

"What do you think?"

"I think I should have ordered an aquavit. You texted the drink order. Just before."

"Maybe."

"But to whom was the text addressed? The waiter? The bartender?"

"We'll cover that next time. This is a process. What I want to make clear tonight is that despite the hits my portfolio has taken, I am committed to exploring the possibility of a serious give. Now might be an appropriate time for one last question."

I was halfway to the morning's hangover. Boozewise, fatherhood had bounced me to the bantam ranks. But I wanted to keep going. I wanted to know things, like what Purdy really thought of our former friendship, whether he sensed how much he'd changed, or if he believed this was what he'd always been. Also, did he happen to know the whereabouts of the vintage Spanish dueling knife I lost in college?

"Why did you insist on me?" I said.

"Sure," said Purdy. "That's a suitable closing question. And here's the answer: because you're my pal. Because, like I said, I held you over the toilet a few times. Was it liquor or smack? I can't remember. Did you call it smack?"

"But you don't need me for this."

"Yes, I do."

"Why?"

"Because I trust you. Because you're not the only one with an ask. I'm going to ask you to do a few things for me. And you won't betray me."

"I won't?"

"You're the opposite of Judas."

"You're the opposite of Jesus."

"So, we'll be fine. You okay?"

I've never been much for drunken wakefulness, always admired those blackout artists who seemed perfectly alert while entirely unconscious, who rode trains and conducted real estate deals and pleasured lovers in a technical sleep state, who woke up in the Cleveland Hilton with inexplicable amounts of river silt in their pants cuffs. My overhooched evenings tended to expire with a lone ax stroke to the motherboard. Lucky nights I'd get one last surge of consciousness, like those precious seconds of life savored, if certain movies are to be believed, by severed heads.

"Anybody there?" said Purdy. "Let's get your ass home."

"Hell, no," I said. "Let's drink! Let's get some coke! Text it to me! Text me some fucking coke!"

I remember saying this, anyway, and I remember Purdy's laugh, his trademark trace chuckle. I remember digging in my pockets to see if I'd be able to cover the dinner, the imaginary blow, expense it later. Of course, I didn't even have carfare, which was rather unprofessional. This was my party, my check, my ask. Purdy pushed some buttons on his handheld again and I wondered if he might be ordering an eight ball, or dumping shares in Singapore, or calling Melinda, or calling a call girl, or calling a car, or checking a West Coast baseball score.

Next thing, I awoke alone in a cab rocketing over the Queensboro Bridge with fifty bucks in my fist like it had been wedged there with great fuss, which I figure it must have been, because even a piker like me knows you don't cadge cab money from the ask. It's a central tenet of development.

You don't even have to research that one. You just feel it in your asking bones.

Of course, there was a credit swipe in the back of the cab, but we both must have known my card would be denied.

Six

Once I could drink all night and, if not spend the next morning charming a potential donor over low-fat scones, or better, reinventing the color field with my best sable brush, still manage to pass the morning vaguely upright in my Aeron. Now, as I slumped across the sofa and watched my child play and my wife dress for work while I sipped my Vitamin Drink from a Bernie-deceiving coffee mug, the best I could do was suppress a decent percentage of the moister retches and wonder how long this hangover would last.

Maybe the hangover would never leave, just fade from immediate detection, hide like a deep-cover hitman, some human killbot who works the graveyard shift at American Smelter, takes his family to mass every Sunday, until the moment the baddies flip his switch. Then my hangover, "activated" by further alcohol consumption, would return, step out of the shadows in surgical galoshes, press the muzzle of its silencer-engorged Ruger to my skull.

The Milo Sanction would be complete.

I made like I was picking my teeth, dropped another of Maura's pills onto my tongue.

Bernie flew by on his wooden scooter, one of those beautiful Danish objects the Danes must foist on the world out of spite.

"Watch it," I said.

My son flung a wet wedge of fruit at the wall.

"Mango attack!"

"Bernie!"

"Togsocker! Macklegleen! Ficklesnatch!"

Nonsense words had become impromptu mantras for the boy, just pleasing bursts of Anglo-Saxon sound, though occasionally he'd hit on one with inadvertent resonance. The last word just uttered, for instance, did describe his mother at certain regrettable points in her history.

"Ficklesnatch!" he said again.

I went to fetch a rag for the wall.

"Bernie, no throwing!" said Maura.

Today was an emergency vacation at Bernie's school, another of those hasty cancellations of service we had come to expect from the dingy neighborhood basement where some young people with fancy education degrees and a tin of Tinker Toys had founded Happy Salamander. We did not understand their dense pedagogical manifesto, emailed to us upon acceptance, but had enrolled our son anyway.

"It's like a student haircut," I had said, and Maura laughed, a new, slightly apocalyptic tinge to her snicker.

So far, Bernie seemed no more miserable than he did anywhere else, and the school was close by. But the Salamander people canceled class quite often. They gathered, rumor had it, for retreats on somebody's father's farm, to debate amendments to their manifesto, snowshoe.

Now we waited for Christine, the neighborhood babysitter. Any moment she would roar up in her minivan and I would take Bernie downstairs, stuff him inside the vehicle with the other kids Christine watched, or maybe abandoned to watch each other while she scouted fiesta-mix specials at Costco. We knew the price of Christine's criminally low price, namely that under her supervision, or lack thereof, Bernie was becoming a criminal. Child care was like everything else. You got what you paid for, and your child paid for what you could not pay for.

We hoped his school's fuzzy fervor might afford some balance. Still, even now, after so much Salamanderine propaganda about kindness and cooperation, no peer encounter began without a toy grab or a gut punch.

I would despair, thrill, each time.

A few seasons in Christine's cement yard with Queens County's puniest toughs and Bernie had the strut of an old-time dockside hustler. It was hard to imagine the boy completing kindergarten, remarkably easy to picture him in a tangle of fish knives and sailor cock under some rot-soft pier.

Now Bernie continued his mango-slickened Danish circuit. Maura did her primps, her mirror checks, her grooming despotic through the scrim of my hangover.

"What are you going to do today?" she said, whipped her wet hair, buttoned her blouse.

"I've got errands. Might try to get some stamps."

"Don't overextend yourself."

"I'll be careful."

Maura pointed to her skirt, her nearly assless habitation of it: "Does this make you look fat?"

An old joke. I mimed my old-joke chuckle. Maybe it was some version of Purdy's.

"What are *you* going to do today?"

"Whatever Candace tells me to do, that bitch."

Candace supervised Maura at the marketing consultancy. They were currently working on a memo about need creation for a women's magazine. I'd never met Candace but I'd often found myself with a need to create a picture of her. The picture was different each time. Sometimes Candace was a little dumpy, or knobby. Sometimes she was muscular and sleek. Sometimes she licked Maura's knees in a supply closet, though I had no idea if their office had a supply closet.

"Sorry?" said Maura.

"Nothing. I love you, that's all."

"Ficklesnatch, you bad ones!"

Bernie had more mango wedges.

"Make sure you clean the walls before that stuff dries," said Maura, kissed Bernie, ducked out the door.

It was just me and my destroyer now. I looked for signs of human feeling in his dead, wet eyes.

Let go, let go.

We both jumped at the honk. Christine's corrections wagon idled at the curb. I walked Bernie out, strapped him into a car seat just notionally fastened to the seat back. They were only going a few blocks. Why be rude? A little girl in a tank top, with a washable tattoo of a monster truck on what would some-day be her bosom, put Bernie in a headlock, bit down playfully on his carotid artery.

"Young love," said Christine. "Say goodbye to Daddy, Bernie."

My son whimpered and Christine laughed, fired up a DVD for the backseat screens. It was sacrilege in these precincts to drive even a few minutes without cinematic wonders for the passengers. What played now appeared to be that movie about the crucifixion, the one everybody got so worked up about, so heavy on the blood and bones and approximated Aramaic.

"Do you think the kids are ready for this?" I said.

"Was *He* ready?" said Christine, shot from the curb.

"I'll pick up at four!" I called.

Seven

The deli near Mediocre had a new wrap man. He rolled my order too tight. Turkey poked through the tan skin. I studied the damage through the translucent lid of the container. It was a bad way to begin my first day at my old job.

I rode the elevator up with Dean Cooley.

"A new start," I beamed.

He nodded, appeared unable to place me.

"Milo Burke," I said. "Back in action."

Cooley stroked his mustache. The door slid open and he stepped off, glanced once over his shoulder as he went.

The development office looked about the same, with certain modifications. My desk, for example, had disappeared, or else been annexed in some office furniture Anschluss orchestrated by Horace. There he lounged now near the window, spread out in an L-shaped command nook of his own, eating ribs from a foil bag.

"Dude," he said into his phone, "I just know I'm going to bag this old biddy. She's got to be good for some serious paper heroin . . . Yes, I mean money . . . Dude, I don't know if that's the latest slang, it's my slang. We all have our own nowadays . . . Anyway, I'm deep in her geriatric ass. I've sort of become her protégé. Her son died cliffsurfing a few years ago and I'm like her new son. No offense . . . Well, it's sort of like base jumping. But more radical."

I could tell Horace was talking to his mother. He spoke to her daily. I had always been a little envious. My mother and I hardly conversed. Since Bernie had been born, we had not gone often to the house in New Jersey where I grew up and where Claudia now lived with her partner, Francine, but things had decayed before that. I traced it to the year my father got sick and we argued about his treatment. Though I was the first to admit I resented the man, preoccupied as he was with his pleasures, adrift in some dream of sleaze, he was still my father, and after the diagnosis I championed all the heroic measures, the experimental chemos, the scalpels and rally caps, any long shot on tap. Maybe I demanded those things precisely because I resented him. But my mother had his ear, convinced him to go gentle into that shitty night. They had caught the cancer late and it had spread quickly, but I wondered if he agreed to slip away out of weariness or a sense of penance.

Meanwhile, the liberation Claudia had felt since the death of her mother and her husband, the nearly Bataan march terms with which she described the slog and heartbreak of her pre-Francine existence, grated. My father had been a scumbag. There was no counter-argument. He cheated on my mother, bragged about his "nooners," seduced my babysitter, sold her quaaludes. Between work and infidelity, he hadn't even been around that much. Mostly it was my mother and I in that house on Eisenhower Road. We'd had hard times, but also some beautiful ones, full of oatmeal cookies and scary stories, the floor covered with butcher paper and us painting murals of pirates and dragons and roller-skating wraiths. We spent hours curled up together with books on her husbandless bed. Did she remember those occasions at all? Were they no consolation? Was I an ass to think they could be?

Yes, I'm sure I was an ass. Maybe I was jealous of her bliss. She took terms like "self-actualize" seriously, or even actually, had a toned senior body, a monumental sense of certainty. She trained for ultra-marathons. I got winded on the Mediocre stairs.

She was not much of a grandmother, refused even the name.

Claudia and Francine, that is how Bernie was to address his grandmothers those rare occasions he saw them. I didn't mind this. I liked Francine, appreciated any instant granting of progressive status. Less work for me. But I guess I just craved, in my twitching little-boy heart, for my mother to want us around, to maybe even nudge and nag the way grandmothers did in advertisements for stewy soups.

Now she came off more the charismatic aunt. Maybe she had actualized into my father. Perhaps a magic portal existed that I needed to step through, too, so I could leave the planet of the weak and whiny, which I imagined at this moment as a humid orb stuffed with pinkish meat and warmed-over chipotle dijonnaise, though that could have been my lunch talking, or imagining, for me.

I pulled a chair up to the far edge of Horace's elongated workstation, popped my wrap lid.

"What's the matter," said Horace. "Your pussy hurt?"

"What?"

"You look like you just got kicked in your pussy. Or like some commandos kicked down the door of your pussy and just rushed in there with machine guns and concussion grenades. Or like your pussy is being used against its will as a staging area for a large-scale invasion by a nation with which your pussy has long had strained relations, even if certain markets have opened up in recent years."

"What the hell are you talking about?" I said.

Horace had his desk phone pressed to his chest. He put it to his ear again.

"I've got to go, Mom. Burke's here. You should see him. Such a sad case with his little wrap and a few gherkins in a ketchup cup. I know. Cornichons. I was going to say cornichons but I bailed. I got nervous. Yeah, I'll tell him. I just asked him if his pussy hurts. He's mulling it over. Okay, love you, Mom. See you later. Around seven. Okay, bye."

Horace hung up the phone, tipped the rib bag into his mouth. A rivulet of greasy sauce ran down his chin.

"Hello, lover," he said. "Come for your desk?"

"Horace, look, since I'm working here again—"

"I heard it was just provisional."

"Since I'll be around the office some, I think we should try to communicate better in the future."

"I think flashing your fuzzy nip at me was communication enough, Wolf Man."

"Horace, I'm sorry. I think I misread some cues or something."

"That's one way of putting it."

"No, really, I never meant anything untoward. I just thought we were goofing around, being jackasses together. I never meant anything sexual, or imagined you felt harassed."

"Who said I did?"

"Vargina."

"Crafty. Divide and conquer. All Gaul, baby."

"Didn't you complain about me?"

"Yeah, I guess I did. But more like as a joke."

"Did you make an official written complaint?"

"Yeah, but in a jokey way."

"Those go on record, Horace. Those are in our file. As soon as a company hires you they begin plotting the paper trail with which to fire you. Didn't you know that?"

"Sort of."

"Okay, let's just shake and start again. Congrats on the new position. I hear you are really doing well on a big ask."

"Thanks, Milo. But you'll have to find yourself another desk. I'm wedded to this configuration."

I found a Plant Ops guy and an IT guy and by the end of the day I had a desk, a chair, a computer, an internet connection. I had a password to the server, though my only access was to an empty folder marked "MiloStuff."

Now that I had the desk I wasn't sure what to do. I only had the one ask. Also, I was on probation. I sent Purdy an email, thanked him for dinner, told him how thrilled I was to be working with him on this tremendously exciting project. I used all the dead language. Dead language would keep me alive. Besides, tone was tricky. I had to sound like a man who unexpectedly discovered himself in a professional relationship with an old friend. Just because it was true didn't mean it wasn't tricky. That was usually when I started to crack—when I told the truth, especially to social betters.

The night before I left for college, my father gave me his Spanish dueling knife. This was huge, the kind of intimate bestowal for which I'd always yearned.

"Take this," said my father, from where he stood at the edge of my basement room. I had moved down there, near the gas meter, to become a man. Soon I would depart the cold cinder walls lined with Scotch-taped postcards of my icons, Renaissance thugs and alcoholic crybabies from the Cedar Tavern. My own boozy, plaintive triumphs awaited, surely.

"Wow, thanks," I said.

The blade bordered on sword. We studied its Castilian chasings.

"A beaut, right?"

"I never knew you had this."

"Didn't want you to know about it. Thought you and the neighbor boys would sneak it out, behead each other. Then I'd really be screwed."

"Probably a good call. Where did you get this? It really is something."

"If I told you I won it in a card game in a cathouse in El Paso, would you tell your mother?"

"Do you think she'd want to know?"

"She always seems to want to know. Maybe it's better if you picture me in a gift shop near a hotel."

"Okay, that's how I'll always remember you, Dad."

"You must be nervous about driving up to school tomorrow. Sorry I can't make it. Got a lot of work, though I'd love to switch places with you. All that moist young stuff up there. Have you gotten laid yet?"

"Dad."

"The few girls you've brought home, they seem like nice girls. But you've got to learn how to reach the dirty glory in them."

"I'll try to squeeze that into my schedule. Thanks for the advice."

"Shit," said my father. "You can read books and paint your splotches at home. Make the most of the scene up there. And I'm not saying this just because of the money. Your grandparents put some aside for you, and I'll kick in some, but there will be debt on your head. It will pursue you like, I don't know, some sicko pursuer. But that's not what I'm talking about."

"What are you talking about?"

"Take the knife."

"Not exactly sure what I'll do with it in my dorm."

"Get drunk and wave it at some stuck-up assholes. Brandish it. Show it to a girl. Girls who can really fuck will appreciate a work of exquisite craftsmanship like this. Or just put it in a drawer and whenever you open the drawer and see it, think of me. In a cathouse in Brownsville."

"You said El Paso."

"What?" said my father. "El Paso. Sure."

I did keep the knife in a drawer, in a series of them, as I moved from dorm room to dorm room to off-campus apartment. I would put it in my desk or under the clutter of utensils in the kitchen drawer. My father died during my junior year and every time I caught sight of the knife a warm charge of grief shot through me. That knife was my talisman of bereavement. I never spoke of the thing unless somebody spotted it, digging for a garlic press or a slotted spoon. Usually it would be a girlfriend sifting through the drawer while we cooked and I would tell her it was my father's knife, bequeathed to me before his death. Everyone knew about my father. I made a habit of getting blotto and cornering people so I could describe the exact nature of his monstrosity. Now I winced when I recalled the bathos, the drool. I was a raincoat perv with my wound. I guess I was working on some stuff. Some moist young stuff.

Senior year I moved into the House of Drinking and Smoking, took the cheap room, almost a pantry. It had a futon, some books, a desk, a chair, a Fold 'N Play record player. I screwed a blue bulb in the ceiling and slept there, mostly alone. I listened to old records and stared at the blue light. I worried I might go crazy, but I also felt on the verge of something important, the final touches on the permanent exhibition—*Father, Fucker, Human: The Dreamtime of Roger Burke*—I was mounting in my heart. I stayed many hours in that room.

Otherwise I studied in the library or painted in my studio or drank in the living room with all the people who either lived there or sort of lived there or might as well have lived there, though the core stayed fairly stable, a crew that included Billy Raskov, Maurice Gunderson, Charlie Goldfarb, Purdy, Constance, Sarah Molloy, and a guy named Michael Florida, who may or may not have been a student, though by dint of his meth addiction could have counted as an apprentice chemist. We drank local beer, smoked homegrown and shake. We used words like "systemic," "interpolate," "apparatus," "intervention." It wasn't bullshit, I remember thinking at the time. It just wasn't not bullshit.

But the blue bulb was healing me.

I moved out at the end of spring term. My plan was to stay in town for the summer, perhaps beyond, to work at a restaurant near campus and finish up some paintings. Maybe I wasn't ready for New York City, even if Lena thought so, had made some phone calls on my behalf. But to what end? To be some pompous impostor's assistant? To stretch canvas, fetch sushi? It sounded pretty admirable, in a strange way, as though in lieu of the atelier you might learn something ferrying hunks of rice-couched toro, but I also wanted more time in my little world. Maybe more time with Lena.

I found a cheap studio above a dry cleaner and moved everything out of the house. A new group took over the Drinking and Smoking lease. One of them was the daughter of a reactionary governor, a girl who'd become notorious for denouncing her father's policies at campus demos. We admired her greatly for this.

Sometime early in the semester I found myself at a party at the house, stood in the kitchen with a can of beer and watched everybody shout and flirt. Already I was the older fellow, suspect. Why had I not gone bounding into the surf of destiny? Why did I still lurk on this sorry spit? Somebody brushed past and opened a drawer near my hip, poked around, maybe for a bottle opener. That's when I saw it, my knife, wedged in the wires of a whisk.

I had forgotten to take it when I moved out. I had no idea what this lapse could mean. Or maybe some idea. I hoisted myself up on the counter, unsheathed the knife. The party got louder, crowded. Somebody tapped my shoulder. Somebody tugged my shirt. A few of the new tenants gathered around the counter. Constance stood with them, smiled. We'd ended things, but we still mattered to each other. She had understood about the blue light.

"Hey," I said.

"What are doing with that thing?" one of the others asked.

"Nothing," I said.

"It's a great knife, isn't it?" said the governor's daughter. "We found it when we moved in. Kind of makes us nervous right now, though, with the party and all these people. Could you put it back?"

"Sure, sorry," I said, nodded sagely to signal my concurrence with the notion that huge knives and parties did not mix. I sheathed the blade, slid it into the back of my jeans.

"What are you doing?" said the first girl.

"What do you mean?"

I scooted off the counter, stood before them.

"We asked you to put the knife back. Not steal it."

"It's my knife," I said. "My father gave it to me. I just left it here when I moved out. By accident. But now I found it. I can't believe I left it in the first place. I'm going to need some therapy to figure it all out."

"That's the lamest story I ever heard," said the governor's daughter.

"Totally," said one of the others.

"Why should we believe you? Do you have proof?"

"Proof?"

"I don't think he has proof."

"It's my knife," I said. "My father won it in cathouse in El Paso."

"A cathouse?" said the first girl, though we knew then to say woman, even if none of us were women or men.

"Is that the word he used?" said another. "Cathouse? Not rape factory? What a pig your father must be. Are you proud of him? Paying to rape underage women of color?"

"They have agency," said the governor's daughter to the first girl. "They are sex workers in a marginal economy and there is agency there. Though not much. Especially if they are underage."

"Who said underage?" I said, tried to recruit Constance to my cause with a glance, but she glided behind the others. Somehow I couldn't blame her.

"Okay, maybe they were eighteen," said the governor's daughter. "Who cares? It's a bullshit story. It's not your knife. And anyway, possession is nine-tenths of the law."

I wondered when she had first heard that sacred charm. Had the governor cooed it into her newborn ear? I could not believe I was not believed. I wanted to laugh. I could just walk out with the knife, nobody would stop me, but still I would not be believed. I would be known as a thief.

I shook as I handed over my father's knife. Such shame. The governor's daughter, who cared so little for this object, would get to keep it. She was from the people who kept everything. I was from the people who rented some of everything for brief amounts of time. I knew I deserved no pity, would get none from the people who kept everything. They only pitied the people with nothing at all. I also knew that because I was leaving without the knife, I did not deserve the knife. A part of me did not want to deserve it.

Brownsville or El Paso.

Wave or brandish.

So it was all very tricky, telling the truth. It wasn't really about the truth. It was about being believed. It was about Purdy believing that he'd chosen right when he'd chosen me. It was bad form to hound him by telephone this soon after the email. I surfed art blogs for news of newer art blogs, food blogs for news of food. A new joint downtown seated eleven. The pork belly tart was divine. Reservations were impossible, and if you got one, it didn't guarantee dinner for your party, just you.

I logged off, swung my knapsack to my shoulder. I'd had a hard time deciding whether to carry a knapsack, a messenger bag, a canvas book bag, or a briefcase. Each seemed to embody a particular kind of confusion and loss. But the knapsack did the least spinal damage. I'd also noticed more people on the street with those briefcases on wheels. Nothing depressed me more than these rigs, this luggage for people not going anywhere, having their holiday at work. Sometimes I imagined those squat cases full of bondage gear or hobby trains, some secret glee, but you could almost be certain they bulged with files.

"Tough hour?" said Horace, swiveled from his monitor.

"Just sort of setting up today. Need to pick up Bernie soon."

"Right. Well, nice to have you back. On a probationary basis."

"Thanks, Horace."

Vargina popped her head up out of her command nook.

"Milo?"

"Hey," I said.

"So, everything working here?"

"Think so, yeah."

"You know, given the nature of your situation here, how it's just this one project, please don't feel you have to come in that often. We're more interested in the outcome than the process."

"Right," I said. "But since, if this works out, I'll be back here long-term, isn't it better if I re-integrate now?"

There was a blankness, and within that blankness an odd flicker of what I took to be pity, in Vargina's expression. The pity part, plus the idea that the tips of her nipples might be brushing the synthetic weave of the cube wall, put a thrum in me. Or it might have been my cell phone.

Eight

They held up the N train at Queensboro Plaza for a medical emergency, somebody maybe stroked out on the car's sticky floor, mistaking for a celestial communiqué the guarantees of Upper Manhattan's number one pimple doctor, or the public service announcement about condoms targeted at Spanish-speaking men who believed they were not gay. The victim's eyes might even have alighted on the new Mediocre subway campaign: *Knowledge and Discovery: A Better You. A Better World*, the words stenciled below a beautiful Polish exchange student in a lab coat. This could be what the admissions folks called a change-of-life opportunity. If Strokey lived he might quit his job, go back to school, become what he always wanted to be, namely, somebody standing next to a beautiful Polish exchange student in a lab coat.

Still, why stop the whole train just so paramedics could board the car and pull some poor slob back from the white light? We couldn't waste time like this. Not for an individual life. We were losing our superpower superpowers. Would they stop this train in China?

I got off and waved down a livery cab, rode out to my Astoria Boulevard stop, took the shortcut through a playground beneath the tracks. The playground was empty except for a burly man coaxing his daughter down a slide. The sight of them startled me. He looked like a man I'd known on my block, a man who was dead now but who in life boasted the same huge shoulders and shaggy dreadlocks. But really this man looked very different, his skin much lighter, and he wore jeans and construction boots powdered with drywall dust. The man I remembered favored tatty T-shirts and checkered chef pants. Whenever I thought of him I thought of those pants.

Often, out with Bernie in the stroller, I'd pass his house. His two young kids, a boy and a girl, would putter around a dirty plastic playhouse, the man on his stoop, smoking, reading the paper. I'd wave, dad to dad. Sometimes we would talk, the weather, the fish at the Greek place up the street, the dilapidation of the swings at the river park.

I liked talking to this man who could somehow pull off the role of loving and attentive parent with a lit cigarette in his mouth. He was a throwback papa, reminiscent of another time, another texture, his affection gruff, or else a bit reined in, but all the more palpable, that full-hearted but fatalistic love from before people used "parent" as a verb, when you might sit on the stoop and watch your children play in your barren rented yard and believe that life could work out. It was horseshit, of course, nostalgia for a nonexistent past, but it warmed the cheap parts of me.

Yet we were also, the both of us in our way, the new dads. This fellow was the real McCoy, a stay-at-home hero, but at least I was a quality-of-lifer, a knock-off-at-fiver, who would rush back for hours of child care if Maura needed to finish a project or just needed free time, a pedicure, a treadmill run. Often enough this man and I both put our kids to bed, our wives still at work, doing the work of their type in this era, the conferencing, the teleconferencing, the brainstorming, the liaisoning. Sometimes the work of their type meant drinks at the bar with other men and women. Sometimes they just needed to get away from us. Enjoy yourself, we said. Heaven knows you deserve it. We meant this and did not resent them for being better than us. New dads still respected what was best in the old ones, but had maybe abandoned the fear, the silence, or else the gabby cruelty of our fathers, grandfathers.

This is how I liked to think of us, anyway, me and this large man with his good laugh and the Marlboro Light in his teeth or between his stubby fingers, which he'd hold with such care away from his daughter's braids when she charged over to collapse in his lap and file howling grievance against her brother's style of playhouse play.

I even imagined a life for this guy, figured him for a chef, because of the checkered pants, home until he could find another high-end organic gig or else raise the cash for his own place, living off scant savings and his wife's administrative job. Then one afternoon, sitting in the playground I crossed now, while Bernie napped in his stroller, I noticed an item in the paper about an entire family wiped out by a beverage truck on the Brooklyn-Queens Expressway, and studying the article and the photograph of my neighbor there beneath photographs (and diagram) of the wreck, I saw I had not been far off.

James "Jimmy" Easter had been a chef in the East Village. Probably knew his way around a pork belly tart. His wife was in sales, medical supplies. Jimmy Easter, there was the name, Jimmy Easter, the missing piece that should have connected it all, me out with the stroller, always the lighter-framed of our two Maclarens, not because it weighed less but because it was cleaner and there was something unmanly about pushing the filthier stroller, with its crumbed seams and yogurt-smeared handles and pockets stuffed with rotten apple cores (not that I ever cleaned the thing), and the friendly neighbor with his cigarette and his children and their mud-crusted playhouse. Except the name connected nothing. Easter was too much. It crowded out what mattered.

There was also the question of the car, the compact Korean-made tomb of the Easters. Had I ever seen it? Probably parked out back. Maybe Jimmy paid his landlord for a space. A monthly strain, this extra. And Jimmy with his cigarettes, even after the mayor jacked the tax, Jimmy still with his cigarettes and the smoke he tried to wave away. What kind of father would smoke around his children, or smoke at all? Not the kind of father the mayor would consider a father. Nobody committed to effective parenting. Did Jimmy have life insurance? Would his death from lung cancer at least pay out?

But these questions, these accusations in the form of questions, they really stopped being pertinent one blue afternoon in October in a southbound lane on the BQE. The semi took care of these questions, or really issues, let's call them issues, much as many of us not my mother claim to despise the word. It took care of the unemployment issue, the parking space issue, the smoking issue, and it took care of James "Jimmy" and Barbara Easter's issue, Devin and Charlene. The truck, the sleep-starved Croat at the wheel of it, took care of everything. Jimmy Easter might just as well have taught his children how to blow smoke rings, or steal cigarettes. Jimmy Easter was off the hook. He would never go down in history, or case history, as a shitty father.

Whereas me, I still had a decent shot.

Nearly every day now I passed the man's house, that yard. The playhouse was gone, but there were still some ancient cigarette butts wedged between the sidewalk and the first flagstone of the walkway, and often as I passed I whispered, "Jimmy Easter, Jimmy Easter, Jimmy Easter," until the name conjured nothing, failed to spook. But then I would very nearly see the boy and the girl in their sweatshirts, climbing through the grimed window of the playhouse, and I would feel a jangled shiver, like shaves of ice in the blood, which was maybe just my nerves trying to shield me, to throw up some farce of hauntedness, of spirits lingering, to save me from the brute fact of their oblivion.

Nine

Late, I sprinted through drab, tidy streets toward Christine's. Her
brick two-family was an exact replica of every other house around
here, including mine. Much as I feared the advent of the me's,
architecture alone was against it. There weren't enough lofts or
factory floors. Kids needed big, decrepit spaces for their parties
and orgies and suicidal Sunday afternoons. The buildings in these
precincts had been designed for only one thing: to house, and
disguise, the fester of families.

When I reached Christine's I was sweating, heaving. I could
have used a nice vomit. I should join a gym, I thought. But then
I'd just vomit in it.

Christine's brother sat in a canvas chair in the driveway. Nick
had the build and the hair of a picture-book giant, a merry bi-
polar glint in his eye. He worked occasional construction jobs and
sometimes held down the day-care fort while Christine cruised
the borough in her minivan.

Nick nodded, waved. The pink plastic rifle in his lap had
leaked, wetted his tracksuit pants. Frantic children danced
around him, screamed, struck Nick with lengths of garden hose.
Nick raised his rifle, launched dark ropes of liquid at the more
brazen tykes.

"Gun me!" said one kid.

"I'm poopy man!" called another.

Bernie appeared to be absent from this frolic.

"Milo," said Nick. "How you doing?"

"Good," I said, ducked a late burst of crimson spray. "Just here for Bernie."

"No, I know," said Nick.

"Have you seen him?"

"What?" said Nick. "Yeah, sure. But first, I was just thinking. How would you like to make some money?"

Nick lowered his rifle, looked over at the boys still cowering from his fusillade.

"Go play with those wood scraps near the garage," he called.

"Sure, I'd love to make some money," I said. "Money is one of my favorite things to make. But I should really find Bernie right now."

"Yeah, no, go ahead, guy. Just that I got this deck job at the end of the week and my assistant crapped out on me. I need a helper."

"Deck job?"

"I build decks. Like off the back of a house?"

"Got it."

"Interested?"

"Ah, maybe," I said. "I'm pretty busy. Can I let you know? I'll let you know."

There was a whiff of the volatile about this man that always put me in modes of appeasement, of friendly deferral.

"Yeah," said Nick. "Let me know."

"I will, I promise. I'll let you know."

"Good. It's a deal."

"What's a deal?"

"You letting me know."

"Yes, that's a deal. Have you seen my kid?"

Nick tilted his head, a new shine in his eyes.

"Your kid? Is it one of these little homos?"

He swiveled in his chair, opened up once more on the boys where they crouched near the ruins of a doghouse.

"Soup's on, motherlovers!"

What he shot at them, I realized now, was some variant of Vitamin Drink. The children squealed and dove into the splintered wood.

"No, not one of these particular little homos," I said, jogged past Nick and climbed the side staircase.

The house was low-ceilinged and dark and as I crept through the kitchen I could almost have been some Hollywood SEAL with a pistol in my hand, an avuncular sergeant in my earbud. I could almost have been any one of the righteous manhunters I'd portrayed in cramped hallways since boyhood, but I was not, felt the dull sear of that notness now.

More howls broke through the roar of a television as I turned into a carpeted parlor, slunk past a flimsy rack of cut-glass bowls, china dolls, and other sad lady collectibles, toward the light of a dusty bay window.

I knew this room from past pickups and now I felt an odd flutter in my gut. Bernie could be facedown in the shag, choking on a cherry sucker from that quartz dish on Christine's coffee table. No longer the high-tech avenger, I'd end up a different character in the same Hollywood movie, the stunned father with his kid's limp corpse in his arms, the collateral damage cutaway.

But Bernie had not choked on a sucker. Bernie was not dead in the shag. Bernie was chewing another boy's penis. The boy screamed as my son gnawed denim. Hunched before the giant TV, where a prelapsarian New York Yankees highlight reel looped swank Jeterian feats, the boys, in their backlit shadow-play agon, jerked like Mrs. Cooley's beloved Balinese puppets.

"Daddy!" shouted Bernie, lifted his head from the drool-dark pants of his prey.

"Hey, little man," I said. "Ready to go home?"

Bernie hopped up, did his funny lope across the room.

"Say goodbye to Aiden," I said, recognized the other boy now, the rabbit-eyed only of another Christine regular, a single mom who sold cell phone plans from a storefront on Ditmars Avenue.

"Bye," said Bernie.

"Bye," called Aiden, perhaps distracted by the swell of martial melodies surging from the plasma. Blue Angels navy fighters streaked over old Yankee Stadium, the bond forged between two of the best-funded teams of their time.

I lifted Bernie into the crook of my arm, passed back through the kitchen, snatched our canvas supply bag, stepped out the door.

The children shivered in the grass, their hair and skin faintly iridescent. No longer the lawn chair hunter, Nick had taken a knee, a precarious pose for a man his size. He leaned on the rifle stock, the bright barrel wedged in his mouth. He bucked his head away, mimed the rifle's recoil in slow motion, let the weapon clatter to the asphalt.

"Just like that," he told the children.

"What are you doing?" I said.

"I'm telling the kids a story about my brother."

"Do you think it's appropriate?"

"What does that mean? Appropriate? Is that a fancy word for having no balls?"

"No, it just means—"

"I know what it means."

"Okay, Nick, I'm sorry if I—"

"Don't worry about it. You were not wrong to wonder. Why is he showing kids how to eat a bullet, right? But this is not what it looks like."

"It's not?"

"Not completely."

"Oh."

"And our deal still stands."

"Yes, it does," I said. "Come on, Bernie. See you kids later."

"Bye!"

Nick turned back to his rapt flock.

"See, my brother wanted to plaster the wall with his brains, but the round went through his cheek. Right here, see? Took out a wad of cheek meat, but he survived. After that he started going to this megachurch in Connecticut. We don't talk much."

I hoisted Bernie to my shoulders, carried him across the street.

"Daddy?"

"Yeah, Bern."

"Is Nick bad?"

"No, I don't think he's bad."

"Is he sad?"

"Maybe he's a little sad."

"Is he angry?"

"He might be a little angry."

"I bit Aiden's winky and mashed his face."

"Yeah, Bern, I saw. Why do you think you did that?"

"I wanted to."

"Why do you think you wanted to?"

"I didn't want him to have his train."

"Was it his train?"

"Yeah."

"Did he share it with you?"

"Yes."

"So, what was the problem?"

"He had it."

"Okay, Bern. Maybe you should have been happy he was sharing it with you, though. That was nice, wasn't it?"

"Yes."

"So, do you think it was right to bite and mash?"

"Yes."

"Why?"

"I wanted to."

"You baffle me, Bern."

"What's baffle? Like waffle?"

"It sounds a little like 'waffle,' doesn't it? You've got a good ear. But baffle means I don't know why you bit and mashed Aiden."

"I told you why."

"I know, you wanted to."

"Daddy?"

"Yes?"

"What's depressive?"

"Who called you depressive? Nick?"

"Nobody."

"Bernie, tell me. Who called you depressive? One of the older boys?"

These poor kids, they gleaned these terms at random, overheard them from afternoon TV, dinner chat. Or else the language of pathology was affixed to them by some shrink Mengele eager to stuff them with Ritalin and Zoloft.

"Who said you were depressive, Bernie?"

"Nobody, Daddy."

"Are you sure?"

"You're the depressive, Daddy. Mommy said. On the phone with Paul."

"Who's Paul?"

"Paul from work. He's an artist."

Paul did design for Maura's firm. Some animation websites also featured his cartoons. I'd met him in midtown once, when I picked up Maura for her birthday dinner. He seemed pleasant, if not a little bland, a tan, lanky guy who wore expensive vintage clothing. I'd kept waiting for Maura to tell me he was gay—she'd declared herself a devoted fag hag when we started dating, said it might even interfere with her quest for heterosexual companionship—but she'd never said anything about Paul's preference. I knew better than to ask.

"Right," I said. "Paul from work."

"Paul is going to make me a whole little movie of superheroes. On his computer. That's what Mommy said. Are you a pansy, Daddy?"

"Wait," I said. "Did Mommy say 'depressive,' or 'pansy'?"

"What's a pansy?"

"It's a flower, Bernie."

"I love flowers. I pick them for Mommy but she gets mad because other people need to enjoy them."

"That's right. Mommy's right."

"You're a nice pansy, Daddy."

"Thank you, Bernie."

"You're welcome."

•

Most nights after dinner Bernie and I retired to his room to play guys. We'd each grip one of his grotesquely proportioned action mutants, bash them together, growl.

"I will defeat you and meal you, Wolfsquid, Scourge of Decency," I might say.

But now Bernie appeared at the threshold of a new phase. The last time I had offered up my services, he shrugged.

"I just want to go to my room and unwind," he said.

Later I went in to tell him a story. He'd become critical of the saccharine bent of my bedtime sagas.

"Don't forget the evil," he said now.

I worked up some woods for him, some trolls, some berry-picking children. I put the evil in there. Finally a hippo ex machina rescued the children from the castle of the Lanky Animator.

Soon Bernie was asleep, or down, in the parlance of our suffering set.

We cooked pork chops from the corner butcher. Maura patted the meat with a Cajun rub. I made the salad, stirred in the vinaigrette. This was our time. The sacred hour of our sacred institution. I sipped some sour Malbec Maura had brought home from an office party and decided not to prod about Paul, instead told Maura about Nick's offer, if only for the chance to launch some jokes at the giant's expense, get my girl to cackle again.

"Maybe you should do it," said Maura.

"Are you serious?"

"Well, this Purdy thing can't take up all of your time. Seems like you're just waiting around for the next meeting."

"He's been out of town."

"Okay, so, maybe you can try doing the deck. You might enjoy the exercise."

"If I can handle it. Could kill me."

"If Nick can do it, you can do it. That guy's not exactly fit."

"Maybe I will," I said, and maybe meant it. A day in the sun, some hard-earned under-the-table cash, it sounded promising. I'd once been a painter, after all, a fellow who worked with his hands. Now I could be a carpenter, like Jesus. I felt flushed with the idea of Jesus, the Jewish craftsman Jesus, and also the shit wine.

"To decks," I said, raised my glass. "Decks are America. The hidden platform where the patriarchy is reasserted."

"What are you talking about?" said Maura, who knew what I was talking about, had dabbled with perhaps a bit more coherence in the same college theory I had, but probably wanted me to focus on how I salted the salad.

"I'm talking about our homeland, honey," I said, poured more wine, gulped it, flusher now, warm with that feeling of wanting a feeling that maybe had already fled. Where had the feeling gone? It wasn't in the wine. It wasn't in the pork chops Maura tonged from the broiler.

"America," I said, "that run-down demented old pimp. Can't keep his bitches in line. No juice. He's lost his diamond fangs, drinks Tango from a paper bag. A gummy coot in the pool hall. The wolves, those juveniles, they taunt him."

"Gummy coot?"

"Whatever," I said. "You get the point."

"Not really," says Maura. "It's retarded."

"Retarded ha-ha or retarded peculiar?"

"Wait. Be quiet."

We froze, listened for sounds from Bernie's room.

"I thought I heard him," said Maura. "Sometimes I'll be at work, in a meeting or something, and I'll think I hear him crying. It's weird. He's been sleeping through the night for a year but I still . . . Anyway, what were you saying? America is an alcoholic pimp?"

"You used to love my raps. My riffs. I thought that's why you married me."

Had she caught the edge of true panic beneath the joke panic? Did she know it was Horace's riff? You really had to hustle to recruit the right people to prop up your delusions, but the moment somebody broke ranks, or just broke for a protein shake, the whole deal teetered.

"I know it wasn't my soap opera looks," I said. "I thought you loved the way my mind worked. Its strange loops. My sense of humor."

"Shhh," said Maura. "Shut the fuck up."

We froze again, listened for moans, the beginnings of wails. It wasn't so onerous these days, but some moments still brought us back to Bernie's infant months, both of us on tiptoes, petrified we'd wake the baby, lose those seventeen minutes of email catch-up we believed our sacrifice had earned us. We were like the Frank family in their Dutch attic, but with email.

"Okay," said Maura, signaled the all clear. "So, what were we saying? Soap operas?"

"Yeah," I sulked. "Soap operas."

"Don't be such a queen," said Maura.

"Save that terminology for your gay lovers," I said.

"Excuse me?"

"I mean your lovers that are also gay."

"What?"

"You heard me."

"What's your problem?"

"I don't have a problem."

"Is there something you want to say to me?"

Why was I such a diseased fuck? It had to be society's fault. I loved people, all people, except for the ones with money and free time.

"No," I said.

"Are you sure?"

"I know you think I'm homophobic, but I'm not. You're the one who betrayed all your gay friends by having a baby."

"Most of my gay friends have babies now."

"You call them your gay friends. That's homophobic right there."

"You've really lost me," said Maura.

"I don't like animation. I like live action."

"Let me have a little time with that one."

"I don't care what people do behind closed doors, or open doors, or out in the street or in a coffee shop. I don't care what you do. Suck cock in Starbucks all day. Just don't be happy. And don't call me a depressive pansy behind my back."

Maura stared.

"I'm just kidding," I said.

Maura did not move.

"Really," I said. "Please, I don't know what I'm talking about."

"No, you don't," she said.

She looked beautiful there near the window in moonlight. I moved to her, tried to kiss her, let my hand fall to the strap of her dress, but she shoved me, gently, away.

"I'm sorry, Milo. I'm just . . . I'm just all touched out."

"Touched out?"

"I know you understand."

"Do I? Does Paul know that?"

"What?"

"You heard me."

"Don't be paranoid, Milo."

"Don't make me paranoid. Especially to avoid guilt."

"I don't know what you're talking about. Paul's really kind of an idiot actually."

"I'm an idiot, too!" I shouted. "Don't you fucking see it, Maura! I'm an idiot, too!"

Maura's eyes got beady. Bernie's wail, low at first, gathered up for the sonic cascade.

"Yes, Milo," whispered Maura. "I do see that now."

·

Bernie soon returned to sleep, but in that moment we probably both recalled the all-nighters of those first few years, Maura always the one to rise and slip into Bernie's room. Once in a while I'd pretend to be about to get up, even pull the sheets off my legs, but Maura would push me back down in disgust. She'd lost years of slumber. A point came where Bernie had suckled for too long to start a bottle, but I could have intervened, insisted I live my share of nightly hell. But I didn't. I liked the sleep. I still felt guilty about it, but I was not about to let the feeling devour me. I had learned long ago how to refine the raw guilt into a sweet, granulated resentment.

There was, for instance, the lullaby question. Maura sang the boy "Silent Night" almost every night. Operation Foreskin Rescue was one thing, but did she have to fill Bernie's brain with Christian death chants? Someday I thought I might go in there with an X-Acto blade, Jew-cut the little crumb right back into my tribe, my half-tribe.

T.C.B., Abraham-style.

Wonder if it's legal. Be good to do a little time.

It wasn't society's fault, really.

I dozed off worried I had truly unhooked myself from the apparatus of okay. Or maybe it was the Malbec.

I woke in silence. Light from the hallway fell on Maura and I watched her sleep, a lattice of saliva fluttering on her lips. I rose to fetch a glass of water, peeked into Bernie's room.

They were all lovely in sleep, but none so lovely as Bernie. Here in my humble outer-borough home a godlet took his rest, a miniature deity in need of protection until he was strong enough to fend for himself and, eventually, deliver humankind from fatal folly.

This not really working thing wasn't really working.

Ten

Purdy put off our meeting another few days. He'd flown out to Vail for an ideas festival, had gotten worked up over some of the ideas. He was holed up in a suite with a gorgeous renewable-energy guru. He would call when he got back, hoped I could forgive him.

"Of course," I said.

"You must have a lot going on back there anyway."

"Oh, yes, absolutely," I said.

"You should come out here, though. It's really something. I mean, these people, you read their books, their newsletters, see them on TV, but to hear them in person, chat with them. Very impressive. Do you realize that someday we will be heating our houses with trout?"

"Is that one of the ideas at the ideas festival?"

"It's just fantastic here."

I almost asked him why he didn't tell Melinda about it, including the part with the guru. Maybe it was blowback from the Jolly Roger days, but I'd always grown anxious when men confided their infidelity, surged with judgment, until my inner Nietzsche called me simp. Meanwhile, I was too scared to tell Purdy his delays had put the last of our savings in jeopardy. Never let them see you sweat, countless bastards tell us, just to see us sweat.

"I'm not really an ideas man, Purdy," I said. "I'm an action fella."

"Yeah, right," laughed Purdy. "Oh, I've got to go. The prime minister of Norway is throwing a pool party. We'll connect up next week."

"Sounds fine," I said. "I should be available."

I looked at my wrist as I said it, as though I kept a large calendar there.

•

I'd been back to Nearmont enough that I didn't have to plan for nostalgic reveries each time the bus passed my old high school (Go Vikings! Kill Catamounts!), or Nearmont Plaza, where once, behind Scissor Kicks, the local hair salon, I'd received the opening stages of a handjob from Sayuri Kuroki, before prowler lights stabbed us to the stucco.

Sayuri's family moved back to Japan soon after, but from then on, whenever I pictured my penis in her hard little hand, I always made sure to insert that gray pixelated dot over it, like they did in Japanese porn. Honor is important to every culture.

So shy and brilliant, my Sayuri, and nothing surpassed the way her black hair fell against the acid-washed jean jacket she'd adopted for life in New Jersey. While the bus pulled up to the plaza stop, I wondered where the years had led her. Maybe she was a successful businesswoman. Maybe she had a daughter who wrote cell phone novels. Maybe she was attending an ideas festival.

It was a short walk from the plaza to the house on Eisenhower, a yellow split-level with that forbidding bedroom turret my mother had built after my father died. I guess without the heroic measures there was money for turrets, for ramparts and moats, slits for boiling oil and archers from Milan, whatever a widow's castle required. The door was open and I stepped into the foyer, turned for a sinking step into the slightly sunken living room.

Claudia sat in her altitude tent, her body stringy and golden in her Mondrian print bikini. The tent took up a good deal of the room. Her girlfriend took up the rest. Francine was tiny but she spread herself out, her interests, her projects, calligraphy corner here, computer cranny there. Earlier, thwarted versions of this woman wove potholders. This epoch found her oscillating between soapstone carving and online pinochle while my mother toiled to meet her quota of surplus red blood cells. There was a seniors charity race a few days away, sexagenarian whippersnappers whose spirits deserved a good pulverizing.

Francine padded over, pecked me on the cheek.

"Beer?" she said.

"Sure."

But for a moment she didn't move. Together we watched Claudia breathe rather ostentatiously, palms up, eyes shut. The tent had cost my mother a bundle, a seventy-first-birthday gift to herself. I sensed the purchase had less to do with the milestone, more with the recent interment of Claudia's mother. I could picture Hilda at this very moment, a skull with orange fuzz on it, yapping at the Auschwitzers in the afterworld about the temple newsletter atrocity.

"My beloved son," said my mother.

"Your eyes are closed. How do you know?"

"I'm peeking. By the way, the answer to your question, whatever the question might be, is that I wish I could. Pretty good, right?"

"Pretty bad, Mom," I said.

"Pardon?"

"Pretty bad mom."

"Would you like to come inside the tent?"

"No."

"There's room."

"I don't think there is."

"No, maybe not. There was something in the instruction booklet about that, I think. You know, when you were born they put you in something like this. An incubator. Did you incubate sufficiently? I always wondered. I always worried. Are you incubated? Are you hungry? We have some leftover Chinese. There's a fantastic place that just opened on Spartakill Road."

"The sweet-and-sour soup!" said Francine, back in her computer cranny. "I creamed my friggin' Danskins!"

Francine's head poked out over the piles of throw pillows and external hard drives. Through a gap in them I could make out part of the monitor. Two Filipinas had at it with a strap-on. The words "Home Aide Ho's" flashed on the screen.

"Really great," says Claudia. "Right where the hobby shop used to be in Eastern Valley. Remember I used to take you there for your figurines? You were very particular. Very nervous they wouldn't have the Welsh Grenadiers."

"I don't really remember you taking me," I said. "I think Dad took me once. After that I walked."

"Memory is a tricky thing," said Claudia.

"Could I have that beer?"

"Jesus, Mary, and Joseph, I forgot your beer!" Francine fetched two from the kitchen. "They're from Costa Rica. I'm sure the Costa Ricans think it's piss, but I like the bottle. See that eagle on it?"

"Thanks, Francine."

"You're welcome, honey."

"So," said my mother, her eyes open, "to what do we owe this wonderful surprise?"

"What surprise? I called a few days ago and said I was coming out."

"The plot thickens."

"Mom," I said. "Why don't you come out of the tent? We can hug or something."

"I can't, baby. I really can't."

"She can't," said Francine. "She's in the middle. Her cells'll explode."

Claudia rose from her lotus position, an old bony flower.

"It's true we haven't been talking a lot lately," she said. "How's the boy?"

"Bernie's fine, Mom. Why don't you come to see him sometime? He misses you."

"He hardly knows me. How could he miss me?"

"That's why you should come by. Spend some time with your grandson."

"Please don't say that word. It's a cudgel. Come sit near the tent."

I squatted on the fringed rug near the zippered door. Claudia frogged her fingers on the tent's translucent wall.

"You're still my little boy, you know. How's the wifey?"

"Maura's okay, Mom. You know she really admires you."

"Why, because she's too frightened to cross over? Still thinks she needs a man in her life?"

"Something like that."

"She's okay. For a straight girl. She's pretty tough. You guys will be all right."

"Mom, I don't know how to say this."

"How much?"

"I've never asked for—"

"How much? If I win the race next week it's five hundred dollars."

"I thought it was a charity race."

"It is. We're raising money for osteoporosis. But there's always side action."

"Well, we're really behind. I'm not sure five hundred is what—"

"Say a number."

"Excuse me?"

"Say a number."

"Ten thousand."

"Ten thousand."

"You could do that for us?" I said.

"Absolutely not. Francine and I are hitting a rough patch. The settlement from her lye burn is being delayed. Real estate is hell. My savings have been chewed up."

"A rough patch," I said. "Okay. I understand."

"Oh, do you, Milo? You're so selfish. You don't see the bigger picture."

"What's the bigger picture?"

"You're still here looking for handouts. Who's going to take care of me?"

"I'm on my knees here, Mom. Not for me, for my family. For my wife. For a beautiful grandson you have totally ignored."

"He's kind of a brat. I'll be in his life when he gets a little impulse control."

"He's not even four."

"I have needs. I'm tired of this child-worshipping culture. You're just a slave to it, Milo."

"I'm only trying to be a decent dad."

"Don't waste your time. It's not in your genes. Besides, try making some money. That might be a good dad move. For heaven's sake, the system's rigged for white men and you still can't tap in."

"You're right, Mom. What can I say? But still, it would mean a lot to me if you made a little more of an effort with Bernie."

"Bernie schmernie. This is my decade."

"Okay, you wrinkled old spidercunt, have it your way."

Francine sucked in her breath.

"Holy macadamias," she said.

Claudia regarded me somewhat clinically.

"Spidercunt?"

I shrugged.

"Look, honey," she said. "I think you better go. I need to stay calm. I'll call you after I race on Sunday."

"Mom, I'm sorry. I just—"

"It's okay, Milo. I just need a little time now."

"We'll call, cutie," said Francine, hugged me.

"Okay, I'll see you guys later," I said, edged to the door. "And I'm sorry, Mom. About . . . about the thing. What I just said."

"Hell, honey," says Claudia. "I murdered your father when you needed him most. I can take a few impotent barbs from my only son."

"That's nice to hear."

I shut the heavy oak door and walked back down the gravel drive toward the plaza. I glanced back once, spotted Francine through the big bay window, in her underwear, climbing into the tent.

Eleven

The next morning I sipped coffee on my stoop, waited for Nick to pick me up. Women in tight slacks charged past to the subway, supple organic forms supplemented with technological grafts—earphones, telephones, wraparound shades. I watched them and recalled those cyborg liberation essays from the postmodern feminism class I took in college. I'd run home after every lecture, jerk off on my futon in a fever dream of blinking vaginas.

Now an old man with a ducktail haircut and rolled T-shirt sleeves sauntered by, climbed into his wine-dark beater. A retired mechanic, I figured, but not so old on second look, forty-five, forty-seven, tops. His 1950s drag-strip hood shtick had to be retro from the jump, a mid-70s reaction formation, some cold Fonzian rhapsody. The man's hands looked ruined, though, rheumatoid, nicked and pinched by gruesome machinery. I'd done many odd jobs in my life, but hardly any heavy lifting. I stared at my own hands, soft, expressive things, gifted, even, like specially bred, lovingly shaved gerbils.

A corroded pickup slid to the sidewalk. Nick leaned out the window.

"Get in, buddy," said Nick. "Big day ahead of us. You eat?"

"Some cereal."

"Cereal? Never touch the stuff. Too many carbs."

I got in the truck and Nick pulled off the curb, steered with his belly and his forearms, his hands tasked with shoveling up a

bacon-and-feta omelet from a foil container. We turned the corner
and bounced, shockshot, down the boulevard. The cab smelled
of breakfast and weed, and I recalled Christine once letting it
slip—perhaps taking me for a potential customer—that Nick
sold eighths and quarters of a few decent varieties. It was not
clear whether the drugs or the decks were the sideline, but Nick,
I was now to learn, had a grander dream, which he announced
before we reached the next traffic light. He wanted to break into
television. He watched a lot of reality shows, he informed me,
especially the ones about breaking into television. He believed
he had a handle on the business, the lingo. All he needed was a
leg up. He already had the idea: his extravaganza would revolve
around the last meals of condemned prisoners.

"Last meals?" I said.

"That's right," said Nick, slid another ketchup packet from
the dash, squeezed it over his hash browns. "You know how they
often report a con's last meal. There are even websites about it.
People are obsessed. And if you followed this stuff, you'd know
that these guys on death row always order fast-food crap. You
ever look into this? It's always the burgers, the fried chicken. The
fried shrimp. Or fried shrimp product. You know what I'm talking about, Milo?"

"I guess."

"You guess? I bet you know exactly what I'm talking about.
Some guy is a few hours away from the Reaper's speedball and he
chows down on a slab of imitation crabmeat in a hot dog bun.
And fucks like you, no offense, get all sad and superior about
it. These poor slobs could order anything they want, you think,
but they are just low-rent and don't know any better. Because
that's the story they've told us."

"The story?"

"That's the official story: a condemned prisoner's last meal can
be anything he wants. It's the American way, right? Like that

guy, the slow one that Clinton killed to show his *cojones*, that boy didn't finish his burger, his hoagie, whatever the fuck it was, said he'd eat the rest later. *Later*. That broke you up, didn't it?"

"Excuse me?"

"I think it was a veal parm."

I did recall that poor kid, the national cruelty so crystallized in that moment.

"Sure, I remember."

"Anyway, the point is, why fast food? Why the crap? Why not grass-fed Angus or Kobe beef, an '86 Mouton Rothschild? Don't look at me like that. I watch the fucking food shows."

"So, is this a food show?"

"Bear with me, buddy. Bear with me and answer this question. Why do these death row losers always order nuggets and dipping sauce and biggie fries for their last meal? Is it A, they are ghetto or barrio or trailer-park trash who don't know any better, who could never imagine a taste sensation transcending that of a Hot Pocket and an orange Fanta, or, B, something else entirely?"

The truck dipped into a pothole, shot near the curb where an old woman wearing an "I'm with Stupid" T-shirt dawdled in the crosswalk. This lady was about to be with nobody ever again, but Nick righted the wheel with one of his sloping breasts, his fork work undisturbed.

"I'm going to go with answer B," I said.

"Well, you're not dumb," said Nick. "But then again, you've had the advantages. You've got some innate intelligence, passed down from people who probably kicked some serious ass to put you in a position to even function on this planet. Because you don't seem, how can I put this, overly equipped. You seem pretty soft. I just mean that as an observation. Of course, we'll see what we see at the site today."

Advantages? What about Purdy? Or Sarah Molloy and the rest of them? Nick may have known that stuffed-crust pizza delivered in twenty minutes or gratis wasn't haute cuisine, but he didn't know a damn thing about advantages, couldn't comprehend the true machinations of money and power, the nuanced, friction-free nanotechnics of privilege that prevent an earnest, talented boy from doing wonderful stuff with oils. But, of course, I couldn't argue about the softness. For a time I wore only heavy, steel-toed boots because I figured if apocalyptic war broke out, sturdy foot-wear would be a must. Then it dawned on me that the better the boots, the more quickly I would be killed for them. My only shot at survival would be shoeless abjection.

"Thanks," I said now.

"I was complimenting your forebears," said Nick. "Anyway, you went with B. B stood for, if I'm not mistaken, and I'm not, something else entirely. Any guesses?"

"I don't know," I said. "They have no choice in the matter?"

"Damn!" said Nick, accordioned his foil plate with his palms, veered again, nearly halved a spry South Asian mail carrier in a pith helmet. "You are impressing the hell out of me. Of course that's the reason. They have no choice. Prisoners are allowed to order their last meal only from restaurants within a three-mile radius of the prison. What kinds of joints do you think surround death houses? Ever been to Texas, those prison towns? Forget the poor dinguses waiting for the strap and needle. Nobody's doing good. No Michelin stars in those counties. Sad but true, my friend. But don't get me wrong. I'm all for capital punish-ment. I'm a huge death penalty guy. I like everything about it. And don't tell me how it's more expensive to the taxpayer than life sentences. Because if you ask me, we *should* pony up a little more. We *should* feel the cost of our ritual, *revel* in it. It was prob-ably a drain on the Aztec economy to capture and drug all those people and carve out their living hearts, but are you going to tell me it wasn't worth it? Yes, sir, the death penalty is where it's at. Is there a chance innocent people die? I should fucking hope so!

Innocent people die constantly in this world. Why should things be better for those scumbags in lockdown?"

"But you said they were innocent."

"Innocent? Please. No thanks, buddy. Keep that knee-jerk liberal crap on your side of the aisle. I'm not ashamed of the sacrifices a balls-out civilization must make to survive. But we're way off the food-and-death track. This show is a winner. You won't regret your involvement."

"My involvement?"

"Well, my sister says your wife is in marketing, and this idea, when it hits the tube, will need some all-pro marketing. And you seem like the kind of college boy who may be a broke screw-up but is ultimately part of the vast conspiracy of movers and shakers who shake and move our society. Jewish, right?"

"Here we go," I said.

"Okay, scratch that. All I'm saying is I need to make the right connections to make this thing happen."

"Make what happen?"

"You repeat this to anybody, I will make a deck, a beautiful Mission-style deck, out of your bones. Weatherproof that shit, too."

"Of course."

"Dead Man Dining."

"Excuse me?"

"Working title."

"I'm lost."

"Be found. The world's top chefs prepare exquisite last meals for condemned prisoners. Stuffed quail for the auntie slasher. Baked Alaska for the office party Uzi sprayer. Chicken à la Berkowitz. Death and food. The only things we can be certain of, right? What's it like to be sitting next to a future billionaire?"

I wondered then if Nick's stomach could also brake the truck. Because in that moment I wanted very much to climb out, hike home, or maybe just stand on the Boulevard of Death, huff exhaust.

"We better get started on that deck, no?" I said.

"Deck?" said Nick. "Sure, but what about my idea? Do you know some people? From the city? People I could talk to? Do a deal memo with? I read about deal memos. I've got one of those books for dummies. That tells you about the Hollywood business for dummies. A deal memo is before you actually sign the contract, right? So everybody's protected? I'm not some jackass they can pat on the head, send on his way, and then rip off."

"I don't know deal memo," I said.

"Of course you do."

"No," I said. "I'm just a regular guy. I don't know all these people you think I know."

"No, I guess you don't," says Nick. "I'm sure you don't. I'm sure none of your college buddies are at all involved with the media."

"Really, I wish I could help."

"Really, I bet you do."

Nick laid his hands on the wheel, perhaps for the first time the entire trip, drove us into a giant parking lot. We looped around some superstores to a loading bay, parked near a pallet piled high with lumber.

Nick nodded over to the pallet.

"Load that shit up, Mr. Regular-Guy-No-Connections-Working-Stiff."

I studied the pallet, the area around the pallet.

"Is there a hand truck or something?"

"A hand truck? What's that? For jerking off? For jerking off trucks? Load the wood, Joseph Fucking Sixpack."

I hopped out of the cab, barked my shin on the runner. I limped over to the woodpile, looked back at Nick, shrugged, yanked the lightest-looking beam to my shoulder. My knees buckled. I staggered to the truck bed. Nick sat bent over the steering wheel, heaving. For a moment I thought it might be a coronary. Then I saw him wipe the tears from his eyes, roll down the window.

"Hurry up, you prick!" he said, his voice breaking.

I rushed back to the pallet. It took me an hour to load the truck. My hands peeled and bled. My shoulders burned, my legs quivered, my vision grew blurry. I puked on Nick's grille.

It was time to start work.

•

"I'm so sorry," said Maura.

She rubbed ointment into my neck, some over-the-counter heat cream, and I recalled how much I'd loved this very scenario as a child, that commercial about an aching jackhammer operator and his masseuse of a spouse. I'd always figured the secret to life had something to do with brutal vibratory stress and a wife handy with balms. This crap, however, did nothing but crank up my nausea.

"It's okay," I said, kneaded my hands together, my wounded gerbils. "I guess I'm not cut out for this kind of work."

"What kind of work?"

"The physical kind. You know, the kind that all humans once had to be capable of."

"I believe in you. You will be a mighty deck builder yet. Just pray to the spirit of the spirit level."

"That's good," I said. "But how can you believe in me? You don't believe in God, but you believe in me?"

"I had certain expectations with God. Come on, let's go to bed."

She laid her hand on my shoulder, slid it down toward my crotch.

"I thought you were touched out," I said.

"Maybe you could touch me back in."

"You mean an appointment? A real appointment?"

"Yes."

The fluttery ear kisses, the sweet pull and bend of Maura as I tugged on the brass hoop of her belt buckle, the downslide of her jeans, the up-peel of her sweater, the sweet chalky stubble under her arms, these are the things I wanted to remember when memory was all I had left, besides catheters and hospital lasagna, awkward visits from stunned progeny. There was no God and being was just a molecular accident, but I still hoped my crawl through the illusory tunnel of retina-annihilating light would end with my face buried in some post-life facsimile of Maura's ass.

Our lives hinge on these moments of quiet tenderness. We stand or fall on them. I passed out on mine. Even as I slipped off my sock I dropped into soft buzzy sleep. A deck builder's slumber. Maybe Maura kept the appointment with herself.

I woke up with a heart attack. It was definitely a heart attack. Death was definitely a battering ram. My fortress doors creaked with each strike. I was really dying now. Death was a punch in the chest. Death was also, strangely enough, an odd slurping sound, a rustling of sheets. There was no tunnel, no annihilating light. No ass, even. Maybe it was not a heart attack. Maybe, in fact, it was Bernie, lying between us in bed, nursing, firing mule kicks into my sternum with each suck.

Kid had rhythm.

"Baby," I whispered. "What the hell are you doing? You weaned him. He's weaned."

"I know he's weaned."

"What are you doing?"

"We're snuggling."

"He's sucking."

"No, he's not."

"I'm not," said Bernie.

"Maura, come on, stop it."

"It's okay. It's just a little regression. It's normal. I read about it. I don't have any milk anyway."

"That makes it worse."

"Go back to sleep, Milo."

"Yeah, Daddy, go back to sleep."

I rolled to the edge of the bed, listened to the soft, wet noises behind me.

My phone throbbed on the nightstand. Purdy's name glowed in the sea green display.

Twelve

An hour later I stood in a bright, enormous candy shop on the East Side. It was late and the clerks seemed eager to close. Purdy shuffled down rows of bins, sampled the designer licorice and mocha clusters, scooped all manner of lacy goo into baggies. He was unshaven, his linen shirt soiled, limp. The look rather suited his ravening.

"Try the caramel turtles," said Purdy.

"That's okay."

"Really. Try them. They melt in your mind. Do you like that? That's funny"

"Purdy."

"Ever been to this place? It's amazing, right? I come here every few months. Whenever I'm just itching to score some blow, which I know would be a bad thing, and really piss off Melinda, and fuck me up for like three or four days because, let's face it, I'm not a young man anymore, even though I look like one, I come here instead. You've been here, right? This place is famous."

Purdy tacked down another aisle, tossed handfuls of chocolate-dipped filberts in his sack.

"I've seen it before," I said. "From the outside it looks like that giant makeup store in SoHo. They are both like these overlit oases of—"

"Sonofabitch."

Purdy stood before one of the last bins with a queasy look.

"It's that marzipanny shit. I don't like it."

"Skip it," I said.

"My flow is broken. I won't get it back. Let's go to the register."

We walked back up the gleaming aisle. Purdy's mania seemed to subside, the dope scorer's calm after the dope has been scored. He clamped his hand on the back of my head.

"What's that you were saying about oases? I love it when you rip into those eighties pomo raps."

"Oh, it was nothing."

"No, really, I enjoy them. They bring me back. I remember, I couldn't sleep, I'd just track you down, feed you some bong hits, and you were good to go. We kept it hyperreal, didn't we?"

"Don't forget Charles Goldfarb," I said. "That guy could talk your ear off."

"Pretty dry. All theory. No poetry."

"Billy Raskov was the true king of bullshit, though," I said.

"Billy Raskov! I just saw Billy Raskov!"

"Yeah? How's his Parkinson's?"

"Huh? No, really, he was just in town. He had a gallery show. I'm helping him make his movie. Shit, we should all get together, Milo. I should call him now."

"It's two in the morning."

"Bet the fucker's up. He's not a sleeper. He's like me. You're a sleeper, Milo. That's the truth about you."

"Lots of people sleep," I said.

"It's okay," said Purdy. "The main thing is you got out of bed. You came."

We reached the counter and Purdy dumped the candy on it, tossed a credit card onto the pile.

"So," said Purdy. "Should we talk?"

We walked the night city. Purdy gorged on his sweets. I outlined some ideas about his give, careful not to corner him on numbers. We needed a new screening auditorium, maybe a digital art center. These could be significant naming opportunities for Purdy. We wanted to get global, create programs in Europe and Asia and the Middle East, establish alliances with other mediocre universities around the world.

"Sure," said Purdy, pinched a mass grave's worth of gummy frogs into his mouth. "We can do that."

"Which?" I said, waited for him to finish chewing.

"I don't know. All of it?"

"All of it? No disrespect, but—"

"You don't even know, man," said Purdy. He sounded a little sugarshocked. "My pockets run deep. Even these days."

He turned out a pocket and a few loose red hots popped to the pavement.

"Did I pay for those?"

"I think so," I said.

I had to take him at his word about the give, at least for now.

"This is great news," I said. "This is fantastic. We can go into greater detail later but it sounds like what you're saying is—"

"Shit, Milo, don't give me the boilerplate. Let's be people. I didn't hear you say anything about painting. Figured that'd be your interest. Need new studios or something? How about a huge prize? Don't be bashful. You want a sour worm?"

"No, I'm cool."

A police cruiser slowed beside us as we made our way down Madison and I wondered what the cops made of us, if they could see how much fucking candy Purdy was eating, if there were any laws about that. The cop peeled away and Purdy coughed. Dark gobs sprayed out of his mouth.

"Sorry."

"Won't that stuff keep you up?" I said.

"I can't sleep."

"Right."

We'd been walking in endless rectangles and now we were

near the candy store again. The lights were out, the security gate down. We leaned up against the wall of a bank and I could feel the cool stone on my back, the billions of dollars thrumming through wires beneath and behind me, or on the night waves above. I wasn't quite sure how they traveled. Or how much they got out anymore.

Now a town car pulled up to the curb. The driver had one scrawny arm out the window. Something about his frizzy hair and enormous eyeglasses seemed familiar.

Purdy pushed off the bank wall.

"Hi, Michael," he said, turned to me. "Can I drop you anywhere?"

"I don't think so, no."

"Please, Milo," said Purdy. "Our meeting isn't over."

"Okay."

I slid in after him. We sailed down the avenue.

"Michael," said Purdy. "Do you want some chocolate or licorice? I know you don't approve of the gummy stuff."

The frizzy head shook in front.

"Your loss. So let's head down to the Fifty-ninth Street Bridge, take this man home."

"Good idea," said Michael.

"Really," I said, "you don't have to."

"I know," said Purdy. "But I want to tell you something."

"What's that?"

"I want to tell you a story."

"I don't like stories," I said.

"Everybody likes stories. It's part of being human. We tell each other stories."

"Then I guess I'm not human. Maybe I'm descended from ancient astronauts."

"Please, no ancient astronauts. No crop circles. Let's leave Maurice out of this."

"Maurice Gunderson?"

"He's a prophet, haven't you heard? A pied piper for the psychonautic Mayan rapture set."

"I heard him talk about this once. I didn't understand it."

"Forget Maurice. You were telling me why you don't like stories."

"They take so long," I said. "Most of them are a waste of time. I like jokes. Can you tell me your story in joke form?"

Purdy grinned.

"What is it?" I said.

"Nothing. You just reminded me of the way you were back in school. It's been a while."

"We had dinner last month."

"It's been a while."

Purdy tossed down some jellybeans, stared out the window where the towers on York shot past. This had always been my favorite part of driving over the Queensboro Bridge at night, catching sight of the lives in those lighted boxes, the chandeliers and paintings (always the same art-boom disaster in a shit brown study), the custom shelving, the enormous video screens, the well-off dozing on their leather thrones.

"Well, what's your fucking story then?" I said.

"So aggressive. I'm trying to put it in joke form here. Give me a second."

"How about just an elevator pitch?"

"Elevator pitch. Nice. Very 1989."

"What do you call them now?" I said.

"Stories. It's all about stories, man. Stories are money. Money is a story. I actually once hired a Ghanaian griot for our Friday meetings. It was great."

"Fine," I said. "Tell me the story."

"You don't like stories. Let's stay with the pitch."

"Wonderful."

"Good. Here we go. A rich boy goes to college. He makes a lot of friends. They all think they are special and that they suffer in distinct ways, but they are all hurtling down the same world-historical funnel. They will attempt to professionalize their passions, or else just get jobs. Some will do better than others. Some won't have to do better because of their trust funds. Despite what are often radically different fashion aesthetics, not to mention politics, they are all fundamentally the same."

"Elevator's nearing the lobby, pal."

"I do this for a living," said Purdy. "I know when the lobby comes."

"Sorry."

"They are all the same except for one girl, or woman, though, really, at this point, girl. Her name is Nathalie. Nathalie Charboneau. Scholarship kid. They meet in the library, the rich boy and the scholarship girl. In the smoking lounge of the library. That dates this, doesn't it? Anyway, they meet. They talk. They smoke. They keep talking. She's reading Schopenhauer. She tells the boy about Schopenhauer. He explicates some economic models he's been studying. They don't really converse so much as listen to each other. They like listening to each other. They agree to meet for coffee. She tells him a bit more about herself. She's from the area, a few towns away. It's a crappy town, the kind of town the town the college is in would be if there were no college in it. She lives in a crappy apartment above a crappy pharmacy with her mother and sister. Her bitter mother. Her junkie sister. But not quite those things."

"They fall in love," I said. "I think I remember her."

"You don't remember her."

"I think I do. I think I remember her, or saw her once."

"Trust me, you don't remember. You never saw her because I—I mean, the boy, not me, the boy—"

"Whoa, there, storyteller!"

"Fuck this," said Purdy, jerked back in his seat. "I thought you could do this for me. Help me."

"I'm sorry," I said. "Really. Please. Finish."

Purdy stared wordless out the window. The river glittered.

"Melinda's pregnant," he said.

"Congratulations."

"Thanks," said Purdy.

"Aren't you happy?"

"Yes."

"The drugs worked. You didn't have to go to Mars."

"That's true."

"You're going to love fatherhood."

"I don't need the line," said Purdy.

"Sorry."

"Let me finish my story."

"Your pitch."

"Yes," said Purdy. "My pitch."

It took a while. Maybe it had been designed for a very slow elevator. Or maybe it was really a story, no joke.

The rich boy, who of course became Purdy as the telling continued, fell in love with the scholarship girl. They had no secrets from each other, but Purdy kept her a secret from everyone else, from his country club set and his jet-set club and even from the faux-bohos he visited to cure his insomnia. The clubs and sets would never accept her, especially in lieu of one of their own. The arty types would, but in a manner that would be despicable, and he also might run the risk of losing her to somebody, like the ridiculous but faintly charismatic Maurice, or, more precisely, something, such as Billy Raskov's tremulous hunt for authenticity. Even Constance's revolutionary socialist pigtails seemed a threat.

"Shit," I said. "You were even more mysterious than I could have guessed."

"It wasn't a game," said Purdy. "I really cared about her. But I was too callow to handle it. She didn't want anything to do with my friends, though, so it was easy to just disappear together. We spent some time with her family. Her mom was sweet. Her sister was a little whacked. Of course, it ended after a few months. I didn't see it then, but the time limit was built into it. I'm not sure if that makes sense."

"I think it does."

"Whatever. She dumped me. Sent me packing. Did it wonderfully."

"What do you mean?"

"It was no-fault. She was sending me back to my kind. It felt like science fiction. You must return to your planet. Please tell them of us, we who live in crappy towns and struggle to get by."

"I'm on that planet right now."

"But you're not quite a native, are you?"

"But she was on scholarship. She was going to get out. Better herself, right?"

Suddenly I wanted to see this girl, this woman, Nathalie, place her somewhere I had been, the House of Drinking and Smoking, one of those theory seminars, the refectory, but I couldn't find her anywhere. How was that possible? How could you evade all overlap? I guess that was one of Purdy's gifts.

"I didn't know it then but she was planning to drop out," said Purdy. "Her sister was sick. Nathalie was going to have to take care of her, work. Her philosophical investigations would have to wait."

"Sad."

"You say that with such haunting conviction. So she sends me back to my galaxy. None of you ever know about any of this, but it eats me up for long time. I feel as though I've failed at something crucial. And I miss the hell out of her, at least for a while. But that fades, of course."

"It does, doesn't it," I said. I was ready to nudge this conversation back to vague and more comforting terrain, the creeks and dales and low rolling slopes of universal disappointment. Something about this story, its specificity, bothered me, more so now that I seemed part of it, part of the future of it, or why else would I be hearing this?

"Time goes by," said Purdy.

"Having no alternative."

"Don't be cute. Time goes by. Nathalie recedes in my mind."

"What about you in Nathalie's mind?"

"How the fuck would I know? Just listen, Milo."

"Okay."

" 'Recede' is a weird word. This isn't so easy. So linear. But I do, on some level, just ball up the memory of my time with her, throw it on the sentimental-education heap. Then, a few years ago, I got a letter. It was sent to the company, before I sold it. She'd read something about me in one of those new-media magazines. Of course, the article she mentioned was already years old. I was a business hero in that issue. If she'd read the takedown they wrote later, maybe she wouldn't have contacted me."

"That piece was bullshit."

"No, it wasn't, Milo. But thank you. Still, it doesn't matter. Anyway, the letter wasn't very long. Chatty, even nostalgic for a while. Then she caught me up. She was living somewhere upstate. Working in what sounded like a sweatshop. Taking classes somewhere inane. Still reading Schopenhauer. I remember she used to say she read Schopenhauer because he hated women so much. She said it was instructive. But the letter. There's a kicker at the end of the letter. She has a sixteen-year-old son. Do I need to elaborate?"

It took me a few seconds but he did not need to elaborate.

"But how could you be—"

"Trust me, I submitted the kid to tests."

"What was it like when you met him?"

"Who?"

"Your son."

"I never met him. Nathalie wouldn't let me. Didn't tell the kid anything, either."

"That's ridiculous."

"It's fair enough."

"No, it's not. Nathalie should have told you."

"It was her call. A dumb call, given my resources, but hers to make. Anyway, I started sending them money. Set them up. Lee handled it all for me. Lee Moss. Lee's the only one who knew about this. Except for Michael here, of course. Lee was my father's lawyer, a mensch. But he's been very sick. Cancer. Pancreatic."

"That's one of the worst. A killer."

"Yes, the ones that kill you are definitely the worst. Anyway, Lee's still doing a bit of work around the office. Putting things in order. He noticed that the last few checks were never cashed. He tried to contact Nathalie. When he couldn't find her, he called around up there, found out . . . well . . . found out about Nathalie."

"Found out what?"

"That she was . . . it's hard. It's really weird how hard it is."

Purdy pinkied away a tear. There was something actorly in the gesture, but at least it seemed improvised.

"She died, Milo."

"Died?"

"Car crash."

"Oh . . . I'm sorry."

"Yes. Well. Thanks. Or . . ."

"Melinda doesn't know?"

"No."

"About any of it?"

"I just never saw a reason to tell her. Maybe I could have told her before. But I didn't. Now it's too late. She's kind of into the whole trust thing."

"So, you want to keep a lid on your history."

"Isn't that what we all want?"

"What about the boy?"

"Don?"

"Don?"

"I didn't name him. It's Don. Don Charboneau. Well, this is the really fucked-up part."

"Oh, there's a fucked-up part?"

"Don's been in touch. Don is just back from Iraq. Can you believe that? He's only twenty-one. And now he's got titanium legs."

"What?"

"You heard me."

"Jesus."

"Usual roadside shit. And both of them."

"Man, that's bad. But there's that guy, that runner—"

"This kid's not there yet. Moves around like a drunk cross-country skier, according to Lee. It's pretty sad. I mean, I feel for him, I really do."

"He's your son."

"Right. He's my son. We think so."

"I thought you did tests."

"Science isn't everything."

"How did he find out about you?"

"We wondered what had happened to him, but he'd sort of dropped out of Nathalie's life for a time. I think she was mad at him for enlisting. Then she dies and he comes back. I guess he went through Nathalie's stuff, figured some things out. He started sending itemized bills for his expenses to Lee. Even showed up at his office once."

"Really?"

"Yeah, pretty aggro, right? Then he sends me a letter with a return address in Jackson Heights. Says he looks forward to the healing."

"Jackson Heights. That's near me."

"I know."

The car was turning onto my block.

"How did you know where I lived?" I said to Michael, the driver.

"What," said Michael, nodded at the navigation screen on his dashboard. "You think you're living off the grid? You have a listed phone number."

There was something in the tweaked amusement of his voice I recognized. It made me think of late nights over a CD jewel case, razor blades, long-winded denunciations of world banking cabals.

"Michael Florida," I said. We had always referred to him by his full name. I never knew how it started but the nature of the name and the nature of the man made it seem correct.

"Long time, brother."

Michael Florida's eyes shone in the rearview mirror. Even in the dark of the car I could make out his face now, the pocked cheeks, the pointy chin.

"How have you . . ." I said. "How did you—"

"Figured I was dead by now?"

"Or working in a halfway house in Arizona."

"Nice." Michael Florida laughed. "But it was Missouri."

The car slid up to my building. I looked up and saw the front room lit. The lamp near the sofa threw light on the ceiling cracks.

"We'll have to postpone the reunion," said Purdy.

"Seems like my life is one big reunion these days."

"I'm sure it seems that way," said Purdy. "Me, when I make a friend, I try to keep him."

"Point taken."

"Don't take it too hard, Milo. You're a good man."

"You think so?"

"I'm betting on it. Michael?"

Michael Florida twisted around and slid a large envelope between the bucket seats. Purdy handed it to me.

"I could have sent you an email and wired some money, but this is more fun, no? Fun's hard to find. You have to make your own. Look this material over."

"I will," I said.

"Goodnight, Milo."

"Goodnight, Purdy. Michael."

I ducked out of the car. The sofa lamp went dark.

Thirteen

The next morning I found a note from Maura in the kitchen. She'd written it in the margins of an unpaid cable bill, slipped it beneath a kiwi. I'd always loved Maura's handwriting, its swoops and swells, its queer collapses. She wrote like somebody half trapped by her bubbly grade school script, still trying to un-girl it:

> *Milo—Working late tonight. Please pick up Bernie at*
> *H. Salamander. He can have the other cupcake in the fridge, but*
> *only after he eats his dinner. He can have one show before his*
> *bath and two books after. Call if there's a problem. Please don't*
> *have a problem.*

The absence of a sign-off did not seem strange. Once she might have written one of our pet names, along with a coded reference to some salacious act. But those names, like most of the acts, had vanished. Bernie had begun to suss them out anyway, and it could be rather unnerving to be addressed by your son as "Smoof" or "Turbs" or "Provost Cavelick," to hear the words wedged so unevenly in his mouth, the way they must have been in ours. That the pet names harkened back to lost years of sustained laughter and lovemaking made me somewhat grateful for Bernie's interventions. Besides, I knew who wrote the note.

I made some coffee and took the envelope Purdy had given

me to the stoop. The envelope was thick, and the first thing that slid out was a packet of cash. I shoved it back in and tugged out some stapled papers, printouts of email exchanges between Purdy and Don Charboneau. Most were terse and cautious hellos, information about whereabouts, fund transfers, but a few let loose, went "aggro," to use Purdy's word, achieved a register that Purdy maybe even secretly admired. The longest, and latest:

From: buckcharb@earthweb.net
To: Purdy.Stuart@GroupusculeMedia.com
Hi Dad. Just moved down to the city to be closer to you, my dad. I'm in Jackson Heights. Ever heard of it? Some good curry around here. Lots of dotheads, too, though Mom would have killed me if she heard me say that. Weren't so many dotheads in the service, but there were a few. Cool guys. For dotheads. Most of my unit was just niggers, black niggers and brown niggers and white niggers and Christ niggers. So, now that my mom is dead and my aunt is dead and even the only close friend I had in the Army is dead, and I have nobody in the world but you (and my girl, Sasha), I am really looking forward to us hooking up and doing father/son things, like going to baseball games, and movies, and you can teach me about sex and how to tie my shoelaces and wipe myself or maybe you can just send me more of that money. Yeah, do that. Don't they call it hush money? That's a funny phrase. Where's Lee, your Hebrew friend? Can you get him to send more hush money? Or maybe you can do it yourself. I know how much you want to see me. Come out and we'll eat some dothead food or there's also really good Salvadoran. I knew somebody from San Salvador in my unit. Another light-wheel mechanic. The close friend I mentioned before. Her name was Vasquez. Fucking Vasquez. Got an RPG right in the teeth. Can

you picture that? Probably not. Yeah, so, that was what
happened to Vasquez. She was right ahead of us and I saw
her head explode off her neck, about three seconds before
our Humvee blew. I bet you really care. There was a lot
of brain and bone in the road, and pieces of a paperback
book by Roque Dalton. Ever read Roque Dalton? I
actually have. I'm the one who told Vasquez about him.
See, I'm not quite the guy you'd think would be the guy
who wrote most of this email. I'm kind of a mystery.
That's what Sasha says. But then again, she's not always
the sharpest card in the deck, if that's the saying for it.
I'll take that money now. Love, your loving son, Don

Along with the money and the emails were directions to Don's
apartment. My mission, so to speak, was described in a brief note
from Purdy. He wanted me to deliver the money to Don, but more
important, get some kind of read on him, figure out whether he
seemed to have a master plan or was just, as Purdy put it, a "hurt,
confused kid with no legs (probably the case)." The "deal," Purdy
wrote, was this: Purdy would be ready at a certain point to get
involved in the boy's life, be a better secret father, if Don wanted
that, to help in ways beyond these relatively paltry payouts, but
he needed a more reliable sense of the kid, if he could be trusted
to not divulge Purdy's broken trust to trust freak Melinda. This
was Purdy's ask. I was going to be his bastard son's minder, his
mind reader. It couldn't be as bad as building decks, and given
what Purdy had intimated at the candy store, the payout would
be better than paltry. Already in my mind I was curating the
opening show in the Milo Burke Gallery at the Mediocre University at New York City, where, in a maneuver without precedent,
I had been promoted from part-time development officer to full-
time chair of the painting department. It seemed right, if only
a tad egotistical, that the first exhibit include a few of my more
representative works.

The morning glided by on daydreams and coffee and decadent sessions at stool. I read poetry for the first time in years, put on loud sludgy music, did a few sit-ups, rolled over with a heavy cramp. I crawled to the computer and hoisted myself into the chair. It was time to catch up on the state of the world. I'd start with the Middle East. I found the report of a recent debate between two professors at the Ivy League college uptown. One of the experts said the Palestinians were irrational and needed a real leader, like maybe a smart Jewish guy. The other professor said that the central paradox to all of this was that Jews both were Nazis and didn't really exist. But how could they be both? He was still working on it.

I clicked onward to *Home Aid Ho's*. This was actually part of a larger constellation of niche sites, and I searched some other scenarios until I found one that catered to my particular deformity. *Spreadsheet Spreaders* featured men who pleasured their female employers for raises of up to twenty percent. I started to rub myself and, remembering I would have to retrieve Bernie soon, recalled that I'd once done what I was doing with Bernie in the room. He'd been a few months old, and though sex in his vicinity was deemed okay, or, more than okay, beautiful and natural, Maura and I had never covered the masturbation question. Was jerking off in view of your mewler any different than making sweet slow love? I'd always meant to start an anonymous thread about this on one of those parenting resource sites. Things got away from me. Now it was no longer a concern. Bernie was too old. I was too old. It took me a good while to banish this memory, return to the hermetic joys of *Spreadsheet Spreaders*. I rubbed on valiantly, shot what was doubtless, at my advanced age, some sullen autist into a superannuated tube sock.

•

Happy Salamander, the physical space, as opposed to the educational concept, took up the basement of a private home off

Ditmars Boulevard. You walked in the side door, dipped your head beneath a sagging heat duct, and descended a short staircase to the low, bright chamber. The fluorescent lights drove Maura mad, but I didn't mind them. It was the filth beneath the tidiness that got to me, every bookcase and table and chair smeared with an odd, thin grease. It must have been some pedagogical lubricant.

Otherwise, you really couldn't argue with Happy Salamander, or you could, but you would get nowhere with its idealistic and adamantine young educators. They had a smug ideological tinge about them, a minor Red Brigades vibe, which often angered Maura, but which I chalked up to an abiding love for children, or an abiding hate for what children eventually become.

Splotched toddler art pocked the walls, the usual stick figure families standing in green yards under multi-colored skies, as though to assure the anxious customer that here, despite rumors to the contrary, a healthful focus on heteronormative rainbows obtained. Posters of butterflies and chipmunks curled damp from tacks, along with Polaroids of the kids on their various excursions to the nearby playground, or the local handball court, or the cracked fountain near the subway where bums liked to sun themselves and smoke. I'd seen the kiddie-diddler there, snarling and remonstrative with his duller peers.

Today the seven or eight kids in Bernie's class were scattered about the room at various stations, or, in Salamanderspeak, activity nodes. Some played office, shuffled telephones and scraps of printer paper across a squat table in approximation of future misery. Others stood smocked at easels, or hovered over wooden puzzles. A few teachers fluttered from cluster to cluster, mother sparrows with their beaked seeds of approbation. I spotted Bernie's pal Aiden sitting alone in a corner. He wore the bitter look of a boy dealt a time-out, a bad baby bird.

Bernie sat nearby on a pink mat. His shirt was off, his eyes closed. He hummed quietly. Maddie, his slender, slightly elfin teacher, knelt beside him, whispered in his ear. I watched as she lifted a chrome-colored clothespin, seemed about to affix it to my son's nipple.

"Hey!" I called.

Soft faces swiveled.

"Daddy!"

Maddie smiled.

"Hi, Bernie's Dad!" She knew my name, but this form of address was protocol, meant, if I remembered the manifesto correctly, to maintain contextual integrity for the other children.

"Hi, Maddie!"

"Bernie asked me about Indians. Or, as I explained, Native Americans."

"Oh?" I said.

"Yes, and we started talking about the Plains tribes in particular."

"They're the fun ones," I said, regretted it at once.

Maddie seemed to waver between confusion and scorn.

"Yes, well, Bernie wanted to know about the lives of the Plains tribes, and we touched upon the famous Sun Dance."

"Sun Dance?"

"Yes."

"What's with the clothespin?"

"Well, Bernie's Dad, it was all I had on hand. I wanted to give Bernie a sense of the ordeal. The piercing of the skin and the looping of rawhide straps through the wounds. They would fasten these straps to the sun pole. The young warrior would have to tear through his own flesh to free himself."

"Oh," I said, "like that movie."

"Movie?"

Maddie seemed unfamiliar with the medium.

"Before your time," I said. It was a phrase I was trying not to rely on so much these days. "Anyway, I hope you weren't going to make Bernie tear through his flesh."

I chuckled, caught a trace of Purdy in the sound.

"Daddy, I don't want to tear my flesh."

"You don't have to tear your flesh, Bernie, I promise."

Maddie made a stern face. I grinned, felt somehow chastened, though for what I couldn't be sure.

"No, obviously we wouldn't tear his flesh."

"I was just joking around."

"But I hope you've read our newest Statement of Pedagogical Goals. It was emailed as an attachment over the weekend."

"I don't think, well, now, not all of it, no."

"Oh," said Maddie, "because we assumed no response meant tacit agreement with our change in direction."

"Change in direction?"

"It's in the attachment, Bernie's Dad."

"Right."

"We believe that many of the problems children suffer from—sensory integration issues, boundary instability, lack of impulse control—stem from our collective refusal to expose children to certain dark edges of experience."

I felt my phone pulse in my pants again. I wondered if it could be Purdy, or Vargina. It was probably important. I couldn't answer it down here because the reception was sketchy, and besides, it was bad form. But I was just here to pick up Bernie, not to listen to Maddie prattle on about child development theory. I was in a hurry, and anyway, Maura handled the theory. I just wrote the checks. Or used to write the checks. Maura had borrowed from her folks for the last installment.

"Yes, edges of experience," I said. "Sounds good."

"I'm glad, because it's what we voted on at Blue Newt. A parent rep was present."

"Blue Newt?"

"Our upstate retreat."

"Right. Sure."

"I hope you'll read the attachment in its entirety."

My phone pulsed again. I lifted Bernie into my arms, carried him to the stairs.

"I definitely will!" I called. I wondered if I should try to get Nick a job here. He had the dark edges down.

"Bye, Maddie!" called Bernie.

"Bye, Bernie and Bernie's Dad!"

Out on the sidewalk I took out my phone. My carrier had called, probably with some intriguing amalgam of offer and threat.

"Dad?" said Bernie.

"Yeah?"

"Is Maddie going to tie me to the sun pole?"

"No, Bernie," I said. "Not if you're good and take your bath without screaming tonight."

"Okay," said Bernie.

"How about some pizza?"

"With torn flesh on it?"

"What about pepperoni?"

"Is that torn flesh?"

"Yeah, there must be some tearing involved. There's definitely some grinding of flesh, not to mention slicing. But I'm sure there's some tearing."

"Are there eyeballs in it?"

"Do you want eyeballs in it?"

"I do."

"Then eyeballs it is."

"Raw eyeballs?"

"Absolutely."

"Thanks, Daddy."

"Hey," I said, remembering now a tip from one of the parenting manuals Maura and I had read a few months ago. "I really liked how you just said 'Thanks, Daddy.' That was wonderful."

"Pansy," said Bernie.

Fourteen

Bernie fed, bathed screamlessly (perhaps for fear of Sioux pain), read to, sung to, and tucked in, I poured a glass of Old Overholt, turned on the TV. It was not often I had the run of the remote this early in the evening, but after a few moments I stopped clicking and settled in with a romantic comedy from the late nineties, the rare thing Maura would have maybe lingered on, caught up in some memory of watching this movie with old friends. It was strange to sit here and watch it alone. A few years, or even months ago, I would have scoffed, begged Maura to pop up the dial for some punditry or playoff scores or a breakdown of cavalry tactics in the Crimean War.

This wasn't just some macho reflex. Stuff me in a tutu and let's screen experimental videos all day, I always said, because I believed in Art (I harbored a secret capital, like a secret Capitol), but don't ask me to endure the corporate weeps. When it came to cinema, I sold out my aesthetic principles only for zombie flicks, monster mashes, jelly-tentacled beasts who lived in toilets, slurped out our kidneys the hard way (watching Bernie get born, that angry purple mango plunging out of Maura, only further lubed my oozing worldview, my drippy grid), or else those special-ops terror soaps, the nutter mullahs and Glock minuets.

I'd never conceded to the rom-com pone, the coffee bars and turtlenecks, all that greeting card ontology. We were all garbage eaters, but there were too many varieties heaped. The idea was to limit yourself to one or two, or else you'd become an American.

But just like one, I'd cheated, changed. Or maybe it was just the way of things, in line with the theory that the older men get, the more they become old women. Now I preferred the feces the wardens of our souls dolloped on the fem trays. Just a little more texture. I couldn't remember if I'd seen *Caller I Do* in a theater, but I'd watched it piecemeal over the years. B.B., Before Bernie, Maura and I spent frequent Sundays on the sofa, shades drawn, soaking ourselves in the healing springs of bad television.

This particular movie took place in Hollywood's New York, a wonderland of pensive latte-sipping and meaningful strolls through Central Park. The city looked crisp, exquisite. The citizens lived like simple millionaires. Our principals were a lonely man and a lonely woman, each with a buffoonish, homely sidekick who would have been thought attractive in real life, and a fascinating, but finally unfulfilling—because there was nobody to "share it all with"—career. They sought each other, missed each other, at cocktail parties, in train terminals, at flower shops, their fin de siècle Nokias gaining symbolic power with each scene. Sucked into the vortex of high formula, a slow sob rose in my body. Just like porn or bang-bang, this was the pure stuff, concocted for the baser circuits, the lizard board.

Now the climax arrived, the charmingly improbable half-nude chase through the gallery district of Dumbo, the couple finally reunited in embarrassed ecstasy as pretentious art aficionados punctured their skeins of cynicism and cheered (had they just exited the latest Billy Raskov exhibit?). The sob rippled up, burst in my throat. Maura and I had already found each other. The desperate, emboldening quest for love, the beautiful, electrifying unknowingness of it all, was forever gone. (Unless we divorced, started over, which would surely be disastrous. She'd find happiness with some curt, sporty banker. I'd live in the laminated basement of a Cypriot retiree near the airport, never talk to a woman under seventy-five again.)

"Fucking pussy," I wept, sipped my drink. "Fucking pussy-hurt pussy."

They sped the credits but I did catch a name. The governor's daughter. An early producing gig. Maybe a favor from one of her father's liberal Hollywood foes? She'd gone on to become an important person in the business. Once, I'd watched her hold up a statue, make a speech on television about film and justice. I thought she might apologize to the nation for stealing my Spanish knife.

Good old Constance, she had hid behind the others that night the governor's daughter claimed her nine-tenths of the law. Her black pigtails doubted me, indicted. Constance knew it was my knife. I'd shown it to her in my room, under the blue light. But that night at the party she made no sign she remembered. She just stood there in her tank top, pink with tequila and summer, watched me squirm. Maybe she believed I had it coming.

Maybe I did. The previous spring I'd been briefly inhabited by the ghost of Roger Burke, sneaked around the whole semester, cheated on Constance every chance I got. The hate in me was huge, but I had always wanted happiness for Constance, still did, years later, when a thick cream envelope arrived in the mail, the names of her mother and father in fancy ink in the corner. Maybe getting hitched wasn't the most Marxist thing to do, but she had found somebody she loved enough to hire a calligrapher. I tossed out the envelope unopened, didn't need to know, for example, the name of the groom, or the wedding site. I had no intention of seeing these people again until I could boast of an accomplishment beyond my failed attempt to sell wallet-ready oil portraits of people's children online. Yes, this had been my home business.

Everything went off, went bad, or so I told myself, though I knew my crucial role in the spoilage. I had skipped my last meeting with Sayuri Kuroki behind Scissor Kicks. Even then I could feel myself doing the dumb thing, as though I wanted to guarantee I had memories to haunt me, feared I might lack a good reason to wince. I should never have worried. I could still picture Sayuri standing there near the Dumpster in her denim jacket, fiddling with the scrunchies on her wrist, maybe worried I'd been knocked off my BMX by a lumber truck. Though maybe she never reached the rendezvous, either.

Constance, I'd just turned abruptly away from her, seeing something better in whatever Lena's adulterous hunger could deliver. I'd almost let Maura drift off a few times, too, before Bernie reversed the inertia. We'd been together off and on for ten years, Maura and I, had tried very hard not to be the love of each other's life. It was like the stupid movie, without the cute bits.

Not one of the cute bits, for instance, was the night we had a foursome with that lascivious couple whose Greenpoint loft, perhaps because of the hillocks of cocaine on the coffee table, we found ourselves the last to leave. After some preliminary dialogue that wanted so much to parody the clunky verbal vamping of vintage porn, but had veered into grim, jaw-grinding consequentiality, Maura and the other woman had stripped and entangled themselves on the bed, all pinches and strokes and theatrical licks. Even through the fog of powders and booze, the sight of them aroused me and I turned to grin at the other guy. He smiled back, held up a palm for a louche, almost Wonderlandish high five. I shoved my tongue in his mouth. Really, I just meant to be friendly, to complement the writhings beneath us, complete the servicing circuit, but suddenly it seemed I'd broken the sacred swinger's code.

"What the fuck," the guy said. He pulled away, wiped his lips. Then he stuck himself in my wife, glared as he pumped.

"I'm not into that," he said. "You had no right."

I crawled off to the coffee table, decided then and there I had no fondness for Greenpoint.

So, things hadn't always been perfect, or even hygienic, but Maura was my love. I wanted to ravish almost every woman I saw on the street, regardless of age or body type, but if I ever did picture myself not married to Maura, never did another woman hove into view, just a taxing still-life: a handle of chilled domestic vodka and sick-making amounts of Korean barbecue.

But now I kept thinking of Constance and Lena, those early confusions. I got up and made my tipsy way to Maura's desktop. I'd kept tabs on Lena before. She taught painting at a state school in Connecticut now, must have been near retirement. I hadn't run a search on Constance lately. Soon I had a photograph of her up on my screen. I'd entered—the invasive quality of the word was not lost on me—the website of an elite girl's academy in New England where Constance served as headmaster.

She looked older, of course, glancing up from her tidy and morally instructive escritoire, her pigtails gone, her still-black hair shorn with sour elegance. It was hard to detect the plump, glowing, self-righteous coed in this dour professional. I had no doubt she was still a feminist. Marxist was debatable. But maybe she was waking up the rich girls to the crimes of their kin. Wasn't there a tradition of that in such places? She did look wiser, happier. But I grieved for her lost radiance, which is just to say I was weeping for myself again.

Lena was another story. Lena shook me with old shame. Lena was another name for my failure to become what I'd once believed I already was. But tonight, strangely, when I thought of her, a different face floated past, a background ghost.

It was one of the last times Lena had visited my campus studio, a corrugated shed near the biology labs. The room got good light, but whenever I opened a window the stench of burnt rats wafted in. Often I'd light a cigarette, let it smolder for the stink, but this day Lena stood there smoking, studied my canvases.

I'd gone in a new direction. It hadn't turned out well, but I thought there was an idea there, a gesture, I could salvage. I'd be graduated in a month, was headed into the savage, supercilious world. This was my last shot at an uncompromised critique. Though of course it would be compromised. But only by lust.

Still, who knew? It was easy to forget Lena was also an artist, that she hadn't been put on earth just to mentor me. She made it easy to forget. She didn't linger in her past, and her triumphs were in her past.

"Thoughts?" I said. "Feelings? Pangs?"

Lena stood with her hand on her head, cigarette between her fingers. She singed her hair often this way.

"I think you've lost your mind, Milo."

"Shit, really?"

"No, not really. Finally. You were close, but now you've gone crazy. Controlled crazy. They're funny and sly, like always, but they've got this turmoil now, too. A newfound urgency. God, listen to me. That stuff in the corner, is it wax?"

"Rubber cement. Treated. I treated it."

"Treated it with what?"

"Trade secret."

"For what will you trade the secret?" said Lena, put her cigarette in my ceramic frog ashtray, and slid her hand into my shirt.

"I thought we weren't going to do this anymore."

"Do what?"

"We weren't going to . . . Oh, fuck you."

"We weren't going to fuck me?"

While we made love on the paint-caked workbench, I watched the cigarette burn in the clay lip of the frog. Why couldn't she just crush the damn thing out? The smoke curled up to the cement ceiling and Lena had an orgasm, or some approximation thereof, and I pulled out, spilled myself on her belly and the tails of her striped button-down shirt, a man's shirt, maybe her husband's. It felt good to do that, like that eureka moment when a child discovers just how, precisely, to be a shit. Lena's face flushed and she blew at her bangs. There was something sulky, unlikable, about that upgust of breath, but I couldn't pin it down. I had the sense I couldn't pin it down because I was too young, and suddenly felt my youth as a form of impotence. I snatched Lena's wrist, turned her toward my paintings.

"Now," I said. "Tell me true."

"I already told you, Milo. I don't lie about this stuff. I'm not that desperate."

"I think you are."

"You little bastard."

"Please, Lena. Who's going to tell me?"

I could see her soften. I was just a dumb, scared boy. I was also a demon, junior precious division. Lena lit another cigarette, sank into a squat.

"I don't know, Milo," she said. "You have talent. It doesn't seem to be outrageous talent, but who knows about these things."

"Compare me to Billy Raskov."

"I don't do that."

"Sure you do."

"Okay, fine. I know you think you're a better artist than Billy Raskov, but you're just a better draftsman. That's something. But there are mentally handicapped people who draw and paint with far more technical skill than either of you. So, like I always say, it all comes down to how much you need to inflict yourself on the world. You're good enough. If you kiss the right ass, you could certainly make a career. Get some shows. Teach. Like me, for instance. I'm not a failure. I'm in a very envied position. You have some big-dick fairy-tale idea of the art world, so you don't understand this yet, but hanging in, surviving, so you can keep working, that's all there is. Sure, there are stars, most of them hacks, who make silly amounts of money, but for the rest of us, it's just endurance, perdurance. Do you have the guts to perdure? To be dismissed by some pissant and keep coming? To be dumped by your gallerist? To scramble for teaching gigs? It's not very glamorous. Is this what you want? You're good enough for it. You're not the new sensation, but you're good enough to get by. But you have to be strong. And petty. That's really the main thing. Are you petty enough? Are you game? Are you ready to screw me again? You must be."

Lena reached for my crotch. I swatted her hand away, stumbled out of the smoky shed. The sun was high and warm, the grass lush, spongy. Some students talked beneath the portico of the biology building. There was a humming sound, which I tracked to a vent in the bricks. The stench of the experimental dead blew out of it. I thought of the rats and guinea pigs and gerbils in their cages, studied my hands.

Soon I would not remember what Lena had said. Already it seemed kind of jumbled. Lena just really made no sense. Past the biology building, on a bench beneath some poplars, I could swear I saw Purdy. Was that Purdy? Yes, absolutely, it was Purdy, on a stone bench with a woman I did not know. She was pretty and sat straight with her hands on her stomach, as though protecting it, and she looked up at Purdy, who seemed to be laughing, laughing incredibly hard, so hard that even from this distance I could see a vein rise in his neck. Though maybe Purdy wasn't laughing. Maybe he was shouting. I had never seen Purdy shout.

What the hell had Lena been talking about back there? Loopy slut. But she had a good eye for my work. Couldn't deny that. Funny and sly, she'd said. With a newfound urgency. Wasn't that the gist of it? It was Art. I was an Artist.

Fifteen

I took the train out to Jackson Heights, didn't even bother to call. If Don wasn't home, I'd grab some samosas at one of the Indian buffets on Roosevelt, read some general-interest rag, chortle at the lurchings of the normie mind, hate myself to the very core, choke on fennel seeds. I hoped he wasn't home. The prospect of loafing in a different Queens neighborhood excited me. But when I reached his building, a grim brick five-story near the subway, and pressed the bell, I got buzzed right in. I didn't even announce myself. I guess Don Charboneau didn't care much who dropped by.

The heat was thick in the hallways. Pipes clanged in the walls. A young woman stood at Don's open door, a redhead in a purple halter. She held a slim metal canister, some kind of sprayer, or mister, pointed up toward her chin. Mist rose, enshrouded her. Her cheeks and freckled shoulders shimmered. Her eyes rolled back, drugged and piggy. It was sexy, but then I'd always considered piggy women sexy. Because of Muppets, maybe.

"You're not the food," she said.

"No, I'm not the food."

"Who are you?"

"I'm Milo," I said. "You must be Sasha. Is Don home?"

"Don's out. Hey, how do you know my name?"

"I'm a friend of Don's dad. I've heard nice things about you."

"Like what?"

"Oh, lots of things," I said.

"Don thinks I'm stupid."

"I don't think that's true."

"How would you know?"

"Just based on the conversation we're having now."

"I have an IQ of 136. That's verifiable. If anything, I'm on the autism spectrum, just a trace of assburgers, which is fairly rare in a girl. Do you know what assburgers is? Anyway, Don's dad's friend, come in. Sorry it's so hot. The boiler just goes crazy sometimes."

I followed her into the cramped studio. There was a futon on the floor, a card table with an old laptop on it that looked more learning toy than computer, some folding chairs. A breakfast counter split the main room from the narrow kitchen.

"I'd offer you some food," said Sasha, shut the pitted door behind us, "but I don't have any. I thought you were the food."

"Right."

"Oh, I said that already."

"I'm sorry I wasn't the food," I said.

"Have a seat."

I sat down at the table, rested my arm on a stack of papers.

"Hey, watch those," said Sasha, slipped the stack from under my arm. "The Todd Wilkes files. Can't mess those puppies up."

"Oh, some important paperwork?" I said.

Sasha did not seem to notice the sneer in my voice. Maybe she was further along the autism spectrum than she realized. She still stared at the papers.

"That Todd Wilkes," she said.

"I don't know him."

"You don't? I thought everybody did. Don thinks everybody does. Don collects everything he can on Todd Wilkes. He went to high school with Todd. They both went to Iraq but Don just hates him. Hated this whole act he put on when he got back. Writing articles in the newspapers about how proud he was to be an American. Shaking everybody's hand. Going on TV. Saying the soldiers shouldn't whine. It was five years ago, but Don's still got a big bug in his butt about it, says Todd Wilkes will be president someday. And that when that happens, Don will have to shoot him."

"Well," I said, "I don't really know about any of that."

"What do you know about, Mr. Not-the-Food?"

I couldn't tell if she was flirting or not. It could have been the heat, or the spectrum. She misted her neck, her knees.

"Do you think Don will be back soon? I have something for him."

"Yeah," said Sasha. "He should be back. He's out pounding the pavement. The pave-o-mento. He said he was going to go out and pound it. He says it every morning. He made me lick his legs the other day. They tasted like a Barbie doll I had when I was a girl. Do you think that's weird? Maybe Todd Wilkes is right. Maybe the vets all whine too much. I don't know where Don goes, but he's usually home around now. It's hot out there, right? But hotter in here. Nabeel, the super, he says the boiler is possessed. He's pretty funny, Nabeel. Mind if I smoke? Even though it's my own motherfucking apartment?"

"Go ahead."

"Thanks. For the permission."

"Maybe I should come back another time."

"How much is in the envelope?"

"Which envelope?"

"The one you must have brought."

I slid it out of my pocket.

"I should really give it to Don."

"I just want to know how much is in it."

I told her how much was in it.

"Good. That's a nice number. Tell me, for real, how long do you think Don can keep this up? Because he's starting to freak me out a little."

"Keep what up?" I said.

"Come on," she said.

The door buzzed and Sasha went to the intercom. She did not speak, pressed a button.

"You know," I said, "it's probably a good idea to ask who it is first."

"I know who it is. It's the food."

"You thought I was the food."

"How many times can I be wrong?"

A moment later a delivery kid was at the door with a plastic bag. Sasha asked him the price a couple of times. The kid shrugged, pointed to the receipt. Sasha handed him some bills and he stood there and stared as she closed the door.

"It's like they want a tip," she said.

"They do want a tip."

"Fuck that. What did that guy do to deserve a tip?"

"He bicycled across the neighborhood to bring you your food."

"That's his job. Don drove a Humvee across fucking Iraq to bring you your freedom."

"They don't really pay them that well around here."

"Like they did Don? You got some kind of bleeding heart? My heart bled out a long time ago."

"I'm sorry to hear it."

"Do you want to squeeze my tits?"

"Excuse me?"

"It's from that show."

"Which one?"

"I don't know. Everybody's in a room or something. And it's real."

"Oh."

"They look fat but they are very firm."

"I . . ."

"He's speechless."

I looked down at the stained carpet.

"He doesn't know what to say. Well, I'm hungry."

I listened to the rustle of the food bags. Paper *and* plastic. You could recycle the paper, slip the plastic over your head. Recycle yourself.

Now the door rattled and a man leaned into the room. He wore a sleeveless black shirt with green letters that read "Thank You for Not Sharing." His greasy hair flopped out of a blue bandana. A pair of artificial legs curved out of his cargo shorts. He just sort of bounced there on the linoleum, scowling, loutish, kangarooey.

"What the fuck is going on here?"

I wondered if the torn boat shoes came with the prostheses.

"No, okay," he said. "Let's rephrase: What the fuck is going on here?"

"This is your dad's buddy," said Sasha. "He has some kind of name."

"Milo Burke," I said.

"My dad's buddy? My dad doesn't have buddies. He has associates. Employees. Clients. Counsel. Which one are you?"

"I'm just helping Purdy out a little," I said, put the envelope on the table.

"Flunky," said Don.

"Same as last time," said Sasha, nodded at the envelope.

"I don't mean to be vague," I said.

"What, you're like some fixer?"

"No, I'm a development officer."

"You don't look like any officer to me. What do you develop?"

"It's been a bad year."

Don shuffled to the table. I'd seen the amputees on TV, the ones who parasailed and played extreme badminton and were paragons of positive thinking, who never let their calamity stymie them. I presumed this Todd Wilkes was one of those sorts.

Watching Don move now I was struck by how utterly impossible and aggravating it must have been to walk on these things, let alone do Tae Bo, no matter how advanced the technology. How easy it would be to say to hell with it all, to lie on a cot with your titanium legs and curse your fate and soil the cot you curse your fate upon and not want to learn how to do anything all over again. I was on the verge of such behavior with my original legs. Don picked up the envelope, thumbed through the bills.

"Ulysses S. Grant is always welcome in my house," he said. "You, I'm not so sure about. What are you eating, honey?"

"Rice and beans, baby. I ordered from the place. Our friend here says I should have tipped the guy."

"Tipped him for what?"

"Riding a bike."

"Riding a bike? Try delivering the fucking beans in a chemical suit. Then I'll tip you. Nobody tipped Vasquez."

"Who's Vasquez?" said Sasha.

She's the one who got an RPG in the teeth, I wanted to say, figured it for lousy spycraft if I did.

"She was my friend," said Don, stumbled over to the futon, flung himself down. "I've told you about Vasquez a million times."

"Oh, yeah."

"Shit, honey, can you take my girls off? I'm whipped. Been pounding the fucking pave-o-mento. It's goddamn hot in here. We've got to get Nabeel to turn the boiler off. Sahsh, my girls."

Sasha pushed her plate away, crouched over the futon, and unstrapped Don's prostheses.

"Feel free to gawk at a total stranger during a private and painful moment," he said.

"Sorry."

"Just fucking with you. You can look. So, you here to give me the money?"

"And say hello from your dad. He'd love to see you sometime."

"Oh, so now I'm his son again. Good. He was hinting he wanted more tests. I'm sure he wouldn't love to see me. But I suppose we'll have to bro down one of these days. Wait, can a dude bro down with his dad? I guess he can. Where's Lee Moss?"

"Lee Moss is very sick."

"Sick like he's going to kick it?"

"I don't know, Don. I'm new to all of this."

"New to what?"

"To working with your father."

"I thought you were old friends."

"We are. But we haven't worked together before."

"Worked together," said Don. "That's funny. My fucking humps are killing me."

"Don calls them his humps," said Sasha.

"Excuse me?"

"His stumps. He calls them his humps. Everything is girls and humps around here."

Don rubbed the rough knobs just below his knees.

"Tikrit," he said.

"Saddam's hometown."

"We've got a CNN watcher," said Don. "How inspiring."

"I tried to keep up," I said.

"Yeah, must have been a real sacrifice."

"I must sound lame," I said.

"No, I think I'm the lame one," said Don.

"You move incredibly well," I said, "considering, you know . . ."

"Considering I'm a double transtibial amputee," said Don. "I'll tell you, man, some things I do better now. Right, Sahsh? Sahsh loves my humps. They're all-American humps. Can-do mission-accomplishing humps. Is my bitterness too obvious? I grew up watching those Vietnam movies on TV. There was always that bitter vet in the ball cap. I think I identified with that guy long before I went into the fucking army. Maybe being a pissed-off, paranoid, maimed war vet was my goal. I bet Nathalie thought so. How could such a smart lady have such a stupid-ass son?"

"Don," said Sasha.

"Mr. Burke," said Don. "Do you know where I can score hard drugs in this neighborhood? I see a lot of curry and lot of beans out there, but no dope."

"No, I really don't."

"You must think we're the lowest scum on earth, right? Regular old dude like you."

"We all have our pasts."

"I'm sure."

The near-knowing, not-knowing snarl in his voice, it reminded me of so many kids from college. Myself then, too. I wondered if that's what Nathalie sounded like. Probably not. Purdy would never have been so smitten.

"I'm sorry about your mother," I said. "I know Purdy is. It really shook him up."

"So much he had to finish her off, right? Wasn't going to keep meeting her in that motel, so he wasn't going to pay those fucking hospital bills. His little upstate authenticity piece just a slab of sleeping meat."

"Listen," I said. "I really don't know what you're talking about."

"Are you sure about that?"

Don rocked forward on his knobs.

"Extremely."

"Did you know Don was an interrogator?" said Sasha. "Just for a little while."

"I took a couple of classes. Online. But my instructor called me Don Juan because in all the simulations I used my masculine wiles instead of, like, a waterboard. When the situation allowed for it. Arab men are attracted to me. They have a whole different take on buttly rapaciousness over there."

"Don."

"Sorry, baby. And what I mean is virtual Arab men, anyway. I'm not a racialist."

"Racist," said Sasha.

"Racialist," said Don. "They're different words."

"Not for the people who use them both," said Sasha.

"Touché, douche," said Don.

"These simulations," I said now, "this class, was this through the army?"

"Not really."

"No?"

"It was on the fake internet."

"The fake internet?"

"Ask the fellow you supposedly work with."

"I'm not sure I follow."

"That's the kind of thing a guy who knows all about the fake internet would say."

"Really, I don't."

"Your ignorance is duly noted. Got that, satellite?"

"Got it," I said.

"Wasn't talking to you. But now that I am, do you have any questions you want to ask me?"

"I didn't come to ask you questions," I said. "I'm not exactly sure why I'm here. I think I'm supposed to make sure that you're okay. To find out how your father can help. He really does want to see you. Do you have a message for him?"

"Yes, I do, Mr. Burke."

"Milo, please."

"Okay, Milo. I certainly do have a message for my father. Please tell him that my mother, his precious Nathalie, the woman he loved so much he let her fester for twenty years in nowhere towns, was better off without him. And that the son he cares for so deeply that he tried to make sure he never found out about him really just hopes that someday soon he, Purdy, goes for a checkup, and the doctor tells him he's dying of cock cancer, and then he, my wonderful father, goes out into the street, stunned by the news, and gets hit by a bus, and lives, only to spend the entire following year rotting from cock cancer and in horrible pain from getting just crushed by that bus, one of those huge kinds with the accordion middle, and him just begging for somebody to feed his mouth a gun. Tell my father that."

"Okay," I said. "I'll try to remember it all."

"And also tell him that the envelopes will need to get much thicker. And that I look forward to joining him for some wonderful father-son time very soon. It may sound corny, but I'd like him to take me to the Bronx Zoo."

"That's the fun one," I said.

"Tell me," said Don. "Was there anything you wanted to be before you became some rich dude's bitch?"

"An artist," I said.

"So you wanted to be some rich dude's bitch all along."

"I guess," I said.

"He guesses."

"By the way," I said. "And don't take this the wrong way."

"What's that?"

"You sound a little like your father."

"I never had a father."

Sixteen

Here came the international teens with their embossed leathers, their cashmere hoodies and pimpled excitements. They had traveled from China, Japan, Russia, Kuwait, just to squeeze into the lone Mediocre elevator car and delay my arrival at work. The international teens studied English in the language program down the hall from our suite. Who knew why they bothered? Maybe someday Business English would be the only trace of our civilization left. Bored youth across the global globosphere would memorize its verb tenses, concoct filthy rhymes in its honor. Maybe they'd speak Pig English to trick the oldsters. Pig English would be Latin.

Rumor had it the whole deal was a scam, that the students were gaming us. We sponsored them for visas, and when the paperwork went through, they transferred to one of the online universities, lit out for the territories, Vegas, Miami, Maui. No classes to attend, all their assignments written by starving grad students and emailed for grading to shut-in adjuncts scattered across the North American landmass, the international teens would have a whole semester for the most delightful modes of free fall. Daddy's Shanghai factories or Caspian oil pipes would foot the bills.

But rumor also had it that Mediocre had to somehow benefit, or the practice would have been stopped long ago.

The international teens wore jackets and carried handbags worth half my monthly paycheck, back when I received a

monthly paycheck. They clutched cell phones and cigarette light-
ers shaped like postmodern architectural masterpieces. The international teens rode to the roof to smoke. Later they would gather
in the lounge area, nap. One boy, a handsome kid in rumpled
club wear, could often be glimpsed snoozing on the suede divan
outside Dean Cooley's suite. No other disco napper dared claim
this inviting nest, and I never discovered who the boy was, or
why he merited this dispensation, but sometimes I found myself
unconsciously bowing my head in his presence.

Now the international teens jammed me harder up near the
button panel, chatted in their conquering tongues. Their giggles,
I concluded, regarded shabby me. It felt good to be colonized,
oppressed, a subaltern at last.

You reactionary scumbag, I upbraided myself. But I'm just
being honest, I replied. Your so-called honesty is a weapon against
the weak, I said. Fuck off, I retorted, I am the weak. Look at my
dollar! It's shriveling in my hand! It's like a vampire caught out
by the sun. My dollar is exploding into dust. I'm not the bad guy
anymore! Han brothers and sisters have the wheel of this wreck
now!

"Excuse me, sir," said one of the Chinese students. "I must
ask once again, I do not mean to offend. Is this your stop?"

Another nodded, held the door. How long had they been
waiting for me to leave the car?

"Yes, thanks, *xie xie*," I said, slinked past them into the lounge
area.

The receptionist had gone to lunch, left Horace curled up
in one of the Eames knockoffs with a twist of pemmican and a
paperback book.

"What up, kid?" he said. "How's my home slice?"

A devout ageist, Horace frequently mocked me with anti-
quated slang.

"I'm okay, thanks."

I took a seat nearby.

"You passing the dutchie, or what?"

"I don't know what that means, Horace."

"Sure you don't."

"What are you reading?"

"This book my sister got for one of her college seminars. It's called *The Unfortunate*."

Horace held up the book. It was called *The Infortunate*.

"You sure?" I said.

Horace flipped the book around.

"What the fuck are you talk— Ah, good catch, Meister Po. Anyway, it's an awesome book. It's about this dude back in pre-revolutionary times. Like his memoir. He was in law school and living on the family dime in London, but really just partying and shit. Listen to this sentence here: 'In my Clerkship, I did little else but vapour about the Streets, with my Sword by my Side; as for studying the Law, little of that serv'd me, my Time being taken up with pursuing the Pleasures of the Town . . .' He's like the first slacker. Just saying you're not the boss of me to his whole world."

"Like you."

"Hardly," said Horace. "There are no slackers anymore. Your generation murdered the dream. You guys were lazy pigs. We're more like highly efficient pleasurebots. But this guy, he really sparked something, in his way."

"Sounds interesting."

"Don't be a phony, Judge Holden."

"Your references are all over the place. You know that, right?"

"That's the point," said Horace.

"Oh," I said.

"Got it, Francis Gary Numan Powers? William of Orange Julius and Ethel Rosenberg?"

Our grandchildren would be steeped in some other nation's trivialized history. It would be their salvation.

"Got it."

"So anyway, this guy, Moraley is his name. He's a real joker. Does no work, gets kicked out of school. Finally gets cut off by his mother after his father dies, and he gambles and whores himself into serious debt. As only a true vaporing dude could."

"Wow."

"That's just the setup. He basically ends up with a choice: go to debtor's prison or become an indentured servant in the New World. Ends up working for a watchmaker in Philly. Young Ben Franklin is hanging around there, too. But Moraley isn't the same kind of self-starter, I guess. Plus he's like a slave."

"So what happens?" I said.

"Nothing really. He goes on a little trip in the wilderness and describes what he sees, though my sister said he made most of it up. Total drunk liar."

"Awesome."

"Actually it kind of sucks. It's pretty boring."

"You seemed so excited about it."

"I was excited by the idea of it. But now that I'm talking to you, it's boring the shit out of me."

"I have that effect."

"I know you do. Or, well, it seems that way, anyway. Or well. George Orwell. That's funny. I never thought of that before."

"His real name was Eric Blair."

"Nobody likes a pedant, Milo. How's your ask going?"

I told him some of Purdy's give ideas.

"Digital art shop sounds smoking," said Horace. "And the brilliant thing about that is the whole point of digital art is you don't really need a ton of real estate to do it. So, of course we should build a huge digital art studio. Cooley's really into counterintuitive moves. Like, for example, people will always need to go to the toilet, so let's *not* have public toilets. It's different, exciting. The global stuff could be golden. We definitely need to get something hotshit live in the Emirates. I've heard

Varge and War Crimes talking. We may have some prince's kid in the film program next year. But you'll have to rip this one. Parking lot jack. For real. Varge and Crimes have both said so, in their ways."

"What do you mean? And since when is she Varge? And how do you know all of this stuff?"

"May I answer your queries in reverse order?"

Horace's swerves in diction always amazed. He once explained that like many in this country, he spoke several dialects: Standard American English, Black American English, American Television English, East Coast Faux Skater English, Foodie French, and Drug Russian.

"Sure," I said.

"Okay, let's see," said Horace. "I know all of this stuff because unlike you, I've been taking this career seriously. I don't sit around dreaming of a parallel universe where everybody's speaking about my artistic vision in hushed voices on public radio and I'm home in my Brooklyn brownstone half listening while my young assistant with the bee-stung lips and gesso-smeared wifebeater gives me a world-class perineum-polishing with her chrome-studded tongue. No, I concentrate on the mission of this office and the mission of the arts at this university. Actually, I try to make your public radio rimjob fantasy come true for young people with the talent and drive and, yes, the moral character to realize it, to walk through the door of life's opportunities and seize the future by the ponytail and yank the future's head down to their crotches and just fucking demand satisfaction, not dream about it while sitting in a cubicle. I listen. I learn. I sit at the feet of the masters, soak up their toosh dev wisdom."

"Toosh dev?"

"Institutional development."

"Right," I said. "I guess I should never have shared that stupid little dream with you when we went to that taco joint. I thought we were buddies."

"It's not Shoah friends. It's Shoah business."

"Huh?"

"Work it out. Break it down."

"I thought it was toosh dev."

"It's what you make of it, pal."

"Anyway, I definitely regret not being clearer: I was talking about how I'd outgrown such silly notions. The loft thing was meant to be an example of my long-shed naïveté."

"Is it a shed or a loft, chief?"

"Horace," I said.

"It's too fun with you sometimes. I like you, Milo. You're like the dim older brother I actually have somewhere. Listen, it's Varge because I like saying Varge. And Vargerine. And Bel Biv DeVarge. But I'd never utter these names to her face. So, now you've got something on me. Although she already knows what a little a-hole I am. As to your last question, I've quite fucking forgotten it, dude."

"You said something about Vargina and Cooley. A parking lot jack on the give. Does that mean hitting a home run?"

Horace flicked his eyes past my shoulder.

"Look, Milo, I don't have to tell you things are bad. It's a very fucked time. There is epic, epochal fuckedness. A bunch of our asks have skedaddled. Even with the markets collapsing, they were waving their cash rolls around for a while, wanting to help the arts, but now a lot of them are just gone. If Purdy is truly still on the hook, it's a big deal. And everybody here has total confidence you'll screw it up. If he walks without writing a check, that's one thing. You're back where you started, out on the street, obviously. But to them it would be almost worse if you did a Milo and shepherded Purdy to some dinky give. Remember your big plasma score? Like that. Then Purdy wouldn't even be tappable again for a long time. I'm not trying to insult you, just tell you the truth. They are hurting and need a big one. If you do this small-time, they will dump you hard."

"So, what should I do?"

"Bleed him."

"I'm . . . I'm not good at it, Horace."

I'd never just blurted it out like that before. Horace looked at me as though I'd bitten off my pinky.

"This is a known known, son. But you've got to fake it till you make it, as the alkies say."

"They promised that if I reeled him in I'd get my job back. Period. They never mentioned numbers."

"We're all good on used floor fans from Northern Boulevard. That's all I'm saying. Capice, Cochise?"

"Jonathan Livingston Seagull, I presume?"

Horace stood, slapped me on the back.

"Hopeless," he said.

•

I needed to talk to Vargina, straighten this out, but felt suddenly faint, headed for the deli across the street. Just standing in the vicinity of comfort food was comfort. The schizophrenic glee with which you could load your plastic shell with spinach salad, pork fried rice, turkey with cranberry, chicken with pesto, curried yams, clams casino, bread sticks, and yogurt, pay for it by the pound, this farm feed for human animals in black pantsuits and pleated chinos, animals whose enclosure included the entire island of Manhattan, this sensation I treasured deeply, greasily. Executive officers, up since dawn for their Ashtanga sessions, might pay for pricier, socially conscious salads at the vegan buffets, but this was where the action was, and I, who should have been Tupperwaring couscous from Queens, who could just barely afford this go-goo for the regular folk, these lumpy lumpen lunches, reveled in them, or at least the idea of them. Because the sad fact was I always balked at the last minute, a dumpling, some knurled pouch of gristle, spooned above my tray. This pre-digestive switch would flip and I'd abandon the wonton or rib tips or the shrimp salad with its great prawns like fetal hamsters drowned in cream, scurry back to the clean wisdom of the wraps. I was the food bar orgy's anxious lurker, the smorgasbord's voyeur.

They promised no excitement, my beloved turkey wraps, but no exotic gastrointestinal catastrophes, either. Wraps were elemental. You had your turkey, your cheese, your avocado and leaf of lettuce, and you rolled that shit up tight. What could go wrong? A child could do it. I preferred children do it. But today, the day I needed my old standby in a nearly pre-civilizational way, they had no fresh turkeys left.

"How about panini?" the counterman said.

"What?" I said.

"Panini."

I laid my hands, my forehead, on the deli case. This one held the myriad schmears, the bagel cheeses, like a small city of cups and tubs, all of it under Saran wrap since the morning rush, submerged like a breakfast Atlantis, peaceful and ordered, decorous. What pleasure to push the tubs aside, curl up in there for cool sleep. I envied the food. That lo-cal scallion cream spread had no worries. There were no little ramekins of lo-cal scallion cream spread depending upon it. It just offered itself up to the schmearer's spade, oblivious.

"No," I said. "No panini."

"What's that?"

"I said, 'No panini,' " I said.

I bought an energy bar, and as I ate it a great weariness fell over me. I forced myself across the street and back up to the office. Reception was still empty. So was Horace's desk. I walked down to Vargina's command nook, knocked.

"Yes?"

"It's Milo," I said. "May I have a word?"

"Of course. Pull up a chair."

Vargina swiveled to face me, scooped egg salad from a plastic dish. The egg salad had a slightly redder tinge than the batch in the deli case across the street.

"Want some?"

"What? No, I'm fine."

"You were staring at it."

"Is that paprika?"

"Have a bite."

Vargina held out a spoonful and I leaned forward, let the egg salad slide into my mouth, sucked down the creamy aftercoat of mayonnaise, with its spiced, nearly deviled, kick.

"Wow," I said.

"Pretty good, right?"

"Delicious," I said. "I . . . I hope this wasn't inappropriate."

"It wasn't," said Vargina. "Until you said the word 'inappropriate.' "

"I'm sorry."

"It's okay, Milo."

"This is delicious egg salad."

"My husband made it."

"He's got a gift."

"I'll tell him you said so."

"Please do."

"So, Milo, how may I help you?"

I told her about my talk with Horace. I tried not to betray too much, kept things general. I just wanted to understand the terms of this arrangement.

"I see," said Vargina. "It sounds like you had a very nice chat."

"Come on," I said, "be straight with me."

"About what?"

"Are you guys going to screw me?"

"As far as I know, the terms stand."

"But what are the terms? What's the number?"

"What number?"

"How big does the give have to be for it to be considered a success, or enough of one to earn my job back? Is there a target on this give?"

"It's hard to say, Milo."

"Hard to say?"

"I mean it would have to be big."

"Big."

"Hate speech, sexual harassment, these are horrible allegations."

"I prefer to think of them as challenges for me to meet and overcome."

"That's good, Milo. You're coming around, I can tell. I'm on your side. Among other sides. But I am on your side. Think I like Llewellyn? The pastiness? The arrogance? Please. But he's our rainmaker. Of course we can't count out Horace. But you, this Purdy give, it sounds like it can be something. We need it to be something. I'm sure Horace told you that. This is larger than you. This whole game is poised for a gargantuan fall."

"What game?" I said.

"Higher education. Of the liberal arts variety. The fine arts in particular. Times get tough, people want the practical. Even the rich start finding us superfluous. Well, they always think we're superfluous, but when they're feeling flush it doesn't matter. You pay a whore to make you feel like a man, you fund a philharmonic to make yourself feel like a refined man. But it's a pleasure many don't feel like splurging on these days. Worse is the pain of the tuition payers. They are just small-time enough to really resent the price we charge to fool their children into thinking they have a lucrative future in, say, kinetic sculpture. Fat times it was maybe okay to send your slightly slow middle son to an expensive film program. He'd learn to charge around in his baseball cap, write his violent, derivative screenplay in the coffee shop. Idiotic, right? But ultimately affordable."

"Those days are over?" I said.

"Not yet," said Vargina. "Or none of us would be sitting here. But it's not looking good. Donors are getting scarce. Everybody's worried. That's really my point. The whole deal's in danger. And maybe it should be. Look at you."

"What is that supposed to mean?"

"You were an art major, right? What did it get you? Some egg salad from a crack baby?"

"That was good egg salad," I said.

"I know you liked it."

"You're a good friend, Vargina."

"I'm not your friend, Milo."

"Good colleague."

"So are we straight?"

"You still need to tell me the number. So I have an idea about what to shoot for. Unless you want to come in on this, work Purdy with me."

"No, this is your deal."

"So, what's the number?"

"You're thinking small again. It's not a number. It's a feeling. A great, big, wonderful, gleaming feeling."

"Okay," I said. "I think I got it now."

"I know you can do it. I also know you can't do it. But on some level I know you can do it. Good luck."

"Thanks," I said.

"Now I've got a question for you."

"Shoot," I said.

"Do you know anybody who speaks Mandarin?"

"Maybe. Why?"

"I'm just looking into something in Beijing."

"That's exciting."

"Yes, it is."

"Tell me," I said. "Does it have anything to do with that kid who is always sleeping outside Cooley's office?"

"You need to mind your own business. Especially on the subject of business."

"Will do," I said.

"Here," said Vargina, handed me the rest of her egg salad.

"No, I couldn't," I said.

"Yes, you could. Just wash out the dish when you're done."

Seventeen

One night in the House of Drinking and Smoking we were victims of what I would later call a home invasion. I didn't know the term then. I think I learned it later, from a rap song, or a movie based loosely on a newspaper columnist's fear of a rap song.

Probably they thought we'd be out, which was funny, because we were never out. This night, though, we had turned in early. Eve of a test week, I think. Given the soporifics in our systems, I'm still surprised we ever woke up, or that Maurice Gunderson did, to the sound, he said later, of his dresser drawer sliding open. His shriek roused the rest of us, though by then they, the invaders, had dragged Maurice from his bed, commenced what Billy Raskov would by morning term a "total fucking rampage." One of them banged a baseball bat on the walls and they all barked and shouted, flushed us from our smoky caves, herded us into the main room, where we sat in our underwear among the ashtrays and beer bottles that littered the glass coffee table we'd bought at the Salvation Army.

The invaders seemed quite familiar with the modality of the roust, knew the best ways to terrorize, corral. Later we learned at least one of them had been in the non-salvation army.

They wore ski masks, but we could tell by their hands that one was black and two were white. We could tell by their accents they were local. The largest invader, the apparent leader, the bat guy, as I later dubbed him, drifted about the room with his Easton aluminum, tapped our shoulders, our knees, lightly, with humorless threat, while the others drew the shades.

I shivered on the sofa in my boxer shorts. Christmas break was not far off and the house was always cold. Constance and Charles Goldfarb sat beside me and through my grogginess I felt my arm brush Constance's warm shoulder. Two things occurred to me simultaneously: that she must have been in bed with Charles, and that I missed her. Then the bat guy smashed his bat on the coffee table. Maurice Gunderson squealed from his camp chair.

"Shit, just take what you need and get out," he said.

Glass twinkled in his scalp.

"What was that?" said the bat guy.

"I said just take what you need."

"What do I need, faggot? Tell me what I need!"

He reached into the pocket of his jacket and took out a small pistol. Its diminutive aspect did not offer comfort.

"Calm down, dude," said another invader.

"I'll keep these fairies here," said the bat guy. "You two go upstairs."

"You sure?" said the third invader.

"Just fucking go!" said the bat guy. "I don't have all night."

If he was the leader, he was not a natural one. He seemed more disturbed than the others, twitchier, less clinical in his approach to the burglarious. That they figured we'd have cash and valuables stashed away here on Staley Street was not an indictment of their intelligence, but it did point to a knowledge deficit with regard to the various striations and flavors of capital accumulation at a private university. There were some varsity golfers down the block they would have done much better to rob. Maybe they already had.

I could hear the other two invaders smash around upstairs, pictured them in the blue light of my tiny room. What would they make of the sketches tacked to the wall, the condoms under the futon, the cracked, unstrung Telecaster in the corner (in case the band idea ever blossomed), the scratched record on the Fold 'N Play? Would they see through the pose?

It did not seem odd that I was thinking about this while the bat guy lurched around us and his accomplices tore through our drawers and our duffels full of dirty jeans and jerk-off socks and plastic bongs and mint cookies and *Foucault Reader*s. I was still a little stoned and very tired but I wasn't that frightened. I did not believe that we were in mortal danger, though I sensed some of us could get hurt. The bat scared me more than the gun. I saw it caving a skull, maybe that of Raskov, who sat on the sofa arm near Goldfarb. There was something melon-y and inviting about Raskov's head, I understood that objectively, and despite our frictions the prospect of its stoving did not please me. But the downside of this muted state was that I maybe appeared too comfortable, too fragmented, dreamy, and I suddenly paid for this with a sharp chop to the ribs. I squinted up from the floor into the wool-ringed eyes of the bat guy.

"What!" he said. "What are you staring at!"

"He's not staring at anything, man," said Maurice, his voice high, airless. "Everything's cool. I have morphine. You want that?"

"Fuck your morphine," said the bat guy. "Yeah, give it to me."

"It's in my room."

"Where's your room?"

"End of the hall."

"Go get it. Just fucking stay where you are."

"I am," said Maurice.

"Get back on the couch."

The bat guy turned just as Constance put out her hand for me.

"Don't touch him!" he said. "Shit, you're a chick. Let me see you. You fuck him?"

It's complicated, I wanted to say.

"He's my friend," she said.

"You fuck him. I can tell. You blow him and tell him how smart he is. But he's a dumbshit. Take it from me."

"I can vouch for that," said Billy Raskov.

I didn't take it personally, knew it for some kind of play, a ridiculous one.

"You can vouch for what, potato head?"

"Jesus, Billy," Goldfarb whispered.

The bat guy stuck his bat in the cushions of an armchair behind him, far from our reach, though I noticed Gunderson eye it. Now he snatched a handful of Billy's lank hair, cranked his head back.

"What do you vouch for?"

"Nothing," said Raskov.

"Nothing?"

Raskov snarled as the bat guy bent his head. Constance leaned in and stroked Raskov's knuckles, as though what he needed most now was moral support, the structural integrity of his spinal column a minor matter.

"No," said Raskov. "Just that I can vouch for what you said about the guy over here. Milo. He *is* a dumbshit."

"Oh, is he?"

"Yeah."

The bat guy slammed Raskov's head down on a spindly wooden end table. A leg splintered.

Billy slumped, clutched his skull.

The bat guy turned to me, waved his gun.

"Nice friend you got there. Calls you a dumbshit. He's fucking the chick, isn't he? Or maybe you all are. Maybe I will. What do you think of that?"

I could see Constance out of the corner of my eye. Her lips twittered, as though moving briskly through a sequence of calculations.

"Been a while since I got my wick dipped."

I could tell the bat guy was about to do something ugly with his penis. His pistol would authorize the ugliness. His pistol would have his penis's back. He started to rub himself. We froze, Billy and Maurice and Charles and I, or else we watched the scene as though it were precisely that, a scene, unfurling in the present but with a structure, a destination, already in place. Like a TV show, if TV made you too scared to move. I guess in a sense it does, but this was also something else. I was waiting for some instinct to take over. Fight or flight, I remember thinking. I suppose just sitting there on the sofa was, technically, flight.

The bat guy made an experiment of bobbing his crotch near Constance's face.

Something scraped on the hardwood behind us.

Purdy and Michael Florida squatted behind the armchair. Had they been here all along? Wandered in from the kitchen? Purdy put his finger to his lips. Michael Florida's eyes blazed, flicked around the room. They each crept around a side of the chair. Purdy slipped the Easton from the cushions.

The bat guy cocked his head but did not look back.

"What the fuck took you so long?" he said. "Did you find the morphine? This kid says he got morphine."

"Hey," he said again, "I want to get out of here. You see this chick here? Let's take her with us. She'll have a better time than with these queers."

Then we all heard footfalls from the hallway, the boots of his fellow invaders. I saw fear in the bat guy's eyes and he had every right to feel it, because as he wheeled to see what forms he had mistaken for his friends, Purdy and Michael Florida vaulted over the wrecked coffee table. Purdy smashed the pistol from the bat guy's hand. Michael Florida dove, speared the bat guy in the chest. Together they crashed to the floor. The bat guy rolled on top of Michael Florida, choked him, both men dusted with glass. Michael Florida clawed back and the bat guy's mask peeled off and we saw his face, his brown hair and rosy cheeks. He looked like a thousand young men in this city. But this one was throttling brave, meth-carved Michael Florida.

Purdy picked up the pistol, pointed it at the other two men.

"He's a fucking nut," said one of them. "We didn't even want him with us."

"He's my cousin," said the other. "But I don't care. We just came for the cash."

It was an odd moment, as though the narrative had somehow forked and we were witnessing two possible outcomes, the intruders subdued at one end of the room, our friend strangled at the other. The story had to decide. Or Purdy had to decide, because the rest of us just sat there, and he did, tossed the Easton, shouted, "Constance!"

Constance stood, snatched the airborne bat. The knob slid toward her fist and I remembered her stint on the freshman softball squad as she rocked her hips and swung into the bat guy's head. He screamed, but did not let go of Michael Florida's throat. Charles Goldfarb shouted. Constance bashed the bat guy on the elbow and his grip popped loose. Michael Florida rose, spun out, a practiced wrestler's escape. Many of us, maybe, were secret jocks. Michael Florida pounced on the bat guy, pressed him into the table shards, tugged his arms behind his back, bound his wrists with a leather belt. Michael Florida, more than anyone, would also be practiced in the swift removal of his belt.

Now Purdy waved the pistol at the two economically motivated, mostly non-violent invaders.

"Go," he said. "Get out of here. Run. Nobody's seen your faces. Just run on out of here."

"What about Jamie?" said one intruder to the other.

"Fuck Jamie. He's my cousin, and I say fuck him."

"They'll kill him."

"Don't be stupid," said Purdy. "We won't kill anybody. We want to graduate on time."

"There's nothing here," said Jamie's cousin. "We got nothing."

"You have everything," said Purdy. "The only important thing. Leave with it now."

"Wait!" called Jamie, started to thrash.

Michael Florida cinched his improvised truss. Billy Raskov stood, kicked Jamie in the kidney.

"Shit!"

It was craven, but at least Raskov had bare feet, and anyway I hadn't been cracked with a used end table.

"Billy," said Constance, pulled Raskov off.

"Leave him here," said Purdy to the other two. "You guys deserve better."

The deserved invaders nodded, bolted for the door. I watched them through the window fly down the street, weave off under streetlamps.

Michael Florida sat on the bat guy until the police arrived.

Charles Goldfarb, who had been sitting in stunned lotus on the sofa, rose, paced, cursed, smoked.

A lot happened after that, testimonies and court appearances and a hung jury and vague threats, never made good, from townier parts of town. That summer the newspaper reported the bat guy had been shot dead outside Star Market. He was a local boy named Jamie Darling. He'd drawn down on some cops with an unloaded revolver. I think the term "suicide by cop," like "home invasion," came later, but that's what it was.

A lot happened even after all the stuff that happened after, but years later I couldn't remember most of it, at least not the legal and ethical intricacies that entertained us for many stoned hours back then.

What lingered was that frozen feeling, the paralysis, the unnerving awareness that came with it, my real-time curiosity about the nature of my cowardice, as though I were already beyond any possibility of action, just wanted to ascertain, in the moment of my acquiescence, whether I was going to ascribe it all to moral failure or grant a kinder, chemical explanation. Of course, the bat guy had a gun. Nobody ever blames you for freezing in front of a gun.

But it was still the bat that scared me.

The biochemical states of Maurice and Billy and Constance also intrigued, and then, of course, loomed the indelible fact of Purdy and Michael Florida, the aristocrat and the outcast, hurling themselves over the coffee table like some heroic tandem from the mendacious mythopoetry of another age, one of whistles and human waves and the Maxim guns ripping away. You had to either have everything or have nothing to act in this world, I mused then, to make the move that will deliver you, or cut you to pieces. The rest of us just cling to the trench's corroded ladder, shut our eyes the way I remember Bernie used to shut them, squeeze them hard, call it hiding.

Of course, this feeling, this hysterical read on agency's dispensations, was a lot of what Maura used to term, with the full-bore Midwestern irony she'd somehow absorbed near Brattleboro, Vermont, "hooey," or what Claudia might have deemed a crock of absolute shit.

Still, a final tally, a statistical breakdown of this moment, did exist.

Future Apocalypse Guru: Smidgen of composure, ineffective diplomacy, intractable whininess.

Artistic Provocateur: Ineffectual response to threat, admirable behavior under physical duress, unseemly and gratuitous assault on downed invader.

Larkish Frankfurtian: Frightened retreat into walls of self.

Marxist Feminist Who Fucked: Initial paralysis, subsequent display of courage.

Semi-Brain-Damaged Crystal Tweaker: Valiant and focused response to threat.

Ruling-Class Brat: Remarkable bravery and tactical leadership in face of threat.

Home Invaders: Bold initiative, bad intel, poor battle management.

Painting's New Savior: Utter cowardice, experienced as bodily paralysis in conjunction with what he would later describe, in an effort to steer the conversation away from actual events, a "bizarre floating sensation."

But no matter my conversational machinations, I knew the truth. Nobody ever mentioned it, of course. It meant not much. Physical bravery probably held the same value in our milieu as skill at parallel parking: a useful quirk. But the box score stayed in my wallet, or the wallet of my heart, so to speak, a smeared and origamied scrap to remind me how little I resembled the man I figured for the secret chief of my several selves.

Eighteen

How sick and marvelous an age this was, wherein I could boot up my desktop with a couple of names or notions in mind—Todd Wilkes, William Moraley, indentured servitude, technological advances in prosthetics, toosh dev—and plug them all into various amateur encyclopedic databases. How fucked and wondrous to siphon off such huge reservoirs of community-policed knowledge, funnel it directly into my head. Every man a Newton, a Diderot. Even now I skimmed an article about Diderot for no reason. Bernie was asleep, Maura just a few feet away on the sofa with her laptop and headphones. She might as well have been in French Guiana.

All was peachy and near utopic until I rose for a beer. At that moment the knowledge just disappeared, tilted out my earhole. I'd have to start again, or else concede my memory palace was a panic room. It would be good to exile some items and sensations, some people, even, but how to cull? I could not spare one hamburger or handjob. I wanted to recall all the cigarettes I once smoked, those afternoons I did nothing but sit on a bench and smoke cigarettes, interview myself for major art magazines. I did not want to lose the acoustics of past lovers, the grunts of Constance, Lena's clipped whinnies, or even the tremolo moans the touched-out woman on the sofa used to make. What else? Which stray events did merit deletion? What about the time I demonstrated my karate kicks to the girls in Mrs. Ardley's

Chem I, felt a hot, fierce squirt in my underwear, knew I'd soon begin to stink?

What about Jolly Roger, my progenitor, the cad denied heroic measures? Could I Augean the whole heap of him away?

I'm not certain who called him Jolly Roger first, maybe one of my mother's brothers, maybe Gabe, the office machine salesman who thought there was something morose about my father, that quality I usually took for the quiet of the sneak, but the name fit for more than one reason. Jolly Roger was perhaps an emotional pirate. The treasure was your trust. Also, maybe the sneakiness did stem from sadness. There were times we'd watch television, my father and I, Roger back from his office in the city, or just returned from one of his trips, sitting in his armchair with a drink, and I'd hunch on the rug to watch his handsome moods, the flicker and drift of his face. The play of his eyes and his lips beat out any cop show or even the old Abbott and Costello movies he favored, each twitch and grimace another secret I would never know, a rye neat in a hotel bar, a cutting glance at a meeting, a winter beach somewhere far from his family, the surf's cold froth lapping the feet of a lover. You couldn't say he lived parallel lives, because that would imply he had a home life. Our house was more a transit lounge.

Sometimes, though, he'd drift out of his dream, realize where he was, get pissy, pick fights with my mother, hint at other intimacies, more than hint. He'd boast about a party in Philly, or Dallas, or Spokane, where the women were foxy (I pictured them red-furred, with quivering noses), the lady primo. Claudia might whip a skillet at the wall and the Jolly One would shrug, slouch off to the den. There were a few weeks he took to wearing sunglasses in the house. I don't believe this was a pose. I think the light hurt his eyes.

Most of the time he avoided me, or humored me, or peppered me with blandly supportive exhortations. "Keep it up," he might say, or "way to go," apropos of nothing I could discern.

Sometimes if I walked into the room he'd just say, "Here comes the kid!" Invariably I'd wheel to catch a glimpse of this mysterious presence. Maybe it was clear to both of us we were never going to understand each other, not because we were complicated people, or even at loggerheads, but because of the minor obligation involved. I really couldn't blame him. I knew what churned inside me. It was foul, viscous stuff. It wasn't meant to be understood, but maybe collected in barrels and drained in a dead corner of our lawn.

Still, if I was a study in teen toxicity, this man, as Maura would say, was a total disaster. He was my daddy, though, the man version of me, or so I thought. The few times we went bowling or burned tuna melts together or the day he taught me how to change the tire on the Dodge Charger he said could one day be mine, these were, to borrow a metaphor from Purdy's world, the great emotional-liquidity events of my youth. That they always seemed somehow artificial, cooked up to stand in for something more textured and sustainable, did not sway me from my adoration. The fakeness was fragile and exquisite. It had to be protected from people like my mother, who would judge our bond faulty, a ruse.

Once, when I was thirteen, fourteen, I passed by his alcove study off the kitchen. Jolly Roger called me in to chat. Later, I could almost see the famous knife in its tooled scabbard on his desk, but this was years before I knew it existed. He was doing the bills under his green lampshade, an elaborate ritual in which a pewter letter opener and a fancy red fountain pen vied for the role of lead fetish.

That desk, those bills, there was still something glamorous about credit cards, the perks of average citizenship. American Express paid for your postage. Airlines served salad and steak in coach. America was dingier, more bountiful. My father traveled to factories around the country to consult in the manufacture of movie projectors. This made him, to his mind, and the minds of others, part of the movie business. The edge of a pocket mirror poked out from under a gas company envelope. I saw the white smears.

"Milo, come on in."

"Hey, Dad."

"Come in, have a seat. I won't bite, you know."

It was the only time I thought he might bite.

"Sure, Dad."

I lowered myself into his captain's chair, a graduation gift from his father, with a slash of black paint where his alma mater's logo once gleamed. There had been some last-minute trouble with Jolly Roger's grades. He still held a grudge.

"It's a funny time," he said now.

I thought he meant 1982. Then I realized he meant this time in his life, our lives, his marriage.

"She gets so mad, Milo. I thought she was going to break all the dishes the other week. Remember that? That was something."

Claudia had smashed a good deal of crockery. It was after Roger had left for a week, only to come home and sneer at the state of the house, make some passing reference to the "dynamite" hair of a woman in San Diego, wonder if Claudia might like to try a shampoo that could deliver similar sheen.

Now he shook his head as though he were in a TV movie about a good-hearted guy overwhelmed by his wife's mental illness.

"I don't know," he said. "I just don't know."

"What don't you know?"

"It's strange," he said. "Maybe sometimes the best thing a family can do is dissolve."

"Dissolve?"

"There's no dishonor. Obviously we're all adults."

"I'm not," I said.

"Well, I consider you one," said my father. "That's what's important."

"You don't have to," I said. "I can be a kid for a while longer."

"Don't shortchange yourself," he said, his eyes a bit watery, with feeling, or pollen, or primo lady, I had no idea.

"I won't shortchange myself."

"No, really. I don't judge you. I don't have those hang-ups. You can fuck anybody you want. You can love anybody you want."

Later I realized he believed I was gay, had taken a rather impressive, if premature, position on my sexuality. At the time I thought he was just veering off topic, which I guess he was doing as well.

"Seriously, you can love anybody, and I will love you."

"Thanks, Dad."

"No, really, I mean it."

"I know, Dad."

"Oysters *and* snails. Ever see that movie?"

"Saw it with you. On TV. But they didn't have that part. You told me about it."

"Spahtakus," he said, "I love you, Spahtakus. Remember? That's what's-his-face."

"Right," I said.

"There's no shame in men loving men," he said. "There's only shame if there's shame. You get me?"

"Sure, Dad."

"I don't go in for all that macho crap," he said. "In fact, even though your mother goes to all those meetings, I'm a better feminist than she is. You want to know why?"

"Why?"

"Because I'm objective. I'm not a woman, so I can see it all very clearly. And they are absolutely right. We are pieces of shit."

"We are?"

"Not you. You're a good boy. I can tell you want to be a bad boy but you don't have it in you. Or maybe Claudia drained it out of you. I shouldn't say that. She's going through a lot of changes. So am I. Change or die, they say. And who, you may ask, are they?"

"Huh?"

"I said, 'Who, you may ask, are they?' "

"Who?" I said.

"Who is who?"

"Who are they?" I said.

"Third base," said my father, laughed.

He loved the old routines, even if he never quite got how they worked. Maybe he liked those movies, the spit takes and predictable trickery, because they gave him occasion to dream, to watch the better movie in his head, or even just browse for an interior state. When you did that without a television, people worried, asked if you'd like to see a professional.

"But who's on first?" I said now, tried to get him going.

"You're a good kid," he said. "It's not your fault."

I thought he meant it wasn't my fault that he didn't love me enough. But he probably meant something else. The phrase "good kid" made me shudder now, especially when I looked at Bernie. I'd spoken those words myself on occasion, knew them for the flail scared fathers wielded to fend off the love of their sons.

I think I understood Roger a little more the night before he died. He looked disappointed on his deathbed, a weak, sweet boy, like Bernie with a fever. Hell, maybe Gabe was right, maybe Roger was morose. Heroic measures had been forsaken. He wouldn't sneak out on this one.

So maybe I wanted all these memories, the sorrows and the hollows. Or maybe I was just programmed to want them, to believe I was composed of them, a failsafe wired into me, to keep me eating and shitting and dwelling on what exactly I wanted in a winter lager and not seeing things very clearly. Some argued that the creation of artificial intelligence amounted to cruel and unusual punishment. Consciousness was suffering. Why inflict it on a poor machine? I wasn't one of those people, but only because I believed that AI would someday make good on its promise of astonishing robot sex, if not for us, then for our children.

I was also one of those people who hadn't caught up with the latest social networking site. Maura belonged to most of them. She passed most evenings befriending men who had tried to date-rape her in high school, but I was still stuck in the last virtual community, a sad place to be, like Europe, say, during the Black Death. Whenever I cruised this site, with its favorites lists and its paeans to somebody's cousin's gas station art gallery, I could not help but think of medieval corpses in the spring-thaw mud, buboes sprouted in every armpit and anus, black bile curling out of frozen mouths. Those of us still cursed with life wandered the blasted dales of this stricken network, wept and moaned and flogged ourselves with frayed AC adaptors, called out for God to strike us dead, or else let us find somebody who liked similar bands.

When it came to locating people, I was still an old-timey search engine man, and now I plugged in the name Todd Wilkes. I wanted to know what he'd done to earn Don Charboneau's everlasting ire. There were more than a dozen articles about this Wilkes. They began a few years back when he'd charmed some politicians at a military hospital in Germany while recovering from bomb burns.

The language of these pieces seemed lifted from the *Daily Planet* archive. Todd Wilkes was "plucky," the reporters wrote, a "throwback, a happy warrior." Todd Wilkes was a "sharp cookie" from a "hardscrabble town." "He has no time for excuses," went one profile. "He takes the bull of life by the horns," proclaimed another. Todd Wilkes was going places. He was not to be denied. Also, he was sick of the whining from some of his cohort. "Nobody put a gun to our heads and told us to put guns to people's heads," he told a New York daily. "I don't care if you left your legs in Fallujah or Baghdad, you better suck it up. Nobody is going to help you if you don't help yourself. We are warriors. I follow the warrior code."

Most of the reporters had gorged on the bluster. Todd Wilkes was off to college to study government. He was going to be a senator someday. "The sky is the limit!" wrote one columnist.

"Forget the sky," wrote another.

I could see why Don wanted to shoot him, but these pieces had run some time ago. We had no use for Todd Wilkes now. But maybe Don still did. Once you've tasted the hate, it's hard to forsake that unique and heavenly flavor. It was maybe what got Don up in the morning. Surely it wasn't Sasha, or the promise of another day out on the pave-o-mento, the sun stabbing his scrawny neck, the humps swelling up, the girls on all fucking wrong.

Nineteen

The Best Place was one of those establishments that signaled the end of empire, or perhaps the advent of something much better than empire, at least to those who could afford it: spa facility, birthing center, archery gallery, breast milk bank, coffee shop. Who wouldn't want to quaff a latte, or shoot a few quivers, during prodromal labor? If the mother-to-be wasn't up to it, she could email JPEGs of her dilated cervix to her birthing community while her partner got a peel, or whiled away the downtime role-playing Agincourt in the gallery.

We few, we happy few.

There was no sign on the street but Purdy had texted me the building number and the password: "Ashtoreth." Somebody buzzed me into a chrome-sided elevator, and I slid stealthphallically several floors up, stepped into a light-soaked atrium. The room resembled a rain forest tricked out with designer furniture, or a furniture showroom tricked out like a rain forest. Women, some pregnant, and a few men, milled about in plush robes. Michael Florida stood at a Lucite bar, sipped something beige and foamy.

"There's our guy," he said, waved.

Here comes the kid, I thought, took a stool a few stools over.

Michael Florida winked, flipped a notepad shut.

"Care for a drink?"

"What are you having?" I said, peeked into his frothy high-ball glass.

"I'm digging on this hind milk smoothie."

"Hind milk?"

Now Michael Florida let me in on the details of this place, the Best Place, the luxurious labor chambers, the bottled breast milk chilled in vaults, the mud baths and neo–Swedish massage and compound bows. Purdy was here with Melinda to screen potential midwives, but he wouldn't be long. There was a meeting with some Chinese bridge loan specialists. It concerned Purdy's new project, something to do with Bible stories and mobile phones. But first Purdy wanted a few minutes with me.

"Bible stories?" I said.

"Better than those midget psalms books, right?" said Michael Florida. "But what do I know? I pick this stuff up in dribs and drabs. I'm just a glorified driver, really. This milk is awesome. And great for the immune system. Mine's pretty compromised. So's yours, I'll bet."

"What makes you say that?"

"Your eyes."

"What's wrong with my eyes?"

"They're fucked up."

"Fucked up how?"

"Kind of sludgy."

"My eyes are sludgy?"

"Sorry, dude, don't mean to alarm you. An expert could tell you what it all means. Liver cancer, diabetes, who knows?"

"Maybe they're naturally sludgy."

"That could be. I'm just—"

"I know," I said. "You're just the driver. Michael, can I ask you something? Do you remember me from college?"

"Yeah, sure. You were around. Though to be honest, between the time we all split from there and the other night when I picked you and Purdy up, I hadn't thought of you once. No offense. I mean I'm sure I was that guy for you. That speed freak always lurking around. Did we ever even talk, just the two of us? I don't think so. We only knew each other in a group setting."

"I guess it goes that way sometimes."

"I was always pretty sure you didn't like me. But then again, why would you? I was kind of an animal. Still am. I mean, look at this."

Michael Florida flipped his notepad open. It looked like a list of names, women's names.

"I'm doing some inventory," he said. "But I'm still out there, man. It's a nightmare."

"Sorry to hear it."

"I've been clean and sober for years. But I have not been able to put together any real recovery around my sex addiction. I had a great thing going with this one girl, she was fantastic, a recovering garbage head, used to sell her ass a little, but she was really grounded and cool. Had her own business making vegan snake treats."

"Snake treats?"

"Snake treats. For boas. Save the mice. She was a sweetheart. But of course I had to go to my Everglades on her a few too many times, and she called me out. Sent me packing."

"Everglades?"

"Yeah, you know, because my name is Florida. When I do something shitty, something swampy and wrong, I call that going to my Everglades. Stupid, I guess."

Michael Florida took a tight sip of his drink.

"So, what's with the list?" I said.

"These are all the women I've fucked in the last month. Twenty-seven of them. I'm not bragging about it, believe me. I'm just trying to get a handle on my disease. Because it is a disease. Do you know about this stuff?"

"I think I have a very different disease."

"Which one is that?"

"The one where you don't sleep with twenty-seven women in a month. The one where you don't get laid at all. Ever. Even by your wife. Especially by your wife. You wouldn't understand."

I looked down at Michael Florida's hind milk smoothie. I wasn't sure why I was suddenly confessing to him. I knew why he'd related his problem to me. There wasn't exactly a surfeit of humiliation in confiding to another man that you have been copulating ceaselessly. Although maybe for him there was. Still, I remembered how he talked to everybody all those years ago. Everybody but me. His speech had grown less frantic and drool-specked since college. The cosmic itch seemed intact. Still, what was I doing? Don Charbonneau's T-shirt snapped on a clothes-line strung between mental tenements: "Thank You for Not Sharing."

"Yeah," I continued. "So it's hard for her. Hard for us. We did almost have sex recently, but in retrospect I don't think it was any kind of turning point. I think it was an anomaly. It's the kid, caring for the kid. She's just really touched out."

"Touched out," said Michael Florida.

"What?"

"No, that phrase. What's her name . . ." Michael Florida ran a leathery finger down his list. "Nadine. She said that was what she always told her husband. Touched out. Like 'Sorry, baby, I'm touched out tonight.' "

"What was her name again?" I said.

Michael Florida laughed.

"Oh, man. That's good. Don't worry. It's not your wife."

"I won't worry, Michael. I don't think you're her type."

"No? You sure?"

"I think I'm sure. Anyway, I should congratulate you. Your disease is really putting up big numbers."

"Thanks, man," said Michael Florida. "But really, just to put you at ease, most of these bitches are sad and fat. A few, though,

I would have paid. There was this seventeen-year-old, yeah, this one, Vanessa. She was something. Thank God for Viagra."

"You take Viagra?"

"Only with the kids. The kids are so demanding. With somebody my age, I don't take the stuff. They get what they get. Anyway, how'd we start with all this? Crazy. Purdy told me to keep you entertained while you waited. Hope I entertained you."

"You did your job."

"Yeah," said Michael Florida, drank off the rest of his milk. "I do my job."

"Remember," I said, "the night those guys broke into our house?"

"Wait, when?"

"Back in college. Those guys came in with ski masks. Tried to rob us. That one guy was getting up in Constance's face—"

"Jamie!"

"Right," I said. "They called him Jamie."

"Fucking idiot, that guy. I couldn't believe what a tool he was. His cousin said he was okay."

"What are you talking about? You knew him?"

"No, I knew his cousin."

"You mean you were in on it?"

"I needed money, dude. I had a disease. I made amends to everybody that was there. Except you, I guess. Forgot about you. That you were there."

"I was the guy experiencing a bizarre floating sensation."

"What?"

"Nothing. Purdy knows?"

"He forgave me a long time ago."

"But you guys came in together."

"Well, he'd come in from outside. I was hiding the whole time. I'd told those guys where stuff was. So, I pretended to Purdy I'd just stumbled in there, too."

"They didn't find anything."

"No. I was pretty stupid. For some reason I thought Gunderson had a lot of cash in his room. Nobody was supposed to get fucked with. But that guy Jamie was disturbed. You know he died soon after that."

"Suicide by cop," I said.

"Sure," said Michael Florida, grinned.

"What?"

"That phrase. It's funnier than 'touched out.' Jamie was a fuckup and a pervert, but I don't think he wanted the cops to kill him. That was their hilarious idea."

"I see. Speaking of the police, how did you keep out of jail when they took Jamie away? Why didn't he rat you out?"

"We were friends."

"I thought you said you didn't know him."

"Did I?"

"Yes, you did."

"Well, I don't know what to say, Detective. I guess you better cuff me."

"Were you . . ."

"What?"

"Were you actually a student at the college?"

"Of course not."

"Oh."

"What, all these years you thought I was in college with you? Do you remember what I was like? How did you square that?"

"I never could."

"I mean, did you ever see me even reading a book?"

"All the time," I said. "You were always reading."

"I was, wasn't I?" said Michael Florida. "Now I remember. I mean, I remember reading. I can't remember a goddamn thing I read."

"Wish I could help. Anyway, I always remembered you tackling that guy Jamie. I thought it was brave. Now I know the truth."

"It was brave. Weird you don't see that."

Purdy emerged from a lacquered door at the edge of the atrium. He waved, walked over, kept his eyes on us while he spoke into something that resembled a long, shiny bullet.

"Then we won't do Susannah and the Elders," he said. "It's no skin off my back. It's not even a Bible story anyway . . . What's that? . . . It's in the Apocrypha . . . What? . . . Okay, you're a talented kid, so I'm still going to let you make some of these movies even though you don't know what the Apocrypha is. Your generation is pathetic . . . Huh? . . . It's got nothing to do with being religious. It's cultural knowledge. Which is the glue of a society. Which is precisely what has come unglued. Which is part of the reason we are all working for the Chinese to produce biblical content for cell phones. Okay, later."

Purdy twisted the upper segment of the bullet.

"Sorry, fellas."

"Nice phone," I said.

"Thanks, though I am not even sure it's a phone. I don't think they've decided. It's a prototype."

"But you can talk into it."

"Yes, that's true. So, what's up? Did you get a load of this joint?"

"Starting to."

"You try the archery yet? It's kind of random, I know, but one of the founders used to shoot competitively. It's like a Zen thing for her now."

"Cool. I'll have to go down and check it out."

"Melinda is back there having deep talks with badass midwives. This morning they finished up a fifty-seven-hour labor. Can you believe that? A breech vee-back with a flat cord, double-looped. I have no idea what that means, but I want to film one and put it on a cell phone. So people can watch it on their cell phones. Did you get a smoothie?"

"I'm fine," I said.

"You could probably use one."

"I'll manage."

"Manage what? Manage to die? Two Hind Kindnesses, please."

The bartender, a young woman with skuzzed hair and a mahogany disk distending her lower lip, nodded.

"So, thanks for waiting. I guess you had to deal with all of this stuff with Abner."

"Bernie," I said.

"Sorry, Bernie. Bold name, by the way. You just definitely want him to be an accountant?"

"We like the name. We named him after my grandfather."

"I'm all for it. There are definitely too many Elis and Olivers and Broncos around."

"Bronco?"

"We know a couple that went with Bronco."

"What are you guys thinking about for a name?" I said.

"Oh, I don't know. How about Don? That's a solid name."

Purdy pinched out a smile.

"I met with Don," I said.

"That's why we're here."

"In your email you mentioned something about further exploring the give."

"Due time."

"Okay, so."

"What did the kid say? Did he pass along a message?"

I told Purdy most everything, left out the soliloquy about cock cancer and the accordion bus. I didn't mention Sasha's offer of a fondle, either. I had never considered it genuine. I think she was just afraid of silence. I described the apartment, Don's legs, his humps, his girls.

"I almost want to cry," said Purdy. "Poor kid. I can't believe what we do to them. Fucking hell."

"Well, maybe someday we can finally—"

"Oh, screw that," said Purdy. "It will always be this way. We do war. That's what we do. We can't be babies about it. I'm a liberal hawk."

"Swoop!" Michael Florida giggled, but I took it for synaptic misfire. He turned back to the girl behind the bar.

"But it's just not right how we treat our guys," said Purdy. "My guy. What we need is a draft, that's all. Why does Don have to do all the fighting? Why not the sons of privilege?"

"I don't know, Purdy."

"What else did he say?"

"He's really angry. I guess that's my point. He's really angry with you. And with the world. I think it gets mixed up for him."

"Did I ask for a diagnosis? Are you licensed?"

"You said you wanted my take."

"You're right. I'm sorry. I did."

"He wants more money."

"How much?"

"He didn't specify. He said the envelopes need to be thicker."

"Thicker."

"And he said he'd like you to take him to the zoo. But I think he was kidding."

"No shit."

"Look, I'm sorry if—"

"No, no. It's me. I'm still raw with this stuff. You can imagine how touchy it is."

"Touched out," muttered Michael Florida.

"There's something you need to know," said Purdy. "He called Melinda."

"He did? When?"

"Yesterday. Hung up. Mel just thought it was a wrong number. But I asked to see her phone and I saw his name in the display. I can't figure him out."

"Maybe you should just tell Melinda. I mean—"

"Milo, you have no idea what you're talking about. Just leave off. That part is not your concern."

His voice had a new cold quaver.

"Understood."

"What is it, Milo?"

"Maybe we should talk in private?"

"This is private."

"Okay. It's just about why Don is so pissed."

"I was a shitty father, Milo. Completely absent. It's not complicated."

"He said something about his mother. About you not paying bills. And something about a motel."

Purdy regarded me oddly. I could not tell if he wanted me to continue. Maybe he was waiting to see what I would say next, and based on that certain irrevocable actions would be taken. It was like those Choose Your Own Adventure books, without so much of the choosing part.

I met his eyes, smiled.

"This is also in that category of stuff that is not my concern," I said. "My bad."

Purdy put a hand on my shoulder.

"You're doing a great job, Milo. I really appreciate this. And your colleagues will appreciate you when this is all over. In the meantime, take this, a sort of goodwill gesture from me. About my seriousness with regard to the give."

He slid an envelope into my shirt pocket.

"I can't take that," I said.

"You already have. You'll hear from me, or somebody, soon. I've got to get back in there with the midwives. You're a good friend, Milo. By the way, we're having a dinner thing next week. Some people from our wasted youth will be there. Should be fun. Michael?"

"Present."

"I need you to pick up a pair of relief chaps for Melinda. Open-toed."

"Relief chaps," said Michael Florida.

"They're compression stockings. They reduce the chance of varicose veins. I'm all for varicose veins. Melinda could use some flaws. But she wants them."

"Relief chaps," said Michael Florida.

"I know," said Purdy. "If I only had a band to name."

Purdy rubbed my head.

"Was there anything else? About Don? Just a little thing. Some kind of detail? I'm curious."

"Well," I said. "He mentioned something about the fake internet."

"The what?"

"He thinks the internet is fake. Or else he thinks there's something called the fake internet."

"So, he's not that dumb."

Purdy wheeled and jogged across the atrium, tugged his phone from his pocket.

Michael Florida and I stood wordless at the bar. I sipped my Hind Kindness. Michael Florida reached over and tasted Purdy's.

"Last time they were creamier," he said. "More hind-y."

Twenty

The hand-scrawled sign over the door to Happy Salamander read: "Closed indefinitely due to pedagogical conflicts. Sincerely, The Blue Newt Faction."

"Fuck," I said, a word I had made sincere efforts to purge from my repertoire of professed displeasure, at least in the presence of my son. It was 8:50 in the morning and Bernie and I were alone on an Astoria side street, not far from a sandwich shop that sold a sopressatta sub called "The Bypass." I used to eat that sandwich weekly, wash it down with espresso soda, smoke a cigarette, go for a jog. Now I was too near the joke to order the sandwich, and my son's preschool was in the throes of doctrinal schism.

"Fuck," said Bernie. "Fuckwinky eyeballhead."

"No, Bernie. We don't use those words."

"Which words?"

"You know which words."

"You used them, Daddy."

"I made a mistake. I am sorry I said that word. It isn't helping with our problem."

"What's our problem?"

"There may be no school today."

"That's okay," said Bernie. "It'll be okay."

We weren't sure where he had picked up that becalming phrase, probably from us, as we tried to talk ourselves out of the awful lucidity certain days afforded. The whole mirthless dwindle of things would suddenly pull into focus, the crabbed, moneyless exhaustion that stood in for our lives, and Maura and I would both start the chatter, the cheap pep: *It's okay, it's going to be okay, we'll get through this.* When Bernie repeated these bromides, he sounded seventy years old. It broke your heart, as did about forty-three percent of the things Bernie said and did. About twenty-seven percent of the things he said and did made you want to scream and banish him to his childproofed room, or do much more heinous and ingenious things, just so he'd get the point, whatever the point could be with an almost-four-year-old, but still, to bury him alive and then save him at the last minute, or tell him that the state had passed a law against ice cream and he would go to prison if he even thought about it, because they now had the technology to detect illegal mint-chocolate-chip cogitation, had, in fact, the chips for it, seemed, if not conducive to his development, at least on some level deserved. Thirty percent of what Bernie said and did was either on the bubble or else utterly inscrutable, just the jolts and stutters of a factory-fresh brain working out the kinks.

"Pedagogical conflicts?" said a voice behind me. Aiden's mother stood with her boy, her red bun blazing in sunlight.

She was sky-charged and goddessy in her pantsuit.

"I know," I said, "like, what the hey?"

I was glad I'd remembered to shucksify my vocabulary in the company of children. I hoped it imparted the care with which I could also create a fluttery motion with my tongue around Aiden's mother's bunghole. I was falling in love with her on the spot, on the sidewalk. I wasn't even an ass man, or ass person. I liked breasts, and the word "burgundy."

It must have been the way she'd said "pedagogical."

"It's a bunch of baloney," said Aiden's mother.

You could tell she was sassy, the skeptical sort. She had opinions. She'd be the first to tell you she had opinions.

"I agree," I said.

"They've got no right. We trusted those little brats with our brats."

"Who are the brats, Daddy?" said Bernie. "I'm not a brat."

"It's just irresponsible," I said. "This isn't the end of it."

"If you're talking about messing those yuppies up, I'm in. Pedagogical, my behind."

Bernie and Aiden slipped from their respective parental grips and commenced conversation about an action hero, something not quite human that maybe transformed or transmogrified but in any event could easily exsanguinate any mother or father or adult guardian, which was the crucial part, the takeaway, as TV commentators put it. It would have been hard to tell, witnessing the boys together now, that one had recently tried to bite off the other's penis. The flipside to the fickleness of children was their ability to transcend grudge, adjust to new conditions. Innocence, cruelty, rubbery limbs, amnesia, successful nations were erected on these qualities.

"Say 'pedagogical' again," I said, a little dreamily.

"Excuse me?" Aiden's mother took a step back.

"I mean, say it ten times fast," I said. "I can't. Why is the school closed? Those crazy kids. I was really looking forward to school today. I had my activity nodes all planned out. I was going to play office."

"Were you now?"

I'd won her back. It had been years since I'd flirted. I felt as though I were snorting cocaine, or rappelling down a cliffside, or cliffsurfing off a cliff of pure cocaine.

"I had a memo all planned out."

"Well," said Aiden's mother, "there's no way I was going to play office. Not when I have to go to one. I was really counting on making a house out of pipe cleaner. Maybe a four-bedroom, three-bath, Italian-style villa."

"That could be tough, with pipe cleaner," I said. "Milo."

I stuck out my hand.

"Denise."

"His legs are the motorcycle, they become the motorcycle or the airplane, but he can't fly like Superman," said Bernie.

Sometimes with peers, and with us, Bernie acquired an authoritative tone that charmed. Autodidactic vigor is darling in a little boy. Give him forty years, though, a beer gut, leather vest, bandanna, granny glasses, and picture him the sad knob known as the Professor in a biker bar off the thruway, the arrogant but harmless turd humored for his historical factoids about extinct warrior societies and mots justes about the bankruptcy of liberal democracy, humored, that is, until a severe, silence-craving patron, maybe some psychotic who made his living garroting people's wives and business partners for high three-figure fees, suddenly didn't find the Professor's disquisitions edifying, kicked his neck in, then it wasn't so charming. Which is why I tended not to picture it.

"I saw him fly on TV," said Aiden.

"He's not real," said Bernie.

"Who? Iron Hawk?"

"No," said Bernie, and I started to cringe. "Superman. He's not real."

"Yes, he is," said Aiden.

"No," said Bernie. "He's just a story people tell to make themselves feel better. That's what my daddy says."

Denise shot me a look.

"It's true," I said.

"I guess it is." She laughed.

Now the Happy Salamander door opened and a bearded young man peered out. This was Carl, a Salamander founder, the heavy theorist with the barn. I'd met him once at a school picnic. Was he Blue Newt Faction? We'd have to tread carefully.

"Hey, guys," he said. "Probably be better if you didn't loiter here."

"Loiter?" I said.

"Right."

"We came to drop our kids off at school."

"I'm sure you read the sign on the door," said Carl.

"I'm sure you have our reimbursement checks cut," I said.

"You tell him, Milo," said Denise.

"Excuse me?" said Carl.

"We're paid up through June."

"Us, too," said Denise.

"There's still a month and a half left of school."

"Yeah, look," said Carl. "This isn't about money, okay? The whole project has been ripped apart. There are former comrades out there spreading intolerable lies about our methodologies. Reputations and friendships are in tatters. And you're worried about reimbursement?"

"Damn right I am," I said.

"We just wanted a nice pre-K for our kids," said Denise. "Blocks and hugs. That's all. We didn't demand Mandarin, or even tumbling. Blocks and hugs. An ant farm."

"And we wanted to give your children the most wondrous educational and social experience ever devised. But we blew it. It's that simple. It's a tragedy. I'm going back to grad school. I don't need this shit. Screw budgets, overhead, trying to compensate for the inadequacies of parents like you. I'm going back to grad school and then I'm going to teach rich kids in Brooklyn. I'll write books. Fuck you, reimbursement. Of course you'll get your reimbursement. But also, fuck you for not contributing, for not helping to make this work, for being a coward in the battle for your children's minds and souls."

"Going back to grad school?" I said. "Didn't you get your degree already?"

"There are many versions of that story, my friend."

Carl shook, his beard wet with spit. He wiped it with the sleeve of his stained French sailor shirt.

"Can we talk to Maddie?" I said.

"Yes," he said. "Maybe it's better if you talk to Maddie."

He disappeared into the house and in a moment Maddie poked her head out.

"Sorry about that. Carl's taking this hard."

"So are we," I said.

"The Blue Newt Faction is talking about starting again. Maybe upstate. If you're interested. The others, I don't know what they will be doing. But we would be delighted to take Bernie back if we get something together at some point. Aiden, too."

"Would you board them? With the milk cows?"

"Excuse me?"

"We live *here*, Maddie," I said. "This school is near our houses. Are you suggesting we all move to a little town upstate? Will there be a cheese collective we can all work at?"

"Cheese collective?"

"Jesus, Maddie. We were depending on you guys. We didn't realize it was just an intense hobby."

"I resent that, Bernie's Dad."

"I'm just being honest, Bernie's immature, self-involved, pseudo-intellectual preschool teacher."

"I'm closing the door now," said Maddie. "For Bernie and Aiden's sake."

"Close away," I said. "Tourist. Honky."

"Honky?"

"Ofay."

"We're all white in this conversation," said Maddie.

"This might be your year abroad, lady," said Denise, "but we live here."

"I really am closing the door," said Maddie, and did.

"Come on," said Denise. "There's a Montessori on Ditmars. Maybe they've got some openings."

We marched off together.

"Daddy," said Bernie. "Is Carl sad?"

"I think so, yes," I said.

"Is he bad?"

"He's young. He's idealistic."

"He's a total disaster," said Bernie.

•

We skipped the Montessori, got milkshakes instead.

"Cheese collective." Denise laughed. "That was funny. You're funny."

I was funny again, the sexy jester Maura could no longer appreciate. Denise's swirling green eyes appreciated all. We'd go to her house, plant the children in front of a longish DVD, *Winnie-the-Pooh*, perhaps, devour each other in the bedroom. She was a single mom, probably no stranger to kid-friendly assignations. (Had she ever listened to a thrusting lover sputter a broken poem of climax into her ear while Aiden moaned with night terrors over the monitor? Might be fun to ask.)

Denise smiled, spooned up her café au lait. The noise of our kin fell away. I pictured days lost in a soft white bed, us rising only to pee or nibble on some olives or last night's stale baguette before our bodies would start to twitch with lust again. I could almost smell the high stink of our clinches.

It might be awkward with Aiden around. It would be better if he didn't have to experience that particular cliché, the naked Mommy Friend, raw whang aflap, washing up in the bathroom or drinking from the kitchen tap. *Hey, kid. Your mom is a real nice lady. You like baseball? You talk at all? Suit yourself.* It would be better, but it wasn't mandatory that Aiden be spared the crushing animal truth, especially if it meant I forgo crushing animal need.

Denise was definitely not touched out. Denise was all touched in.

I watched her wipe chocolate from Aiden's mouth. Then I

looked down at Bernie, the top of his head, peered through his hair at a sliver of pinkish scalp. His tender little scalp. We'd made that scalp, Maura and I, shielded it from the scalp hunters of this world.

There was no way I could go through with this. I wasn't that guy. No matter what had become of my marriage, I wasn't Roger. My life would never be a cavalcade of nooners. Pornography and corn chips would be my mistresses. Maura would be my wife.

I'd led Denise on. Now I'd have to let her down. She'd see through me anyway, the timid husband afraid to act upon his desires, the evader, the deflector, the sublimation machine. She'd find a better man to touch her in and out, somebody capable of real love, real deceit. Maybe a single man, though they said the good ones all were taken. She'd find a married man who could afford another secret family. Some men could pull that off. Purdy never had the choice, and Roger never dared, as far as I knew, but he was a one-off specialist. There were other sorts, however, capacious souls, who yearned for monogamy with several women at once. Their energy was unthinkable, biblical, Koranic. Poor Denise. She'd probably just been horny, wanted dick. Here I was getting sanctimonious and my whang did not even warrant it. But I had no choice, I had to close off this buzz between us. She'd have to learn to live with the spurning.

Denise threw some money on the Formica.

"So, Milo, it was nice to meet you, officially. Guess we may end up seeing you at Christine's. Goodbye, Bernie."

"Goodbye," said Bernie. "Goodbye, Aiden."

"Goodbye, Bernie."

"You're leaving?" I said.

"I just got a text from my boyfriend. He's coming home early with pizza."

"Sounds fun," I said. "Boyfriend?"

I watched her face register what I, and only I, it turned out, had been mulling, saw the surprise there, the disgust, the deeper disgust, the moral judgment, the slight flattery, the steepening dive into new realms of physical revulsion, followed by pity's steadying hand. Denise snapped her purse shut.

"His name is Larry. He's great. Hope you can meet him sometime. He's a trainer at a gym in Manhattan. He trains the guy on the news."

"Which one?" I said.

"The one with the awesome body. Though not as awesome as Larry's. Okay, Aidey, let's go."

Denise stood, hustled her little boy out of the diner.

"Daddy, why did they have to leave?"

Bernie blew sugar across the table through a straw. Normally I would have snatched the straw away, admonished him loudly enough to demonstrate to the dining public my stern but fair-minded parental manner. But now I just sat there, dazed, let Bernie blow sugar and shred napkins, pour ice water onto his ever-burgeoning heap of sugar and shredded napkins, tamp it with a coffee spoon.

"They needed to meet up with Denise's friend Larry."

"Larry, with the muscles?"

"You know him?"

"He once came to pick Aiden up at Christine's."

"Oh."

"Aiden says that Larry is gone. He went to a land called Elmira. He got a pole of violets for it."

"He what?"

"He . . . ladled his prole."

"Violated his parole."

"That's it. You know, Daddy. You always know."

"Aiden told you this?"

"His mommy cries a lot. Aiden saw Larry's winky, too."

"When did he see Larry's winky?"

"In the kitchen. Aiden got up from a bad dream and went to the kitchen and Larry was drinking juice out of the carton, which you said is bad, but Larry does it."

"It is bad," I said. "It's just really wrong to do that, Bernie."

"Larry does it."

"Larry got violated up to Elmira."

"Did he have to go there because he drank from the carton?"

"Life can be very tough on people," I said.

•

I hated to travel into Manhattan with Bernie. The boy figured the sidewalks for a snack spread. Old gum, cigarette butts, bottle caps, petrified turds, even the occasional crack vial or broken syringe—Bernie could work it all into his mouth. Of course he could find such ad hoc oral solace on the boulevards of Queens, but the trash seemed less virulent here. It was the home poison.

Still, I had to see Maura. We could surprise her, Bernie and I, maybe drink some lemonade on a bench in Bryant Park. I knew she took her salads there when the weather was good. Sometimes she told amusing stories about the scene, the ongoing mash-up of tourists, homeless drunks, street clowns, construction workers, and office temps reading their papers or calling their friends or playing bocce ball with the bocce ball hustlers.

I'd witnessed some odd things myself, the few times I'd met Maura for lunch or crossed through to the Public Library before getting back to Mediocre. I always seemed to bump into somebody I knew, people from work, old acquaintances. I'd once seen Maurice Gunderson deliver a lecture about the apocalypse to a large group gathered in the outdoor reading area. It was a warm spring day and he looked golden, prophetic, up at the lectern.

When his talk was over I stood in the autograph line with a copy of his book I'd taken from a display table.

He got into an argument with the man in front of me about crop circles. The man had proof they were pranks. Maurice said the pranks and the proof of the pranks were both part of a cover-up. They went on for a while. I was about to slip away when Maurice looked past the man and called me over.

"Sir, what's your feeling about all of this?"

I stood there, beamed, waited for Maurice to recognize me.

"No pressure," said Maurice, looked back to the other man. "Maybe we can continue this at the party."

"Love to," said the man, and I realized that despite the spat the man was a friend and fan of the Gunderson project. Now Maurice held out his hand for my book, to sign it.

"Whom shall I make it out to?" he said. "Or do you just want the signature?"

"Signature's fine," I said.

"A collector," said Gunderson. "Get it through your head. There's no point in collecting anything, except maybe some good karma."

Gunderson grinned and handed the book back, stared past me to the next pilgrim, a tawny teen in a cocktail dress of skimpy hemp.

Now Bernie and I walked hand-in-hand through the park. He did not wriggle, did not bolt, did not eat garbage from the ground. We strode together in perfect sunlight. I loved my family, my life. We passed a urine-scented lawn-sleeper with a swastika on the web of his cracked hand and I loved him, too. I even loved the bespoke-suited tool on his cell phone shouting at somebody about somebody else's promise that he'd be "getting his beak wet." But mostly I just loved my wife and my son. I almost wanted to shout it aloud, but the men I'd known who indulged in such gestures tended to be divorced.

There was maybe an immutable law about that.

But there were also maybe immutable laws about beautiful moods. Here was the love of my life on a shaded bench with her lunchtime greens. What a turkey wrap meant to me, a bowl of arugula and goat cheese meant to Maura. My heart was full of tender wonder. Maura had a noonday luminescence. Beside her sat a handsome man who laughed and kneaded her thigh with a strong tan hand. It was Paul the Animator. I had a moment to decide: gay touch or straight touch? Before I could, Bernie broke from my grasp, galloped at them.

"Paul!" he shouted. "Hi, Paul! Do you have my superhero cartoon?"

A Spandexed man on a unicycle sliced past me.

"Watch it, fatty," he said.

"Fuck you, clown," I snarled.

The man's arm shot back. A spray of daisies sprouted in his fist.

Twenty-one

We ate dinner in silence, or near silence, as Bernie, naked, wet from the bath, speared disks of Not Dog with his fork and chuckled knowingly at something he most likely knew nothing about. Maura kept her eyes down, sipped her wine. I pretended to relish my Swedish meatballs, which I'd picked up with some other groceries after leaving Paul and Maura in the park.

It had been nothing but pleasantries among us, but the flustered way they had gathered themselves after Bernie called to them charged our exchange. Paul had tried to excuse himself but Maura insisted he stay. They could walk back to the office together. Lunch hour was over anyway. Why hadn't I called? Maura wanted to know. I told her about Happy Salamander, the defection of the Newts. But why hadn't I called? Paul looked shaken, though still wonderfully tan. He promised Bernie he'd finish his animation soon, led Maura away.

"Paul's my grown-up friend," said Bernie.

"What about me?"

But I'm not sure he heard. He'd already darted away, disappeared into a throng of Russian tourists, then just disappeared.

"Bernie!" I dipped into that familiar parental trot, the one that covers more ground than walking but does not yet reek of pure panic. It's important to smile a lot while you maintain a steady pace and call out your child's name in an almost jovial manner, as though it could be a game, and even if it's not a game, you still aren't worried, it's happened before, though not too often, and besides, it's age appropriate, so you don't consider it an issue requiring therapy or, heaven help us, a pharmaceutical regimen. This is no big deal, the trot and the smile signal, though it sure would be great to locate the little scamp. But hey, the kid gives back a lot of love, and usually you're a bit more in control of the situation, though you understand child-rearing throws its curve-balls, its cutters and sinkers, too, but still, this is nothing compared to the hard work the parents of, for example, Down kids must put in, or even the folks with autistic children, where you're doing all that special needs slogging and not even getting those sloppy Down kisses, no, your kid, he's a regular kid, maybe with some impulse-control deficiencies, or dealies, as you laughingly call them with your wife, or maybe, and you're definitely willing to entertain this notion, especially in this era of so much entitled helicopter coddling, or whatever the term is where the children are literally enfolded in cocoons of helicopters that entitle them to do whatever they want, because of the culture, maybe this very normal, regular, active boy, who happens to live in a social strata that condemns masculine energies in all its children, maybe he just needs to have his coat pulled, to be briefed, as it were, in an energetic masculine way, to be boxed or cuffed or whacked upside some part of him in that no-nonsense, simple folkways folk way (because throttling and such, it's worked for thousands of years, no?), or at least persuaded in a compelling and lasting fashion that it is not okay to just dash off into a throng of Russian (gas-rich, reassembling their rabid empire) tourists and ignore his father's cries, yes, it could be that he needs to be squared away on that score in a more visceral sense, though certainly not in the sense of a spanking or a hiding, such tactics, alas, never work, but anyway that is a separate discussion. Really, right now, you just need to get a visual on the little shit, pronto.

After the trot comes the flat-out run, all heaves and stumbles, the smile long vanished, but it never came to that, because

I found Bernie, or he found me, his wrist in the grip of a stout woman in a business suit.

"Yours?"

"Bernie," I said. "You are in big trouble. Thanks."

"No worries," said the woman. "He was just chasing a pigeon."

"Thanks again. I really appreciate it."

"I've got three at home."

"Pigeons?"

"No, kids. Here."

She handed me Bernie's wrist.

"He's a fast one. But I know how to sneak up on them."

"I owe you," I said, dragged Bernie away.

We stood behind a tree near the edge of the park.

"What are you doing, Daddy?"

"I think I'm going to cry," I said.

"Don't do that," said Bernie.

"Okay," I said, picked up him up, laid my cheek on his shoulder.

"Bernie," I said. "I love you so much."

"That's nice, Daddy."

"Yes," I said. "It is nice."

"You want to know something else nice?"

"I sure do, Bernie."

"I love mommy's friend Paul. Do you think Paul loves me, Daddy?"

They weren't like dolls, because dolls had no feelings. Kids had feelings, just not any remotely related to yours.

•

Now we sat at dinner saying nothing. Some families did this every night. Hollywood made poignant movies about them. But we'd always been blabbermouths.

Bernie chuckled again.

"What's so funny?" I said.

He looked up at me with odd fervency. He was holding his miniature half-on between his fingers, thwacking it against the chair seat.

"Daddy," he said.

"Yes, Bern."

"This isn't a winky."

"It's not?"

"It's a video game."

I looked down at my son's lap. An odd benevolence surged through me. I had maybe made peace with Bernie's foreskin. His freak flap, let it fly. If he ever wanted to be a real Jew he could have it snipped. Nobody would ever be able to question his commitment after that. Besides, if he wanted to be a real Jew, he'd probably have to renounce me. Because I was a fake Jew who spent a lot of time on the fake internet rubbing my video game. Because the real Jews scared the hell out of me, same as the real Muslims and the real Christians, the real Hindus. Because they believed. How could they believe? Fine, come kill me as a Jew, flog me to death in a desert quarry, bayonet me in the Pale, gas me in your Polish camp, behead me on your camcorder, I still would not believe. To me that was the true test of courage: to not submit to the faith they assume you possess and will kill you for. So now I loved Bernie's foreskin. Or at least I'd made peace with it.

"I've made peace with it," I whispered.

"Excuse me?" said Maura.

"I said I've made peace with it."

"That was quick."

"What do you mean?"

"Wait a minute," said Maura. "What have you made peace with?"

"You tell me."

"Not so fast."

"What do you think I've made peace with?"

"That's what I'm asking you."

"You tell me," I said.

"I think we're going around in a circle."

"Which means what?"

"What do you mean which means what?"

"It could mean there is something you don't want to tell me."

"No, Milo, it's you who won't do the telling. Don't you see? You won't tell me what you've made peace with. So, I can't tell you what I don't want to tell you until I know what it is that you've made peace with."

"I'm no longer at peace."

"Good. You probably shouldn't be."

This is how I knew my wife was having an affair with Paul. The knowledge arrived with a pressured sensation, a pallet of wood on my chest. Deck wood. For a Mission-style deck. I stood, moved to the door.

"Where are you going?"

"I'm going to get some air."

"Daddy, will you get me some?"

"Air?"

"Yeah."

"I'll try, Bern."

"You can't go out now," said Maura.

It was true. We had the evening ritual ahead of us—the dishes, Bernie's books, his teethbrushing, his pre-tuck-in piss, which often required some degree of cajolement, his stories, his songs. It would be a kind of betrayal of the ideals of co-parenting to walk out now. Then again, sliding your tongue along the seam of Paul the Animator's smooth and perfumed scrotum had to hold formidable rank in the hierarchies of betrayal. Maybe someday a civil court judge would sort through the equivalencies. Most of me hoped not.

"I need some air," I said.

A walk around the block convinced me I could not return home tonight.

I headed for the doughnut shop. I wanted doughnut-scented air. My pain had earned me both a Bavarian cream and a coconut chocolate flake. I was the only customer and I sat and ate my doughnuts, pictured myself that lonely diner at the counter in the famous painting. I'd always studied it from the artist's perspective, the stark play of shadow and light. But to be the fucker on the stool was another kind of stark entirely.

Now the door opened and the kiddie-diddler, his herringbone blazer twined shut with twists of electrical tape, wheeled a plaid suitcase into the shop.

"Good evening, Predrag," he said in that radio voice.

The counter kid nodded.

The kiddie-diddler sidled up, tapped a finger on the napkin dispenser. Predrag slid the old man coffee in a paper cup.

"Predrag, my strapping friend, what are the specials tonight?"

"No specials. Doughnuts."

"What about those croissant sandwiches? With the eggs and sausage?"

"What about them?"

"I'm in the mood for one of those delectable concoctions."

"Microwave's broken."

"Yes?"

"They're frozen. You need a microwave."

"Surely you have a conventional oven back there," said the kiddie-diddler.

"These are for the microwave only."

"I'd be surprised if you couldn't defrost them in a conventional oven. You know, Predrag, and I grant that you may be too young to remember this, but there was a time before the microwave. A better time, some would argue, though I wouldn't. That would be silly. No time is better than another time. It's preposterous. There are always people doing kindnesses and there are always people smearing each other into the earth. To think otherwise is foolish. But I dare say it's not so foolish to suppose one could circumvent the problem of the broken microwave and heat the croissant sandwich in the conventional oven, probably to better overall effect. What say you, my Serbian prince? Couldn't be that much of a hardship, could it? Not compared to the Battle of the Blackbirds, I'd wager. What say you, son?"

"I say you don't have any money to buy a croissant, you old queer. Not a dime."

"The Slavs are a brainy lot," said the kiddie-diddler, swiveled toward me on his stool. "Absolutely crazy, as history bears out, but very smart, very courageous, marvelous poets, and also fine logicians."

"The fuck you talking about?" said Predrag.

"Any coarsening effect, as witnessed here, can be blamed on the West, I assure you. What's good in them comes from their Oriental influences, a notion they detest, but understand in their hearts to be the truth."

"Here," said Predrag, threw a frozen croissant in its wrapper at the kiddie-diddler. The old man ripped it open, sucked on the crystals.

"That's right," said Predrag. "Now give me five dollars."

The kiddie-diddler lowered his pastry.

"Young man, you know I never carry that kind of cash around."

"Damn it," said Predrag. "Do I have to call Tommy?"

"No," said the old man, looked at me again. "We won't have to call Thomas, will we?"

"Excuse me?" I said.

"Sir, I recognize you as a man of this neighborhood. A frequenter of this counter. Surely you could find it in your heart to advance the cost of this sandwich. I am good for it."

"Right," said Predrag.

"I am!" said the kiddie-diddler. "Is there no dignity allowed an old man?"

I threw five dollars on the counter. The kiddie-diddler rose, fixed me with his runny blue eyes.

"Sir, so that I may promptly repay you, with interest, may I enquire as to where you reside?"

"In a fabulous and secret universe of the mind."

The diddler blinked, smiled, patted my arm.

"Lifelong resident myself," he said, walked out.

"Jesus," said Predrag. "Every day with that old homo. I hate him."

"Because of the kids?" I said.

"What kids?"

"I don't know."

"Don't be spreading shit like that," said Predrag. "People get their throats cut, you start talking like that. He never hurt anybody. He's a good man. I just hate him. That's all. He gets in the way of my lie. My lie for myself."

"Your lie?"

"That in America, things can be okay."

"Why do you let him back?" I asked.

"It's his store."

"His store?"

"Well, was. Till he went nuts. Now his brother Tommy runs it. Not a very nice guy, Tommy. Lets his brother roam the streets. That's not America."

"Actually, that is America," I said.

"True," said Predrag, "but I don't want to hear it."

He had his tongs up, somewhat martially.

Out in the night again, below the N tracks, I still didn't want to go home. To slink back into the apartment, yank a blanket around my shoulders on the sofa, it seemed a kind of death.

It was too late for Claudia's house in New Jersey. A hotel in Manhattan would be ruinous. To call Purdy stood for another kind of undoing. It would be a mistake to owe him any more than I did. I still hadn't touched the money in the envelope.

Don Charboneau lived the closest, but he and Sasha just had the one room. I couldn't picture us in a group spoon. Maybe it was time to look into that Cypriot let. Still, I needed a place for tonight. Horace bunked with his mother in Armonk. Or had he not mentioned something about some roommates, a new place in Bushwick?

I called him, was at his door in Brooklyn in an hour.

"Milo," said Horace, shirtless, in dirty corduroys. "Welcome to the coop."

He scratched at his chest, led me into his new home.

•

Horace lived in a huge room filled with cages. Inside each cage was a young person, a futon or cot, a footlocker, a few milk crates. Bare bulbs on wires hung from fixtures in the high ceiling. I'd read about these places. Kids moved to the city, but there were no apartments left to rent to them, or none they could afford. But on a starting salary, or no salary, you could maybe manage a cage. Several dozen people resided here among the drum kits and guitar amps, the antique film editing deck, a few long tables and spindly chairs, a minifridge. Power cables streaked the floor under mounds of black and silver tape. Laptops glowed from the cages. Voices rose and fell, rippled about the room, a dozen conversations going at once, or maybe one conversation replicated over and over by feral and beautiful children.

The place resembled a new model prison, or one that had achieved a provisional utopia after principled revolt, or maybe a homeless shelter for people with liberal arts degrees. The cages brought to mind those labs with their death-fuming vents near my college studio. These kids were part of some great experiment. It was maybe the same one in which I'd once been a subject. Unlike me, though, or the guinea pigs and hares, they were happy, or seemed happy, or were blogging about how they seemed happy.

Horace had a sleeping bag in his cage, a desktop computer on an upturned box. The floor was cold concrete. A net sack of VHS cassettes dangled from the ceiling, maybe to honor the ancients, their antediluvian delivery systems. Underneath stood a stack of office files, the familiar hunter green tabs. He was taking work home, to his cage. He was a stronger, more adaptable kind of human.

"Miss Armonk?" I said.

"Thanks," said Horace, "but I'm not *that* pretty."

"No, I mean—"

"I know what you mean. Yeah, sometimes. I mean I miss my mom. The home-nuked meals. We had a lot of laughs. And she has a good hash connection. But my dad thought it was time for me to venture out into the world. Here's the world. You can crash out on the sleeping bag. Not in it. That would be a little gross. Just on it. I've got band practice."

Horace stood, stepped out of the cage. He fastened a padlock to the door.

"Locking me in?" I said.

"Trust me," he said. "It's better this way. They don't do the most rigorous vetting of tenants around here. Most of the kids are cool. But this place can be a creep con, too."

"What if I have to take a leak?"

"There's a jug over there in the corner. Okay?"

"Okay. And thanks."

"Hey, we're on the same team, right?"

"What team is that?"

Horace walked off, joined a few others near the rehearsal platform. He hoisted himself up behind the drums, laid down some lazy paradiddles. A gaunt woman with a constellation of face studs and a coonskin cap fingered a fuzz-toned bass. A bald guy with a microphone duct-taped to his throat dropped for some push-ups. His grunts and a few hard burps roared through the PA. The bass player looked over at the blinking soundboard near the drums.

"Wait!" she called. "We should be recording this!"

They got loud and I got weary. I had worried they would keep me awake but they functioned like the noise machine Maura brought home a few years ago, the one that blasted the crush of waterfalls while we slept, or did until we produced our own noise machine, one with the opposite function, shoved the store-bought model in a closet with our racquetball gear and my home gravlax kit. I fell asleep as the throat-miked youngster gargled schnapps and Horace bashed away on his snare and the girl plucked a two-note bass line much like the two-note bass line I used to pluck back when I also believed it was more authentic if you could not play your instrument whatsoever.

That night I dreamed I was an indentured servant in colonial Philadelphia. Somehow, even in the dream, I sensed that I had once been a development officer in post-colonial New York City, but couldn't be certain. I wore a leather apron with pouches filled with tools, pliers and awls, heavy iron files. My workbench was heaped with broken video games. I had no idea how to fix them, but I knew my master would not let me sleep or eat until I had. Jaw clenched to stanch my sobs, I jabbed a bellows up against the exposed logic board of a console, pumped.

A summer storm whipped the elms outside the workshop window. I heard a knock on the door and a round-shouldered young man with bright gray eyes leaned into the room.

"Ben," I said.

"I came to see if you needed any help, Milo. I know these contraptions tend to bedevil you."

"I'm fine, Ben."

"Truly, Milo, I am here to offer any advice you require. I have been thinking much on the subject of induction. And I feel I owe you after the incident last week in the tavern. I never knew you possessed any Hebraic blood."

"I never knew you were an anti-Semite," I said.

"Well, we do not have that term yet, but I am chancing that you refer to the prophecy I allegedly deliver at the Constitutional Convention sixty years from now? About how the Jews are insidious Asiatics we must protect against? That was a forgery. Everybody knows that."

"But what about the stuff you said at the tavern last week?"

"I just apologized for that."

"Ben," I said, "get the fuck out of here."

"Please, Milo, forgive me. Not for my sake, but for yours. You must relieve yourself of the burdens of resentment. Such an amelioration of the soul will enliven you. I am loath to see you toil with such futility."

"Sorry it's so painful to watch."

"I just don't understand it, my good friend. I left school at ten but have applied myself assiduously to learning and life. I will refrain from reciting my present and future accomplishments. You can look them up on ye olde webnet."

"I hate that joke. Both of those jokes."

"To each his own," said Ben.

"You made a slave hold the kite."

"Pardon?"

"I read that somewhere. You made a slave hold the kite and then the lightning struck and he got hit."

"Kite? Lightning? I fear I am ignorant of this calumny. But, yet, you may have something there. As I mentioned, I have been cogitating upon certain electrical properties, as found in nature. Kite, you say?"

"Come off it, Ben. You fucking hustler."

"And what, pray tell, are you, Mister Burke?"

"You know what I am, Ben. I'm a piece of shit. A man with

many privileges and zero skills. What used to be called an American."

"Not my kind of American. Fare thee well, Mister Burke. Good luck with that GameCube."

Young Ben Franklin slammed the door shut after him. My master's lucky horseshoe fell from its nail, clattered to the stone floor.

I woke with my cheek pressed into the cage wire. The bass player's porous face, scabbed and splotched at the sites of her various impalings, bobbed inches from mine. She knelt on the stone floor in the next cage over. Horace thrust away behind her. I'd once heard him refer to this position, on the phone with his mother, as "the style of the doggie." Of course, he might have been in her ass. I had no way of knowing from my vantage. It was a phenomenological quandary. Either way he pushed into her, and the girl's face drew up to my tiny patch of world. Our eyes locked. Her sour breath jetted through the wires. I stuck my pinky through the cage, uncertain of the nature of my ask. A suck? A nibble? She seemed to know, precisely, shook her head. I shrugged, rolled over, stood. The place had quieted down. Kids huddled in clots. Some swayed on their haunches around laptop screens. The boy with the throat mike snored on the drum riser, his aural emissions now less tropical waterfall and more the creak of a splitting ice cap, or some ur-continent's ancient riving.

Twenty-two

No messages from Maura arrived in the night. It seemed she had not crumpled with longing and regret, tried to reach through the dark to find me, beg forgiveness, or at least talk me home. Maybe the animator had cabbed out to comfort her, to animate her. Maybe at this very moment she brewed him coffee as he doodled at the kitchen table for Bernie's amusement. Did his cartoons feature an oafish, middle-aged disappointment who'd watched his young colleague fornicate in a chicken-wire cage and now just wished more than anything his wife could love him again, because that was the gruesome truth about betrayal, it was the cheater who had to be coddled, groveled to, convinced?

I hoped he drew me with some mercy, for Bernie's sake.

I checked my email on Horace's laptop. Two new messages sat in my inbox, the first from Don Charboneau, addressed to me, but with Purdy cc'd:

Hey there, bag boy—where is my bag? Daddy mad I called his lady friend? (Are you mad, Daddy? I just want a new mommy. And also I am so excited to meet my new sibling. Is it a boy or a girl?) Anyway, Mr. Burke, I guess this email is to you. I just wanted to see how it was hanging. Since my Daddy doesn't seem to want to respond to my emails I thought I'd get us all on the same screen this way. I'm thinking of starting some kind of

mail order business called PurdyStuarthadasecretfamily
.com, but I'm not sure what I could sell. I really just
want to get drunk and watch television, but my finances
are in a delicate state with this depression and shit. I'm
not sure what to do. I was hoping for some fatherly
advice, if not from my father, then from you. You ever
read *Hamlet*? It's too long, and kind of in love with
itself, but there are some good parts. I feel like Hamlet
sometimes. But I know I'm in a very different situation.
Because nobody poured poison in my father's ear. My
father just fucked my mother long after he'd left her and
married somebody else. Then he killed her, sort of. So it's
kind of a separate story line. What should I do?
Confused in Denmark, or Maybe Northern Queens

The second email, from Purdy, said, *Lee Moss, ASAP*, which I
read as *RIP*, oddly, until my eyes focused.

"Want to ride into the office together?" said Horace. He
walked into the cage, rubbed his hair dry with a dishtowel.
"You're single now, and the morning rush is a great place to
meet women. Or at least stare at them until they get pissed and
change cars. What do you say? Or should we play hooky and get
breakfast? No, wait, I can't, I've got a meeting with an ask."

"Where's your friend?" I said.

"What friend?"

"The bass player."

"Oh, Colleen? She's got the morning shift at her diner job.
What was the deal with your finger last night?"

"My finger?"

"You know what I'm talking about, you freaky polysexual
maniac. I like it."

"Polysexual? Because of my finger?"

"I don't know, dude. Good thing you didn't try to go glory-
hole through the wire. Colleen's not so free-spirited. Though I

would have taken care of you. And I don't even mean that in some sort of jokey crypto-homophobic way."

"Thanks, Horace. I seem to remember some harassment allegations you made about me at work."

"That's all part of it. The deep play."

"Shit," I said, looked at my phone, as though there was a clock on it, which there was. "I should just go now. Have a great commute."

•

The office of Lee Moss reminded me of ads I'd once seen for replicas of some literary titan's study. A faded lion could have paced all that leather and oak with a brandy in one hand and an Italian shotgun in the other, wondered whether his talent had finally fled him, and how long after his death his shiftless heirs would sell his name and likeness to an office design company. The place also boasted a decent view of the park.

Lee Moss himself resembled a faded lemur, frail, fuzz-skulled, curled up in his oxblood club chair, a tartan shawl across his knees. He motioned for me to join him on his throne's twin, poured a glass of water from the pitcher on the deal table between us.

"Thanks," I said. "So, Purdy suggested I stop by. I'm sure you're busy, but he insisted."

"Not so busy," said Lee Moss, his voice a flat rasp. "People cannot believe I'm still coming to work. They think I'm some kind of martyr to my clients. But I like being here. I'm more comfortable here. If I were home, I'd be in my study, which is just a less-comfortable version of this office. So why not be here?"

"As long as you get to see your family."

"My family? I shut my family out years ago. Not that I didn't love them, but I had to rack up the hours, right? That was the understanding. I made the money. I didn't go to the Little League game or the bake sale. You know, when you're a person like I am, you can either sit around and bemoan the fact that you missed all the Little League games, or just accept the fact that you were never really the guy who wanted to be at the Little League games. I think it's better to be honest. I gave my family everything. In return, they left me alone. It was a fair trade. But now I'm supposed to go home and die in the house with them? I'm supposed to lie there and wait for death while they tiptoe around my room a few minutes a day and then go off to shop or watch videos or drink liquor or make babies or price real estate or whatever it is they do? No thanks. I'll finish things out here, in my chair, taking care of business. My due diligence, sir. Now, I'm sure you didn't come here to listen to my speech, but I enjoy giving it, and I don't stint on my pleasures right now, as you can imagine. Thanks for coming to see me. I've been looking forward to meeting you. Purdy Stuart's old school chum. He's a good boy, Purdy. I worked for his father."

"He mentioned that."

"It's funny. I can tell you're a no-account putz, but you and I, we're on the same side of the fence. We serve the same liege lord."

"I didn't realize we lived in a feudal system."

"You must be kidding. If you didn't learn that going to school with the likes of Purdy, what did you learn?"

"I learned about late capitalism. And how to snort heroin."

"That's cute."

"I used to think so."

"You're growing up. All you need to remember is that nothing changes. New technology, new markets, global interconnectivity, doesn't matter. It's still the rulers and the ruled. The fleecers and the fleeced."

"Which are you?"

"I'm a piece of expensive equipment. You, too. Maybe not so expensive. Do you have any other questions?"

"What is Purdy trying to do? What does he want me to do?"

"Containment, I think, would be one word."

"But to what end?"

"I don't think I'll live long enough to make an informed conjecture."

"How about uninformed?"

"You feel caught somehow. You want to honor the terms of your employment. But it's difficult because you've been shut out of the whole story."

"So, what's the whole story?"

"None of your beeswax."

"That's helpful."

"I do what I can."

"Well, if you won't tell me," I said, "I'll just have to go with what I think would be Don's version. It's pretty grisly."

"Are you threatening your employer? Our employer? Why don't you do it like a man? Did they teach you anything about being a man while you were learning about late capitalism, whatever the fuck that is?"

Lee Moss plucked a phone from his suit pocket, angled it to his ear.

"Hello, young Stuart!" he said. "Yes. Yes. Okay, I'll take care of that. He's here, though. Here he is. He has something to tell you. For you."

"Hello?" I said.

"You dog."

"Excuse me?"

"Billy Raskov here just told me that you used to bone that hot art professor, what was her name?"

"I don't know," I said.

"He doesn't remember her name!" Purdy called to somebody.

"No, I remember, it's just—"

"I'm playing with you, Milo. You're always so sensitive. So nervous. Don't be so nervous."

"I'm not nervous."

"You are, you're nervous. Come to my thing next week."

"What thing?"

"Don't eat. I hired this incredible chef. He dehydrates everything into these little figurines. He does a menagerie. The best part is it's not nearly as expensive as it looks."

"What time?" I said, but Purdy was already gone. I handed the phone back to Lee Moss.

"His father used to beat the living shit out of him. Can you believe it? Embarrassing."

"Purdy never mentioned that," I said.

"Of course not. Walter Stuart was a monster. You don't beat your son. You alienate him, distance him from any sense of self-worth, force him toward the womanish and then berate him for latent faggotry, but you do not beat him. That's for people just off the boat. Purdy was a tough kid though. Learned how to be a monster, too. Which is the point of the exercise."

"I see," I said.

"I really doubt you do. Here's a cashier's check. Look at the figure. Ask the Charboneau boy if he accepts. If so, he can come here to pick it up. He will be required to sign a number of documents. Waivers. This isn't to cover up any crime. That's why it pains me to pay out so much. I don't mind paying to cover up a crime. What else is money for? But this is just to protect Melinda's feelings. And she's a goddamn gold-digging twat. But her feelings must be protected. That's at the top of my to-do list. And as long as Purdy pays you, it's at the top of yours. Here's your check. The check for you. Read the amount written on it. You can see it's quite a bit more than you probably expected. When the boy has signed the documents, you will receive this check. And one final thing. Here's a coroner's report stating that Nathalie Charboneau died of complications arising from injuries sustained in a car crash. No foul play. So you can put your mind at ease. No crime. Just feelings. Pretty despicable, really."

Lee Moss closed the folder in his lap.

"I don't need a check," I said.

"Everybody needs a check."

"No," I said. "I need Purdy to reach deeper than this. I need him to make a big give to the university. Then I will get many checks. Paychecks. From my job."

"A sizable give might not be prudent for us."

"But that's what this is all about for me. That's what I've been eating the shit for."

"If you don't like what I'm telling you, you can walk away. This isn't the mob."

"Purdy promised."

Lee Moss dipped his head, reached for his lapel, spoke into it.

"Shatz, some of the Brazil nut carob chip, please." Lee Moss's eyes seemed lit with a new kind of joy. "It's a wonderful ice cream made by some young farming people upstate. It's keeping me alive."

"Of the pancreas, Purdy said."

"In my pancreas, yes," said Lee Moss.

The door opened and a stern young man in a suit carried in a tray with two bowls and two spoons and a periwinkle pint carton that read: "Blue Newt Creamery."

"I hope you'll join me."

"I ate before I came."

"Don't pass up life's treats, son."

"Okay."

"Wonderful."

The sounds of our spoons on bone china mingled with Lee Moss's hard breathing.

"My advice is to follow this through. Follow-through is the most important thing in life. Go see Charboneau. Tell him the number. Report back. We will see where we are. And perhaps, despite the volatility in the market, Purdy will be in a good enough position to make you a beloved man at your third-tier college. My grandson's at Harvard right now. He's a dummy.

But then again most of them are. I went to City College on the GI Bill. This was back when there was America. How is your delicious treat?"

"Delicious."

"We are going to eat ice cream and we are going to eat shit. The trick is to use different spoons."

Twenty-three

A firebird of new need had soared from the ashes of the need creation memo. Maura was stuck late at the office, couldn't pick up Bernie from Christine's. Maura's message made no mention of our trouble. All this searing silence, I worried we might be selling out, going Hollywood.

There was no time to visit Don before I got back to Astoria. The train climbed out of the tunnel, broke into a vista of railyards and brick. I called Don's cell phone.

"The flunky."

"Hi, Don."

"Greetings to you, sir."

"I need to speak with you. Can I make you lunch at my house? I'll have my kid at home, but I can keep him busy with a movie while we talk."

"Sure you want to show me where you live?"

I hadn't thought of that, though this was the first time Don, for all his posturing, had swerved into unadorned menace.

"Why not?" I said. "We have happy things to discuss."

"I have yook in my mouth," said Don.

"I'm sorry?" I said.

"I'm yooking in my mouth."

"Excuse me?" I said.

"I don't know," said Don. "What is it they say now?"

"Who?"

"The people I went to war for."

•

Bernie sat alone in Christine's concrete yard. He was chewing on a chunk of tire. The minivan was gone.

"Daddy!"

"Where's Christine?"

"She said she'd be right back. Told me to wait here."

I knelt to the pavement, put my arms out.

"I'm sorry, buddy. Come here. Everything's okay."

Bernie did not move. He picked up a candy wrapper, studied it.

"Daddy, look, it's a superhero."

"Bernie, I love you. I didn't mean for it to get like this. It'll never happen again. I promise."

"Aiden pooped on his winky."

"When was this?"

"I don't know. A million days ago."

"Please put that wrapper down, Bernie. It's garbage."

"When I'm five can I have the wrapper?"

"Yes, Bernie."

"Are we going home now? Let's say goodbye to Aiden."

"He's still here?"

"He's inside with Nick. Nick is cleaning his underpants."

"Nick's here?"

"His brother died. He fell off a roof in Connecticut. Will I ever die in Connecticut?"

"Bernie. We need to go now."

My boy looked up and smiled.

"But wait right here for a second," I said, took the broken side stairs, pushed into the dim kitchen. Nick squatted near the sink with a tissue in his hand. Aiden stood with his pants at his ankles.

"Just don't see how you got it on your johnson, little man," Nick said. "Well, hello, there."

"Everything okay in here?" I said.

"What does it look like?"

I didn't answer, glanced around the cramped room, the pots in teetering stacks, the econo-sized boxes of crackers and cookies and dried noodles, the bank calendars and rubber band balls and tins of allspice. Aiden's stink mingled with the scent of lentils on the stove.

"It looks like you are holding down the fort," I said.

"This is what I'm doing."

"I'm sorry about your brother."

"He got what he wanted."

"It's a tough thing."

"They found the remains of his last meal. Supermarket olive loaf."

"I've got to go now," I said.

"Look," said Nick, dabbed Aiden's testicles. "We don't need static. Life is short. The world is a bully. You want in on my show, just tell me. The offer still stands."

"Thanks for saying that," I said.

•

We took the back alley way to our house.

"Who's that?" said Bernie.

Don sat on our stoop, a newspaper in his lap.

"That's a friend of Daddy's. When we get inside I'll need to talk to him. You can watch a show."

"But I want to play with you, Daddy. I want to play guys."

"We'll play guys," I said. "We'll always play guys. But I need to talk to this man now."

"His legs are really skinny and there's a shiny part."

"They're made of metal."

It seemed a little chilly for cargo shorts, but then again, what did Don's girls know about the weather?

"Can I get some legs like that?" said Bernie.

We neared the stoop and Don waved. I laid my hand on my son's shaggy head. He was tall enough for that now. I wondered if this gesture, some compound of fond feeling and flight readiness, was hardwired by nature, or maybe television. It felt natural. But so did television.

"Boys!"

Don was doing sunny today.

"Hope you like smoked turkey," I said.

"Sandwiches?" said Don.

"Wraps."

I fixed lunch in the kitchen. Bernie and Don watched a DVD about dinosaurs. I'd seen it many times. The dinosaurs made cooing sounds and laid eggs by rivers and munched the leaves of primordial trees. The movie was for kids, so they never tore open each other's chests. They just growled, pawed the moist earth, marched off into the rainbow ooze.

"Those dudes are armored up, boy," I heard Don say. "Could have used some of those dinosaur hides in Iraq."

"I like this show," said Bernie, "but they don't have the asteroid."

"What asteroid?" said Don.

"Asteroid is what extincted them. It fell on their heads. Their raw eyeballs popped out."

"That's not what happened," said Don.

"What happened?" said Bernie.

"Wheels within wheels, kid. You a truther?"

"What's a truther?"

"You got it in you, I can tell."

"Where in me?"

"Where it counts."

"I can count to ten."

"Can you count to nine eleven?"

"That's a big number."

"It's small potatoes."

"How come you have metal legs?"

"My girls?"

"They're girls?"

"To me they are."

"Why?"

"You ask a lot of questions."

"I don't know a lot of stuff."

Don laughed.

"There was a guy who wrote a story," he said. "It was in a book my mother used to read. A story about a goose."

"I have Mother Goose."

"This is different. Anyway, one time, I was about ten, eleven, my mother was reading this story, and smiling, and she didn't smile a lot, so I noticed it right off. I asked her what she was smiling about. Then she read me the part of the story where the guy is describing this big tall army officer. I can't remember his name. I wish I could remember his name. I don't even have the book anymore. But this officer, he was a real mean guy with these high leather boots. Like up to the thighs. And the guy who wrote the story, he said the officer's legs were like girls coming out of those boots. It seemed weird to say that, wrong. But also right. And it made my mother happy for moment. It stayed with me. So, when . . . well, I call these my girls. And it makes me happy."

"How come you have girls and no legs?"

"Legs got blown off."

"Did it hurt?"

"Hasn't stopped."

"Was it the asteroid that did it?"

"Don," I said, "come on in the kitchen."

I'd laid out a plate of turkey wraps, a bowl of chips, a small dish of cornichons.

"Nice spread."

"Have a seat."

"Thanks. Getting a little sick of the dal and beans. This is nice bland American food."

"Dig in."

We ate without talking, like sad machines, our arms jutting out at robotic intervals for vegetable chips and pulls from our celery sodas. We ate quickly and then just sat.

"Coffee?" I said.

"Why not?"

I'd already brewed it, poured him a cup. Don studied the mug. Maura had brought it home from work, swag from the great swirl of need.

"World's Best Alcoholic Abusive Dad," said Don. "Is that ironic?"

"I guess," I said.

"See, I don't get that kind of irony."

"Maybe it's just glib," I said.

"I defer to your judgment," said Don. "So, you brought me to your lovely home for what reason?"

He rose from his chair, bounced a little where he stood.

"You can take them off," I said, "your . . . things."

Don's eyes went tight.

"I'm real grateful."

"Sarcasm," I said.

"What I was raised on. It's stupid but you can trust it. It's just there to hurt people. Nothing more."

"How's Sasha?"

"You like her? Did you like squeezing her tits?"

"I never did that."

"You think she wouldn't tell me?"

"She lied," I said.

"Doesn't matter," said Don. "Sasha and me, we're done. She went back to Pangburn Falls. Going back to school, she says."

"College?"

"High school."

"High school?"

"She's got a lot of road on her. I'm not even her first army of one."

"Sorry to hear she's gone."

"For the best. I'm not doing so hot, you know."

"No?"

"Not feeling that great."

"Oh."

Don took a sip of coffee. The stomps and shrieks of Tyrannosaurus rex drifted in from the next room.

"I'm not going to the zoo with my daddy, am I?" he said.

He looked almost disappointed.

"No," I said.

"What's the dollar amount?"

I told him the figure Lee Moss had shown me on the cashier's check.

"And I sign a bunch of shit that says I'm never to go here, call there, say this or that to X, Y, and Z. And I stay an orphan. Don't get invited to Vail for the ideas festival."

"How did you know about that?"

I saw a flicker in his face now, another Don, the vengeful one, the sneak, the creep.

"I'm informed. I'm a truther. A Purdy truther."

"What do you want me to tell them?"

"How much do you get?" said Don. "For brokering this crap."

"I get a chance to survive," I said. "It's a bad time. That money you'll get will carry you for years, as long as you don't burn it all in tinfoil."

"How do you know I chase the old dragon?"

"Your eyes are pinned. I figure you think snorting is for amateurs, and you are wearing short sleeves. You sure as shit aren't shooting between your toes."

"You're not all fool."

"Thanks for that."

Don sat back down at his plate, poked at some stray lettuce with his fork.

"I knew for a long time," he said.

"Pardon?"

"She had pictures of him in her drawer. I look like her but there were some things, my nose, my chin, I guess. She'd stare at me funny, like I was somebody else. Or also somebody else. I didn't know the name Purdy Stuart or anything. Just that I had to be related somehow to the guy in the pictures. To me he looked like a wuss. She told me my father had been a man she met in a bar. One time she said he'd moved away to Alaska. Another time she said he'd died. Maybe she had more bullshit ready if I ever said I wanted to find the man's relatives or something. But I didn't. What the hell for? My mother and me, and her sister, and my grandma, I already had a family. Sad fucked-up women, all of them. Dented cans, they call women like that. But I loved them. Besides, what the fuck was I? The most dented of all. But my mother, she was something, on a good day. Smartest person I ever knew. Worked her shifts and read her books. I wish more rubbed off on me. But it doesn't rub off. I always thought there was some big thing she was going to do. Had her acceptance letter from the fancy college. No diploma, just the letter, because she never finished. Hung it on the wall of every shithole we lived in. But she just went through her days. Pretty down a lot, but sometimes just, like, shining. And there were a few years there, at the end of high school, right before I signed up, when she was shining for a week at a time. It would build up for days, her happy, playing her CDs and even baking cookies and shit, and then she'd be off to visit some friends, or that's what she'd tell me, she was visiting friends for the night. She always left me a lot of food. She was only gone a night but the fridge would be stocked. Then she'd come home, be her depressed self again."

I heard a crash from the living room.

"Bernie! You okay?"

"Yeah, Daddy! I'm watching my show!"

"Sorry," I said.

"You're a good daddy," said Don.

"According to the manuals, I'm screwing up in more ways than I can count."

"You're a good daddy."

"I'm sorry. Please go on."

"I've said enough."

"I want to hear this," I said.

"Once I saw them. I was cruising around on a Saturday night and my friend called and he was at a party a few towns away and I took a shortcut I'd never done before, passed this motel right outside Pangburn Falls. Saw her car in the parking lot. I knew it was hers from her fucking lame-ass liberal bumper stickers. Always used to embarrass me. Save the abortionist polar bears and shit. Anyway, I pulled in and snuck up to the window. They were on a bed, it was still made, and they were dressed, drinking whiskey. I saw the bottle on the bureau. It was the guy from the pictures. A lot older, but him. They were just laughing. Easy. Reaching out for a gentle squeeze now and then. I couldn't hear what they were talking about. They both looked really thrilled to be there together in that shit room. I got out of there. Took some pictures and got the hell out of there."

"You took pictures?"

"With my cell phone."

"You have them?"

"She came home the next morning, seemed sadder than ever. That was the last time she went out for the night, at least while

I was around. I joined up and deployed, eventually. You know, my convoy got lit up the day she had her car crash. Nothing happened to me that time, but still, kind of weird, right? Lot of rain up here, they said. She hydroplaned. Hit a tree not so far from that motel. Crash put her in a coma. They gave me leave to see her. It was a nice room, a decent place. They said it was taken care of. I thought she had some insurance from her last job. I didn't even go through her papers before I flew back. Then I get a message she's dead. Died in transit, from the nice place to a state place where they had to take her. Why'd they move her? I wanted to know. But there was nobody to ask. By the time I got home for good, after all that time recovering and rehabbing and learning how to not really get around on the girls, nobody could answer my questions. But I went through her stuff. Didn't find anything. Then the hospital had some papers they sent over. That's how I found out. Purdy had been paying for the nice place. But after a while he stopped. So they had to move her. I guess they didn't really know how to do it right. It's hard to move hurt people. I've seen plenty of that. A lot of people die *on the way*. Look, probably she wasn't coming out of that coma. Probably I would have had them pull the plug. But still."

Don leaned back in his chair, kneaded his legs.

"My fucking humps."

"I have aspirin."

"Aspirin. No. Never touch the stuff. They're scared of me. Purdy and Moss and them. Think I'm a psycho."

"Maybe."

"I don't mind."

"I'm not sure that's all of it."

"Purdy doesn't know a thing about the world I come from. The world his fucking son comes from."

"This is really about his wife."

"Melinda? She's okay. Just another rich bitch. Maybe I should take them all out. I've got PTSD. Got papers on it. Maybe I could do that. Live rent-free in a psych ward for the rest of my life."

"Don't do that."

"No?"

"Would Nathalie want that?"

"Would she want me to take the money?"

"I don't know."

"No, you don't. You don't know at all. Tell them I'll sleep on it. Which means I'll get high on it. Maybe the dragon will whisper the answer to me."

"I'm here, Don."

"That's your problem," he said, winced out of his chair. I followed him into the living room. Bernie clutched a pillow. A pterodactyl soared above some coastal cliffs.

"Nice to meet you, Bernie."

"Nice," said Bernie.

"Look at the man, Bernie," I said. "Say goodbye."

"Goodbye."

"The asteroid didn't fall on their heads," said Don.

Bernie stared up at Don.

"What about the asteroid?" he said.

"It didn't kill the dinosaurs," Don said. "It just killed everything else. The plants. The sunlight. It was cold and dark and there was nothing to eat. The dinosaurs got so sad, they died."

"In Connecticut?" said Bernie.

"Especially in Connecticut," said Don, heaved himself out the door.

Twenty-four

Our world at an end, we watched TV. We'd endured another silent meal, though not truly silent. We had to talk to Bernie, answer his questions about the recent visitor, or I had to, kept things vague, tried to steer the subject back to asteroids, comets, galactic disturbance. Maura did not speak, cut her lemon chicken into rectilinear bites.

"Daddy," said Bernie. "Are you going to see Aiden's mommy again?"

Maura raised an eyebrow, stacked her tiny bricks of meat.

"That was a playdate, Bernie," I said.

"At a diner."

"Right," I said. "So if you want to play with Aiden again we can do that, no problem."

"Okay," said Bernie.

"Eat some more broccoli," I said.

Maura tapped her fork. You weren't supposed to push food, even broccoli. It would make them hate broccoli, you.

"Or don't," I added. "Eat what you like. Those fish nuggets look good."

"They look a little fancy," said Bernie.

This was the kind of adorable that once had Maura and I grinning crazily at each other, but my wife stood now and walked to the sink, scraped her plate.

"Daddy's going to tell you a story and tuck you in, sweetie," she said.

Bernie fell asleep before the evil. The children picked their berries. The trolls slumbered in their caves.

The spires of the castle of the vintage cardigan king pierced the mist.

Maura and I took our places in the living room, turned on the television, moved through the stations of the stations. We still did not own the devices that let you skip the commercials. Would we always be part of the slow television movement? Would we always be a we?

We jumped from pundit to pundit, then on to basketball, Albanian cooking, endangered voles, *America's Top Topiary Designers*, *America's Toughest Back-up Generators*, *The Amazing Class Struggle*, the catfish channel, a show called, simply, *Airstrikes!*

We watched television in the old way and it was good.

Maybe the animator could just scram. No fester, no rot. Maybe we didn't have to talk about it. Maybe that was the problem. We yapped too much. We weren't equipped.

"I love you, Maura," I said. "I don't know what's going on, but I'm also fine with never knowing. If you can end it, come back to me."

"How can you be fine with never knowing?"

"What is there to know?"

"What do you want to know?"

"I want to know what's happening between you and Paul. But I'm saying I can live without knowing if whatever it is stops happening."

"Paul's gay."

"Really?"

"The only person I've ever fucked from the office is Candace. And that was a few years ago."

"Are you gay?"

"Once in a while. Not really. You knew that."

"Well, yeah, in that sense. I mean, like, in Greenpoint, I was gay, too."

"You were a spaz."

"I'm a sensualist."

"Okay, Milo."

"Have there been others?" I said.

"Others?"

"Besides Candace."

"I thought you were fine never knowing."

"I didn't realize how much there was not to know."

"What do you want, Milo? A signed confession? A show trial?"

"What happened?" I said. "I was out there pounding the pave-o-mento! What the hell happened to us?"

"The pave-o-what?"

"Forget it."

"What do you want, Milo? What are you asking for?"

"Asking?"

"What's the give?" said Maura. "A divorce? A stale but stable marriage? A poison one? What about Bernie? Do we stay together for the sake of Bernie? Do we split up for the sake of Bernie? Different websites advise differently."

"You're way ahead of me," I said. "I just love you."

"That's a cop-out, Milo."

"How can that be a cop-out?"

"God," said Maura, "we're arguing like a bunch of pussies."

"Do you love me, Maura?"

"Fine, forget it."

"Forget what?"

"This crisis. It's not worth it."

"What do you mean?"

"I'll stop fucking Paul."

"I thought it was just Candace. I thought you said Paul was gay."

"You're like from another century. Nobody cares what anybody is."

"You're from the same century I am."

"Poor Milo. What are you asking for?"

"From you?"

"From all of it."

"I don't know," I said. "I guess what I really—"

"Look," said Maura. "Look there."

It was *Caller I Do*. This was no surprise. It was on heavy rotation these days, a new classic. The male lead scrunched in a steel-domed turret in a sandbox in Central Park, wept. He'd just seen the woman he loved kiss a much younger man on her office softball team. His cell phone blinked the name and number of the woman, who was calling to tell him the younger man was not a rival lover but the office mailboy, a virgin soon headed to the hospice to die of leukemia. The kiss had been an innocent goodbye gift, but the man was too blinded by tears to see his cell phone display.

"I love this part," said Maura. "I mean, I hate it."

"We used to hate this together," I said.

"Maybe we can get back to that place," said Maura.

"Let's have an appointment," I said.

"I'm touched out."

"I thought you were in."

"I'm out again."

"Oh."

"We'll get there, baby," said Maura. "Not yet. Soon."

"I want to show you something," I said. "A part of my life. I want to share it with you."

I fetched my laptop, found *Spreadsheet Spreaders*. Maura peered over at the screen.

"Is that what you like?"

"I like you."

"Take out your cock," she said.

I unzipped my fly, tugged myself out.

"Do your business while I watch the end of the movie."

I scuttled over to the other end of the sofa, propped the laptop on a pillow. I did what she said, but she never looked over. I wanted her to look over. I tried to keep everything on my hand.

"Done?" she said.

"Yes."

"Okay," said Maura. "I love you, Milo. We are changing, our lives are changing. I don't know if we are finished or not. But we need a little break. Go to your mother's tomorrow."

"But what about Bernie?"

"It's just for a few days. So I can think. So you can think. Figure out what the hell you are doing with your life. With Purdy."

"What does this have to do with Purdy?"

"I need you to figure that out. Now go to the kitchen and wipe your hand."

•

I slept on the sofa that night. It was noisy out here in the room near the street. There were car alarms and the shouting of names. Somebody named Garza was going to get it. Somebody was going to bust a cap in Garza's ass. Somebody, maybe Garza, knocked over a garbage pail. The sound recalled the metal canoes my bunk once had to portage over rocks on a summer camp trip. We caught trout from a stream, ate nuts and berries and M&Ms. Our counselor talked incessantly about the "truth of the land." He did not mention the home heating potential of trout. I saw the side of Wendy Leed's tit, heard an owl hoot. I thought I heard an owl hoot now.

My phone glowed again.

"Did I wake you?" said Purdy.

"No," I said.

"But you're the sleeper. Why doth the sleeper not sleep? Melinda's conked. She sleeps and she hurls. First trimester is an ass-kicker. Who knew about any of this shit? Morning sickness always sounded so dainty to me. A little tummy ache before breakfast. But then you think of what's growing in her. Our heads are too big, you know. I've been reading up on this."

"I know all about it," I said, bent away from the sofa's crevasse. Maybe I would have to exile myself to Claudia's just for the sake of my spine.

"It's because our brains evolved too rapidly," said Purdy. "One minute we're doofuses in trees, the next we're outfoxing mastodons on the savannah, and we have these huge-ass pumpkin heads. Can you outfox a mastodon? Did foxes exist? Were there mastodons on the savannah?"

"I don't know, Purdy."

"They had those midget horses, I think. But anyway, think about it, big baby skulls ripping through the birth canal. It's criminal. It's rape, really. Reverse rape. Nature should do time for it. Melinda says I'm an idiot. She says the female body is designed for childbirth. Have you ever heard of the pelvic floor?"

"Purdy," I said, "how much candy have you eaten?"

"A lot. I'll have to do another ten miles on the treadmill tomorrow. You work out?"

"Not at all."

"You should."

"Why?"

"You'll live longer, better. Don't you want that?"

"I'm not sure, given my present circumstances."

"You'll definitely look better."

"Better than what?"

"Better than a half-melted block of Muenster cheese."

"That's a nice image."

"I rarely employ them. Anyway . . . yumm . . . ginger crystals."

"I'm actually hitting a bit of a rough patch with Maura."

"Rough patch. That's kind of a *dead* image, no? I'm trying to cut down on stock phrases myself. But I'm sorry to hear about your marital woes. Anyway, listen. Melinda wants to do a natural childbirth, but not at that place you met me, the Best Place. She's decided to do it here at home. No epidural, nothing. Fine by me. If she's a glutton for agony, that's her business. I'll be right there, stroking her brow, telling her what a great job she's doing, rah rah. I'll cut the cord. We're banking the cord blood. For bone marrow transplants, stuff like that."

"Do you need a bone marrow transplant?"

"I don't know. Do you?"

"I don't think so."

"Well, this blood won't help you. Oh, and there's also the placenta. Maybe I'll do some kind of face-mask treatment. I'm not eating that crap. Friend of mine slapped his boy Bronco's afterbirth on a Portuguese sweet roll. Ate it with his wife right there on the birthing bed. Did it come with soup? No thanks, I say. Maybe I'll help with the snip-snip."

"The what?"

"The circumcision. We've decided to go with that. It's not a religious thing, it's just that Melinda thinks foreskins are repulsive. Plus they give women cervical cancer."

"Oh," I said. "Yeah. We didn't do Bernie. We went the other way on the question. Maura thinks . . . we think it's mutilation."

"No, female circumcision is mutilation, not male. What planet are you on? What they do to the clitoris—man alive! I mean, especially if it's not even part of your culture, that is some brutal shit."

"I've never heard of that," I said.

"Never heard of what?"

"People doing female circumcision when it's not part of their culture."

"That's what I'm saying," said Purdy. "How insane would that be?"

"Will the midwives do a circumcision in your home?"

"No, but Melinda's doctor has already agreed to be here just for that procedure, so we can get everything out of the way in one shot. The midwives and doulas are cool with it. It will be a melding of opposed philosophies as only a rich motherfucker like myself can engineer."

"I see."

"So, anyway, sorry to ramble. I've just been sitting here watching TV and spinning my wheels. I'm not even forwarding through commercials. You should see the kind of stuff they've got on. I now officially know more about the Maxim gun than I ever thought possible."

"I saw that one."

"I bet you did," said Purdy.

"What's that supposed to mean?"

"Oh, did that sting? Come on, Milo. Don't be so sensitive. And don't take yourself so seriously. We both know what your life has been like."

I stayed silent for a moment, listened for the owl.

"Milo?"

"Purdy, why'd you call me? You must have got word from Lee Moss. Your son is thinking about it. But I think he will sign the papers."

"I know that."

"So, why did you call?"

"Do I need a reason? Don't you work for me?"

"No, I don't. Maybe I do. I don't know."

"Don't worry about that," said Purdy. "I called because I can't sleep. This is when we always used to talk. Like in the house on Staley Street. You'd always be there. You were my friend. Weren't you my friend?"

"Yes," I said.

"I don't have too many—"

"Yes, you do."

"Yeah," said Purdy. "But they're all asleep right now."

Twenty-five

Nobody told me about the noon staff meeting. Nobody told me much of anything these days. I was some kind of bad luck charm. I was somebody's error in judgment all over again. But the energy tides eluded me. I was stranded on a shoal with my turkey wrap. A Post-It note on my computer reminded me to ask for more Post-It notes. But I was afraid to ask. I wasn't even drawing a salary, but I did not want to be a drain.

Nobody told me about the noon staff meeting, or even waved me over to join them now, but I followed them into the conference room anyway, found a chair between Horace and Vargina. There were people from other teams I did not know that well, a tall Asian man who raised money for the business school, a white woman with cat glasses who handled undergraduate gifts. The early arrivers had left chairs between themselves and others, the way travelers on a bus might prop their suitcases on the seats beside them, make a play for solitude. But the room filled up. We'd packed the bus. Now the driver climbed aboard.

Dean Cooley walked in and slapped a folder on the desk. The folder sported the new lime green tabs a recent directive had mandated. War Crimes scanned the room until his eyes appeared to alight on Horace, who wore a tuft of his hoagie's shredded lettuce on his chin.

"In my time," said Cooley, "I have been a combat marine. Trained for combat. Trained to kill. But I never saw combat. I never killed. It was my blessing, and my misfortune, to be an instrument of war at a time of relative peace. So, as I say, I never saw combat and I never killed. In my time I have also been a purchaser and purveyor of bandwidth, not that there was much difference in those heady, early days of bandwidth. We were all for one thing: more bandwidth. Above all, I was an instrument of bandwidth. But I never saw bandwidth. How can you see bandwidth? You can see measurements of bandwidth. But you can't see bandwidth. It does not matter. What am I driving at?"

Some of us slid our lunches off the table, into our laps, or bags.

"Anybody? Nobody? Anybody?"

"We don't need to know?" said the man from the business school team.

"Know what?" said Cooley.

"Who we are?"

"No," said Cooley, "you need to know who you are."

"What we represent?" said the woman with the cat glasses.

"You represent the university," said Cooley. "What about you, Llewellyn? You're one of our franchise players. What the hell am I talking about?"

"I know!" said Horace.

"Go ahead, Lettuce Face."

"We need to know you believe in us."

"That I believe in you?"

"Yes," said Horace.

"But I don't believe in you, young man. That's not my job. I'm not your mommy. I believe in results. Does anyone know what I'm talking about? Vargina? Sean?"

Vargina and the man from the business school development team nodded.

"Anyway," said Cooley. "Llewellyn, you were going to enlighten us."

Llewellyn propped himself up on his palms.

"Well, to be perfectly honest, Dean, I am not entirely clear on your line of thought, but I believe it has something to do with conviction."

"Conviction."

"Yes."

"Very interesting."

"Is it?"

"It is. You're very close."

"I am?"

"Yes, you are," said Cooley, raised his hand as though it held a dog treat. "It's right over here, Quantrill. Come for it. Let's hear that rebel yell."

"Conviction about the product," said Llewellyn.

"Okay . . ."

"Conviction about the product even if it is something of an abstraction. Conviction that we can weave a story, as it were—"

"Story, yes, that's it, keep going . . ."

"A narrative in which—"

"Narrative? Don't get fruity."

"A story . . ."

"That's it . . ."

"A story about all the wonderful things that the give can bring about, a story, in our particular team's case, about the role of culture as both a bulwark of the civilization we cherish and a bridge, an interconnective bridge, to other incredibly and wonderfully global modes of thinking and being, as well as a story about young and diverse and often sexy people expressing themselves through their creativity and in doing so spreading a kind of artistic balm on the wounds of the world, a balm that not only heals but promotes understanding, especially in a world, a globe, as global as ours, where isolation is no option, where the only choices are globality or chaos."

"Globality or chaos?" said Cooley.

"Yes," said Llewellyn.

"You sure?"

Llewellyn squeezed his fists, nodded his head.

"Yes, I'm sure."

"Damn right, you're sure! Because that's what I call a fucking story! You see? You see, Lettuce Face? You hear that, feline and voluptuous secretary from the 1950s? That's the bull's balls, right there!"

"Thanks," said Llewellyn.

"No, thank you, young gentleman. Not only for that cogent and rousing description of what it is we do around here, but for something far more important. See, Lew here is what we call a change agent. He brings in the loose change of the rich folks. It falls out of their pockets and Lew is Johnny-on-the-Spot about bringing it here to us, to our students, to our joint glorious project of bulwarking and bridging. What I'm saying is, the papers on the Teitelbaum ask have finally come through. Guess which students at which university will have a new game design center?"

A shout went up, followed by applause. Llewellyn did his best imitation of bashful.

"So, give that man a potato chip!" said Cooley.

Many of us laughed, applauded anew. I joined them, a shamed heat rising in me. Would Cooley mention that the Teitelbaum ask had once been mine? I'd screwed that one up good at a lunch, made the mistake, in listing the kinds of exhibits that might be mounted in a proposed gallery space, of mentioning the work of a Polish artist who built a model Treblinka with Tinker Toys. The camp guards were freeze-dried ants. Teitelbaum, a Holocaust orphan, was not amused.

"What did he make the Jews out of?" the old man snarled over his salade Niçoise.

"Vintage coins from the Weimar Republic," I mumbled.

"Money? He made them out of money?"

"It was a point about historical perception. The artist is Jewish himself."

But Teitelbaum, who'd made a fortune in optics, was not so intrigued by this notion of perception. He charged off to the toilet. I ate some slivers of his hard-boiled egg.

People still clapped but Cooley had a new stern look.

"No, really," he said. "Give him a potato chip."

Sean slid a rippled mesquite-flavored chip from his bag, passed it down the table to Llewellyn.

"That's your bonus," said Cooley, and the room got quiet.

We did not get bonuses. But something about hearing the word seemed to drive the fact home. I wondered what management technique this was that Cooley had decided to employ, though after some years in this business, I'd come to suspect there were no techniques, or none that really traveled well out of books and conference seminars. The kiddie-diddler was right, it was all just people doing kindnesses, or smearing each other into the earth, usually both at the same time.

"That's your bonus," said Cooley again, and I remembered that I had actually gotten a bonus, from Purdy, half a year's rent in an envelope in my desk. Grounds for dismissal. I'd already been dismissed, of course. But it could also be grounds for a prison sentence, if it constituted defrauding my employer.

"I'll treasure it," said Llewellyn, the chip aloft.

"Frame it!" somebody called.

"Bronze it!"

"Stick it up your butt!"

"That's your bonus," said Cooley, "but that's not your only bonus."

The room hushed down at these last words. This was the original management technique. It was also, if you substituted the word "candy" for bonus, a pleasant way to torment your child on a Sunday afternoon.

"What's the rest?" said Llewellyn. He seemed jumpy, a bit slopped by an overspill of ego fuel.

"The rest of your bonus is your ability to sleep at night, knowing that you have done your part in keeping hope—hope for a great fucking human flowering—alive and well. Darkness is falling, my friends. Our job is to put the Maglites in the hands of the people whose ideas, whether in the realms of business, medicine, law, or science, pure and applied, will lead us through the black hour."

"Let's not forget the arts!" called Vargina, with rare or, rather, meeting-specific cheer.

"Sure, the arts, too," said Cooley. "Hey, we've always made room for you self-involved little people, haven't we? No need to be upset. We get it. Even cavemen needed their cave paintings, right?"

"Hooray," whispered Horace.

War Crimes wheeled.

"What was that, Slick?"

"Nothing."

"I got a question for you. A quiz. Answer this correctly and I'll give you a twenty percent raise right now. In what year did Bertolt Brecht create the vaccine for polio?"

"Sorry?"

"In what year did Bertolt Brecht create the vaccine for polio?"

"No year?" said Horace.

"Say it like you got a pair."

"No year, sir!" said Horace.

"Good work. The raise thing was more of a hypothetical. But keep up the nice effort. Anyway, you all get my point. Though I guess I've made several today. Mainly I just wanted to let Llewellyn here know how much we appreciate his top-notch performance. But he's not the only one. There are others here who deserve singling out. Before we get to that, however, I have some sad news. It concerns a family very close to our hearts. I received word this morning that Shad Rayfield is very ill. Collapsed on his catamaran. We will wish the best for him, reflect on his mighty accomplishments, most notably his design and production of some of the world's best attack helicopters, and in the great works of philanthropy he has undertaken, as well as pray for his speedy recovery. I know Shad considers the Rayfield Observatory the crown jewel of his gives, despite the fact that it's never worked properly, and was unfortunately erected too near a large lime works, so that visibility is a severe problem. Still, the building stands as a symbol of all that is possible, even as we possibly depart the age of the big give. So, let us lower our heads and send good thoughts to Shad Rayfield in whatever mode of spiritual contemplation we happen to choose. Martha, am I to understand you are Wiccan?"

The woman with the cat glasses glanced up.

"Well, we don't have a broom for you here, but we welcome your style of worship. And let us not forget the suffering of poor McKenzie Rayfield as she endures this very fraught time. Mr. Burke, you know her a bit. Maybe you have a few words you'd like to share with us?"

"Excuse me?" I said.

"Got your attention now, haven't I? Nice to have you at the meeting."

"Thanks. I wasn't sure if I . . ."

"Oh, I made sure you didn't know about it. But you're here anyway, aren't you?"

The whole room stared, and it occurred to me that my mishap with the Rayfield girl must have been the gossip item of the year. This had all come together quite nicely, I realized, the Teitelbaum celebration, the announcement of McKenzie's father's collapse. Next would come my crucifixion. But I wasn't dying for anybody else's sins, just mine. I'd get my due, my due diligence.

"Yes," I said. "I guess I am here."

"You guess?" said Cooley. "No, I would say you are definitely here. Do you know why you are here, even though you were purposely excluded from this meeting? Would you like me to tell you why you happen to be here even though you weren't invited?"

"Yes," I said.

"The reason is quite simple, my friend."

"It is?"

"Yes, it is. The reason you are here is that you, Milo Burke, are a fucking development gladiator."

"I am?"

"You say nuts to defeat. You laugh at the grave."

"I do?"

Cooley glanced over at Vargina, who nodded, swiveled toward me.

"Milo," she said. "Maybe you've thought about what happened with McKenzie. Because she is so talented and ambitious, it was hard to remember she is really just a kid, still growing in certain emotional areas, but maybe now you've concluded that despite all of that there was no excuse for the way you spoke to her. And maybe it's even been a kind of watershed for you, a blessing in disguise. Perhaps it's forced you to confront some demons of your own, and now you feel more complete and healthy and happy. You no longer harbor the negativity that was affecting your performance and your general well-being. If you could just find a way to make it up to McKenzie, and you are eager to work with the rest of us to find such a way, maybe the whole ordeal, unpleasant as it was, could be put to rest."

I clasped my hands on the table.

"Milo?"

I heard the click of a salad lid, the scrape of a soda can.

"I couldn't have said it better," I said. "Thank you, Vargina."

The room broke into applause again. Horace patted me on the back.

"Pathetic," he whispered.

"Outstanding," said Dean Cooley. "Give that man a potato chip."

Sean slid another chip from his bag, sent it down. I held it aloft, near my chest.

"First off I'd like to thank my agent!"

Even Llewellyn laughed, or maybe only Llewellyn laughed.

"Listen up," said Dean Cooley. "To cap off this wonderful moment for Mr. Burke, I have one more announcement. We've been a bit worried, to be truthful, because of the lack of updates we've been getting from Milo on his special project, but I guess there was a good reason for the radio silence. Seems Mr. Burke is to your average development officer what a recon marine is to your typical jarhead. He's the cream of the crop, and best left alone to gather his own intel, set his own traps, and take down the enemy like a freaking phantom ninja born straight out of Satan's blazing quim. Sorry, Martha."

"For what?"

"Good girl. Anyway, it's my great pleasure to inform all of you that next year we will break ground for the Walter Stuart Memorial Arts Pavilion, right here on our main campus, which will house facilities for all branches of the visual arts, but with special attention to the construction of naturally lit studios for our painters and a brand-new bronze-casting facility. Burke, looks like even Stonewall Jackson here could learn something from you. Now I hope your spirits are buoyed by all this news. Given the economic situation, most of you will be fired soon, but I want us all to be proud of what's going on around here. Okay, have a great day."

The applause started up again. The potato chip crumbled in my hand.

•

Back at my workstation I clutched the edge of my desk. It wasn't the terrible feeling, the Maxim gun shudders. It was more what coursed through me the night of the burglary on Staley Street, actions of cost taken all around, me in a frozen state, nothing close to floating. A soft hand roamed my shoulder.

"Relieved?" said Vargina's voice.

"I'm not sure what it all means," I said.

"It means you've proved yourself."

"But I never even . . . did you?"

"Shhh," said Vargina.

"Who handled Purdy's give? He was my ask and the whole deal was in a tailspin. Was it Cooley?"

"Purdy handled the Purdy give. Some things came together. There was a Chinese element involved. A few people did favors for other people. An international student, a young man of means, was instrumental."

"The napper," I said.

"This went up to the provost, the president, the board. It was beyond us really. It just fell together."

"Why am I still here? Purdy?"

"It was a stipulation of Purdy's give, yes. But I backed it up. I told Cooley we needed you."

"You don't need me."

"I know that."

"So, I get to stay?"

I didn't really hear Vargina's answer. I'd tried to stand, crumpled to the carpet. I came to with Vargina leaning over me, her breasts brushing up my chest.

"I'm sorry I undress you with my eyes," I said.

"It's okay, Milo. Just breathe."

"I do a lot worse with my eyes. Am I the only one?"

"Of course not, Milo. You just lack subtlety. But breathe now."

"Subtlety," I said.

"Breathe."

"I never wanted to hurt anyone. I just wanted to slide my dick between your breasts."

"A Sabrett man," said Vargina.

"What?"

"Breathe. You're okay, but we've called for help."

"I'm so sorry," I said.

"I'm not offended, Milo."

"Does that mean you are interested?"

"Not at all. Now keep breathing, baby."

"Because I'm married?"

"Sure, because you're married."

"Because I'm white?"

Vargina laughed.

"I'm not very likable, am I?"

"You're likable enough," said Vargina.

"No, I mean, if I were the protagonist of a book or a movie, it would be hard to like me, to identify with me, right?"

"I would never read a book like that, Milo. I can't think of anyone who would. There's no reason for it."

"Oh."

"Hey, here come some friends. Look. Here they come. Look at them. Like angels."

They looked more like muscular men in blue shirts. They laid a large kit next to my head, dug through it.

"What happened?"

"Well," I heard Horace say. "He figured out the world wasn't all about him and he fainted."

"Seen it before," said the other.

"By the way," said Horace. "You guys make pretty good money, right?"

"It's not great."

"What's the training process? I mean, like, if I did CPR in swim class, do I get to skip ahead?"

•

They took me to the emergency room for a few hours of observation. I lay on a gurney beside an old drunk woman with gangrene. She lifted some blackened fingers.

"I used to play piano," she said. "Up in Utica. Up in the hotel there."

"I've never been to Utica," I said.

"Do yourself a favor. Don't go up there. Look what happened to me. Utica spat me out."

"Tough town."

"Utica is pitiless. Used me up and spat me out. I was Piano Patty. Go up there and ask around, they'll know."

"I thought you told me not to go there."

"Do what you think is right. I'm not your mommy."

"You're the second person I've heard say that this afternoon."

"Must have been on the radio. Some kind of giveaway."

The doctor stopped by my gurney with his clipboard.

"We're ready to release you," he said.

"So, everything's fine?"

"I didn't say that," said the doctor. "I said we were ready to release you."

•

That gangrenous wino from Utica was correct. She was not my mommy. My mommy was here in Nearmont, in her living room, sipping peppermint tea.

"When I was young," she said now, "single, working in the city, that was something. Something hideous. But wonderful. I did things that would make your hair curl. The hair on your palms."

"Mom," I said.

We had to shout a bit above the loud, lunging minor chords Francine banged out on her organ. This recital, according to Claudia, was the new post-prandial routine. Francine claimed to have studied at a conservatory in Indiana, though all she ever played was this piece of her own composition, a meandering dirgey thing with sudden surges of dark joy. Francine's performance varied, my mother said, with the quality of her stash.

"Very nice, Francie! Fortissimo!"

"Fortissimo," I said. "You don't know anything about music."

"Fake it until you make it. Now where was I?"

"You were about to inflict me with the details of your youthful peccadilloes."

"Peccadilloes? What are you, an old society dame? You kids today are so uptight."

"I'm almost forty, Mom."

"You must change your life."

"Don't give me your hippy crap."

"That's Rilke."

"Rilke's a hippy."

"I'm not. The fifties were the sixties. For the people who mattered. Not that I mattered. But I wanted to."

"And what were the sixties?"

"Boring. Of course, by the good part I was stuck out here."

"With me."

"Don't sulk. You were an infant. It's not your fault you weren't stimulating."

"Weren't you happy just being a mother?"

"I was happy being a mother. Take out the 'just.' "

"Well, you're still in the suburbs, and I'm long gone, so I can't take all the blame."

"When did you ever take blame? You give blame. To me."

"We're not doing that tonight."

"Right, I forgot. The suburbs are the new bohemia, anyway."

"Judging by what we're hearing right now, you could be right."

"Don't worry, I'm right. Fortissimo!"

•

Later I sat on the patio with a beer and a one-hitter I'd found in Francine's sewing box. I kept calling Purdy. I kept calling Maura. I even called Don. Nobody was home, or near a phone, or answering. I sat out on the patio in a rubber-ribbed chair with the phone in one hand and the one-hitter and a lighter in the other and the beer like a throttle between my legs, and it seemed for a brief moment that I might be the pilot of something, something sleek and meaningful, but I was not the pilot of anything. The night was warm, the night sky blue, gluey. I could smell the neighbor's fresh-mown lawn. New Jersey was a fresh-mown tomb.

Fool, I said to myself. Depressive, raw-eyeballed pansy. Is that all you've got? That's what you had when you still lived on this street, when you were just a budding tristate artist manqué. Now what are you? A botch of corpuscles. A waste of quarks. A carbon-based fuckwad. Purdy is better, Maura more right. Someday you will be a fat, grinning embarrassment to Bernie. Will you still pretend to be a painter? Will you still pretend to be a person?

"Milo?"

My mother's voice carried softly from the kitchen.

"Hey."

"Everything okay out there?"

"Sure, why?"

"I just heard this, I don't know, grumbling."

"Oh, sorry. I stubbed my toe."

"Sitting there?"

"Yeah."

"Oh, okay."

The door slid back and I stood.

"Wait!" I wailed.

·

It's an odd sensation to weep in your mother's lap for the first time in thirty years. It's not the same lap. It's smaller, more fragile. Bonier and tinier. I was afraid my head might hurt her lap. I was afraid her lap wouldn't help my head.

But it did. Claudia cradled me, stroked my hair, cooed: "It's all right, baby. It's all right." It was not all right, not really, but this hardly mattered. My mother was stroking my hair. My mother's lover, at the end of the sofa, kneaded my feet.

"Thanks, Francine."

"My pleasure, Milo."

Soon I was all cried out. I remembered the sensation, felt it frequently as a child, each time I was denied a toy or a chance to play with somebody else's toy or informed that another slice of pineapple pizza was not in the offing. You cried and you cried and then you really couldn't cry anymore. You got wrung, husked. It was that voluptuous emptiness you read about in old books, or old-seeming books that would use the word "voluptuous" that way, a strange, soaring, dead puppet exultation I could never quite explain. I had last felt it a few months after my father died.

Nobody had died just now. The stuff had just welled up in me, up to the eyes, as they used to say, not that I was sure anymore who "they" were.

Who's on first? Self-Pitying Twit. Third base.

More than anything it was just so very good to be stroked and kneaded by my mother and Francine. It was just so very nice to be kneaded in Nearmont. Too bad I couldn't live here with them. But I was not welcome here forever. That's what made me welcome now. I was being readied for release. I would have to drag my botched ass back into the world. Francine was Claudia's family. Bernie, and maybe Maura, was mine.

"I love you," I mumbled into my mother's jeans.

"I know that, honey."

"I'm sorry."

"What are you sorry about?"

"Me. Spidercunt. Everything."

"I forgave you a long time ago."

"And I forgive you, Mom."

"But I don't want your forgiveness, silly boy."

Francine dug lint out from under my pinky toe.

Twenty-six

Purdy's chef wore the sideburns of a Vegas legend. They poked down below his purple toque. He lurched around Purdy's enormous Tribeca kitchen with some kind of digital cleaver, shouted into a wire that fell from his ear. He cursed himself, his food, the kitchen, his crew. He castigated various assistants en route with ingredients, though I wondered how much these outbursts counted as theater for the half-dozen party guests gathered near the cutting boards.

"Leave it to a fucking Turk to forget the tarragon!" he said into his wire. "Soon as you get here I'm handing you a ticket back to Istanbul. Freight. You can go back to work in that fusion nightmare I found you in, though perhaps you'd be better off sterno-braising anchovies for the smugglers in stir, you greasy bastard."

"Must be gunning for his own show," said the man beside me, a handsome silver-haired fellow in a pink polo shirt. He had the collar of his polo shirt up. Maybe he liked it that way, or else it was some kind of comment about people who liked it that way. When it came to sartorial irony, the rich had it tough.

"A cooking show?" I said.

"A screaming show," said the man.

"I have an idea for a cooking show," I said.

"Good for you," said the man, and walked away.

A few more moments of baster-based antics and I followed the him into a space the size of a small ballroom. Purdy's parlor was a design-porn paradise. Here twinkled every chrome and leather marvel Maura had ever circled with affecting sanguinity in her catalogs, all the sofas and chaises and cabinets and floor lamps we could never afford. That was half the room. The other brimmed with mahogany bookshelves and gleaming antique credenzas and Persian rugs. One end was for high-tech pleasures, the other for reading Gibbon while getting blown in a wingback chair.

I walked over to the liquor table, to a young barman in a braided jacket.

"Scotch rocks," I said.

It was not my drink, but then again, this was not my world.

"Okay?" said the barman, pointed to a handle of inexpensive blended whisky beside the silver ice bucket.

"No," I said. "It's not okay."

Always it had been okay, but not tonight. Something had changed. I had demands. Certain people might have called it personal growth. These were the scumbags the new me would learn to admire.

The barman shrugged, squatted, came up with a bottle by the same distiller. The label was another color. This was the good stuff. The better stuff. The kid poured me an important man's pour.

"Thanks," I said.

"You're welcome, sir."

"Do you do this full-time?"

"I'm still a student."

"What do you study?"

"Bartending."

"Oh."

"Mr. Stuart always hires student bartenders."

"What a saint."

"I guess it's a lot cheaper, yeah," said the barman. "But it gives us a chance to practice in an LLS."

"A what?"

"A live liquor situation."

"Right."

"Milo!" called a voice. "Over here!"

Here it was, here *they* were, for to see them stand together, even as they beckoned, made it clear for all time how much I was not of them. There was Purdy, tall, becalmed, nothing like the fiendish candy-store man or the late-night dialer I'd come to know, his taut arm slung over the shoulder of an even taller fellow, bald, with fringes of curly hair: Billy Raskov. Billy looked better bald. Others I did not recognize stood with them, Purdy still the nucleus, the germ seed, the one who could somehow corral us all into a mood of sweet boisterousness, private pangs be damned.

"Milo!"

Another man joined Purdy's group just as I did. We shook hands, but somebody nearby squealed and I caught only the end of Purdy's introduction.

" . . . farb."

"Farb?" I said.

"Goldfarb."

"Of course," I said.

He'd been a messy gangle back on Staley Street. Now he was lean, handsome, with the mien of a racing animal.

"Goldfarb," said the man.

"I know," I said. "Charles Goldfarb."

"That's right, Milo. I'm surprised. I figured if you ever saw me again you'd want to deck me."

"What are you talking about?"

"You don't know?"

"No," I said.

"Come on, Charlie," said Purdy. "Stop teasing. Charlie, Milo, this is Lisa and Ginny. They're friends from the building."

We did our dips, our pivots, our mock-bashful waves. Purdy raised his glass.

"I'm glad we're all here. Dinner is going to be great."

"It better be," said Lisa. "That man in your kitchen is a dick."

"Nice to see you, Milo," said Billy Raskov. His trademark slur was gone. It made me wonder if it ever existed. Maybe I'd imagined it all these years. Maybe that's why I'd always gotten odd looks whenever I brought up his feigned Parkinson's.

"You too, Billy," I said, glanced back at Goldfarb. "I'm sorry, I guess I'm confused."

"Don't worry about it," said Goldfarb.

"Okay, I'll try not to. So, Charles, I think I saw somewhere you wrote a book?"

"Thanks, I appreciate the kind words."

"What kind words?"

"Sorry," said Goldfarb. "Embarrassing reflex."

"Poor Chuck," said Purdy. "He suffers from Post-Praise Stress Disorder. It's left him a wreck. I saw your thing in the paper last Sunday, by the way. Fantastic. Blistering. And thoughtful. Speaking of blisters, did you guys notice what's hanging over the fireplace?"

"Come on, Purd," said Billy.

"Check it out," said Purdy, pointed across the room to a large canvas, a luminous twilit landscape. "The latest Raskov."

A river coursed through a verdant gorge. The sky bled rich reds and blues. In the mossy foreground, a nude woman tongued the anus of an elk. Nearby, a figure in a shepherd's tunic lay disemboweled. A fawn fed on his viscera.

"It's called *Renewable, Sustainable*," said Purdy. "Can't take my eyes off it. Billy's gallerist killed me, but I had to have it."

"I'm impressed," I said. "I didn't know you could paint like that."

"Thanks, buddy. I'll admit I still can't touch your technique, at least as I remember it, but I've been getting better."

"Billy's having another big show next month," said Purdy.

"That's great," I said.

"You should come to the opening."

"I'd like that."

"I was thinking," said Billy. "Are you in contact with Lena? I haven't talked to her in a long time, I'd really like to—"

"Yeah, I really haven't been in contact."

"Not since it was full contact, right, bro?"

"Excuse me?" I said.

"Just joking."

"I think it's hot," said Purdy. "Milo, could I have a word with you?"

"Sure."

"Over here."

Purdy led me away from the group. We passed the barman, who nodded. Maybe this private audience with Purdy confirmed my top-shelf status.

Purdy wheeled near the corner of the room, clasped my shoulders.

"Well?"

"A pavilion," I said.

"Not bad, huh?"

"I can't thank you enough," I said. "Really. It's so amazing. I'm still processing it."

"What's the matter with you?"

"What do you mean?"

"It doesn't seem like a very happy process, judging by your face."

"I am happy. I really am. I'm just spent. You know I collapsed? I collapsed from happiness. I had to be hospitalized."

"No shit."

"So . . ."

"Don't tell me," said Purdy.

"Don't tell you what?"

"You're pissed."

"What are you talking about?"

"You're pissed I went over your head."

"No, I'm really not."

"It had to be that way. For your benefit. Shit, in a way this whole thing has become about you. I care about you. Don't you get that?"

"I do."

"You've got to stop resenting me. It's foolish."

"I know. And really, thank you."

"You're welcome, asshole."

"I deserve that," I said.

Purdy took a breath, gazed past my shoulder.

"Lee Moss died yesterday."

"Oh, man. I'm sorry. I just saw him."

"I know. He took a bad turn that evening."

"I'm really sorry, Purdy."

"He was an old man with cancer."

"I know he was close to you. Like family."

"Let's not get too sentimental. He helped my father defraud the government. Because of that my father had more money to leave to me, the boy he liked to beat senseless. Moss was the old breed. Took care of business. Ethics were for the Sabbath. Just a hardworking shark, a true Jew lawyer. No offense."

A tall woman in white walked up, tilted her Bellini in greeting.

"Oh, hi, Jane."

"Hello, Purdy."

"Jane, you remember Milo Burke."

The gray eyes of the governor's daughter seemed to sparkle as they surveyed the damage.

"Yes, of course, how are you?"

"Great," I said.

"Wonderful. What have you been doing with yourself?"

"Working."

"Very nice," she said.

"Be right back," said Purdy, pecked Jane's cheek.

"How about you?" I said.

"I've been working, too. On a few projects."

This woman's power had always resided in her courage. She'd defied her father, defied him still. She made her films to destroy his beliefs. Whether he also helped fund them was not the point. She'd been given an out at birth, a frictionless existence, refused it. I did admire her for this. But she'd taken my knife. Worse, she probably had no recollection of this fact.

"What kind of projects?" I said.

"I just finished a film about a family in a refugee camp in Chad. And I'm doing something about health care, the uninsured."

"They're being murdered," I said.

"It's true," said Jane.

"There was one woman upstate, our age. She was in a coma in a hospital, but her . . . carrier cut her off. She died in transit to the state ward."

"That's terrible. Did you know her?"

"Not really. Some of her relatives."

"Really? Would they speak to me? We're doing a lot of interviews before we start."

"No," I said. "I don't think so. They're pretty private."

"Well, let me know if you think they would. These stories need to be told."

"I will."

"It was nice to see you again," said Jane.

"Wait," I said.

"Yeah?"

Here was my moment to ask about that night, the party. I didn't want the knife back. I just wanted to know if she remembered, to understand how one event could mean so little and so much.

"No, I just was going to ask . . ."

"Yes?"

"I have an idea for a TV show."

"That's nice."

"Well, it's really my friend Nick's idea, but we're collaborating."

"Nick?"

"Nick Papadopoulos."

"I don't know his work."

"You might. You might have sat on his work. Though probably not."

"I'm not sure where you're going with this."

"He's a builder. A contractor. Builds decks."

"Is it some kind of home repair thing? I don't really do that sort of—"

"No, no," I said. "It's a cooking show."

"Cooking? I think we're full up on those. See that guy in there?"

"Right. So, take that guy in there, Mr. Kitchen Badass. Now put him on death row."

"Pardon?"

"I mean not him. I mean he's there, but he's not on death row. But he's going to cook a last meal for somebody about to die. *Dead Man Dining*. You know why those last meals are so crappy?"

"Because they all eat crappy food in those parts of the country."

"Yes, bingo. Now bring on the Kobe beef."

"Excuse me?"

"I mean . . . wow, Nick is much better at this. It sounded different when . . . oh, forget it."

"No," said Jane. "I'm intrigued. Let me see if I've got you right. America's best chefs come to America's worst prisons to cook lavish last meals for condemned convicts."

"Yes. That's what I was trying to say. Perfectly put."

"I can see it," said Jane, snatched another drink from a passing tray. "First we film the chef on the way to the airport, nervous but excited, and also moved by the gravity of the event. He reflects on crime and fate and society, how lucky his own life has been. Then he arrives at the prison and meets with the warden, who explains in somewhat disturbing detail what the condemned man did. Whether you agree with capital punishment or not, there's no getting around the fact that a court of law found this hick guilty of hacking the girl up in the forest, or mowing down the returns line at the shoe outlet. A sober few minutes. Then the fun. Our chef sits down with the maniac. They talk about food. While the unschooled but unquestionably bright killer talks about the staples he was raised on—chicken fingers, hamburgers, onion rings, cola, processed bread, and peanut butter laced with rat shit, we start to feel for him, his crime recedes, and what we are watching is a boy who never had a chance to taste the better things, to know possibility, to see a way out. It's sad, but a quick cut to the warden will remind us that we should be careful about where our sympathies lie. And what are the families of the victims eating tonight? Commercial."

"Holy shit," I said. "That's it. You're good."

"When we return from the break," said Jane, "we're with our celebrity chef in the prison kitchen. The prison cooks watch with bemusement as the chef's shock at the meagerness of utensils mounts. Don't they even have a paring knife? A goddamn strainer? Yuckety-yuck. So now the chef speaks to the camera about his philosophy of food. Food doesn't need to be fancy. It just needs to taste good. Especially in bad times. It's all about simplicity. Fresh fruit, fresh vegetables, good bread, cruelty-free meats. It's sad how out of reach these things are for so many Americans. As to the prisoner's last meal, well, the chef has been doing a lot of soul-searching. The worst thing would be to take too big a gamble, to prepare something wonderful but too for-

eign to his taste. Those of us not about to be executed can afford
an adventurous though vaguely disappointing dining experience,
the ostrich steaks and persimmon spaetzle not nearly as scrump-
tious as advertised. But this one has to be right on the money.
So, we will work with all the tastes and textures that Clarence—
Clarence, right?—already craves. The only purpose of this meal
is to take him back to maybe the one brief moment in his sorry
life he felt loved. We may have a little fun with presentation,
but the grub will be solid, familiar, though much fresher, juicier,
more savory, than this food-court castoff could ever have imagined. Now come the snafus. The hurdles, the drama. What do
you mean we have to go all the way to Lubbock for thyme? I said
Syrah, not Shiraz! No, they're not the same! The usual diva hilar-
ity, but with this incredibly compelling undertone of impending
death. We intercut the chef in the kitchen with the prisoner pen-
ning his final thoughts in his diary, or kneeling with his prayer
group. The executioners test the straps on the gurney. The warden
stares out his office window at the new moon, ponders the price
of justice. And then the moment we've been waiting for. The
prisoner sits at a cute little table set up in, no, not his cell, but
in a little conference room near the warden's office. White table-
cloth. A rose in a vase. Our chef brings out the meal, explains
what he's prepared and why. The prisoner takes a bite, begins
to cry. He had a mommy once. The chef begins to cry. He still
has a mommy, but he's so busy chasing those Michelin stars he
doesn't get to visit her enough. The warden stares. His mommy
used to lock him in a manure bin. We cut away. We'll let the
man eat his last meal in peace. Commercial. Come back to final
thoughts from the chef, back in his restaurant now. The whole
experience has changed him. But he hasn't forgotten the victim
or the families. He thinks about them, too. He thinks about the
whole sad tragedy of it all. Maybe if everybody could eat well
there wouldn't be so much hate in the world. But he will keep
doing what he's doing, cooking meals with love, doing his little

part to bring peace to the planet, dish by dish. Fade out to words on the screen: Clarence Howard O'Grady was executed on blah blah for the murder of blah blah and blah blah. His last words were these: 'I am sorry for what I did and the pain I caused. I wish I'd had Jesus in my life sooner, and more omega-3s. In my next life I'll wash dishes in Chef Gary's fancy restaurant in New York, so I can have artisanal baloney every day. Sleep tight, you world, you motherfucker."

Jane smiled, drained the rest of her Bellini.

"Is that basically it?" she said.

"That's it exactly."

"Thought so."

"That was amazing."

"Thank you."

"So . . . do you think . . . I mean, could you be interested in something like that?"

"If my name were attached to something like that I would commit suicide."

"Oh."

"But here's my card."

"Oh, okay."

"Please pass it along to your friend. The deck builder. A documentary about how reality television has warped the fantasy life of everyday Americans, that could be interesting."

"Very," I said.

"Case studies."

"Yes, right."

"So, did Purdy put you up to this?"

"Purdy?"

"Pretty funny. He's a sick puppy."

"Well, if you need any help with your documentary. You know, legwork."

"Legwork."

"Right."

"Take care, Milo. Nice to see you."

Jane turned, moved off into the crowd.

"Where's my fucking knife?" I said, but she was already gone.

I went back to the bar for another round.

"The same?" said the barman.

"Yes," I said. "A double."

The kid filled my tumbler to the rim.

"Oh, damn," he said. "I forgot the ice. Now there's no room. I'm really sorry."

"How are you going learn if you don't make mistakes?"

"But I'm in the field. This is live liquor."

"Don't worry. I'll take this bullet for you."

I winked, walked. I was not a winker. This worried me.

"Milo," Purdy called from the fireplace. "Come back over here. I want you to meet somebody."

He stood with a generically stunning woman in a black silk dress. There were thousands, or at least several hundred, just like her in this part of the city, on Hudson and Chambers and Franklin and Worth, perfect storms of perfect bones, monuments to tone and hair technology. Around here she was almost ordinary, but you could still picture small towns where men might bludgeon their friends, their fathers, just to run their sun-cracked lips along her calves.

"Melinda, this is Milo. I told you about Milo."

"Yes. Welcome."

"Great to meet you at last," I said. "I've heard so many wonderful things."

"By all means, begin transmission."

"You look beautiful. Purdy said you'd been having a hard few weeks."

"Oh, it's fine," said Melinda. "I'm not the first woman to get knocked up and puke."

"Well, I think it's very exciting. The home birth, all of it."

"I always dreamed it would be like this. Purdy has been so fantastic about meeting my desires. I'm afraid I've been really demanding. But we worked so hard to get here. I'm not ashamed to say how many times we tried, how many ways. But finally I'm pregnant, and I've never been happier in my life. Really. You are the best, baby. And we are going to have the best baby! Ha!"

"But not at the Best Place," said Purdy.

"I'm just so excited," said Melinda. "And I'm learning so much. I won't bore you with it all. But the doctors and midwives have been tremendous."

"So have you, Mel," said Purdy. "You've been tremendous, the tremendousist, the tremendousiast, of them all. And I speak as a husband and a grammarian."

"Is it weird to say how much I love this man? You have a wife and son, Milo, don't you? You know this feeling."

"Sure," I said. "The feeling. Absolutely."

"Why don't you two enumerate my amazing qualities," said Purdy. "I'll be right back."

We watched Purdy walk away, join Charles Goldfarb at the bar. He glanced back at us, waved.

"Would you like to feel?" said Melinda, tilted the tight swell of her belly.

"You're barely showing."

"It's okay. Touch it."

"Really? Most women I've met hate that convention."

"I never knew this."

"They don't understand why any man would feel enti-tled to—"

"Just put your fucking hand on it." Melinda smiled.

I laid my palm on her stomach.

"So tight," I said. "You could bounce a dime off that."

"Sounds fun. So, tell me, Milo, how is it all going?"

"Well, it's going great. I'm sure Purdy told you about the new arts pavilion and I just have to say—"

"Not that," said Melinda. "The kid. Purdy's other darling child."

"Excuse me?"

"What do you think, I'm just some clueless bitch? Ever been to Elizabeth, New Jersey?"

"Driven past it."

"Exactly. But it's where I'm from. Now I'm here. You want to know something? I really do love Purdy. I was always going to marry for money, but I had choices. I chose Purdy. I wanted Purdy's child. I wanted his first child, but I guess I'll have to settle. He could have told me from the beginning, I would have been fine with it. I would have made a place for that kid in our family. Theoretically. Now that I've met him I'm not so sure."

"You met him?"

"We had a chat. I was sick of his stalkery phone calls. I only told Purdy about one of them, the first, before I started to figure out what was going on. But after a while, I called the boy's bluff. I met him for coffee. He's in bad shape. Still a real spaz on those prosthetics. I gave him the name of a physical therapist."

"That was nice of you."

"I thought it was patriotic. After all, this boy gave his legs so my husband could enjoy the freedom to fuck his trashy mother behind my back."

"So you guys really talked."

"We had a cell phone slide show, too."

"Look," I said. "I don't know what to say."

"You're not to say anything. And you can take your hand off my stomach now. I just don't understand it. Hookers are one thing. We know how these guys have to work off some steam. But what the hell? She's not even that pretty. Wasn't even pretty. I feel bad for her. I have this sense I knew who she was, kind of. I don't blame her, I really don't. It's just, like, she's this black hole in my understanding of the universe. Why her? It must have been something."

"What do you mean?"

"What did they have together? What was it?"

"I don't know."

"The way they talked. Maybe that was it. Purdy and I talk, but I know there's a part I can't get to. I want to know what it was with them. Purdy will never tell me. I'll never ask. Who else is there who knows? Florida? That thug. Lee Moss? Well, not Lee Moss. He died yesterday. Did you know that?"

"I heard," I said.

"I'm just trying to understand, and it hurts all the time. And it makes me worry. About what will happen to us."

"Like I said, I really don't know."

"I didn't think you did," said Melinda, looked down at her belly. "Or maybe I thought you might."

"I'm sorry."

"That's what they all say."

"I don't know if this helps," I said, "but I'm going through something similar."

"You're a man," said Melinda. "You're not going through anything remotely similar. Just tell me this. Everything's going to be fine, right? That boy is going to leave us alone? Because I can't handle this right now. I'm having a goddamn baby."

"It looks that way."

Melinda waved past my shoulder, blew a kiss.

"Idiot," she said. "Thinks it's about trust."

•

Purdy announced we would be eating family-style at a cluster of tables in the main room. Servants, or, in the argot of this crowd, caterers, set our places, decanted the wine. Were they indentured caterers? I found a seat at a table with Charles Goldfarb and the women from the building, Lisa and Ginny. I couldn't decide if they were sisters, or lovers, or just friends. The way they picked food from each other's plate signaled all three possibilities. Every few minutes another platter would arrive, each with its menagerie of dehydrated food. The figures dissolved in your mouth like sugar lumps, but none tasted like sugar. There were olives in the shape of lobsters, lobster in the shape of gazelles, mahi-mahi in the shape of bonobos. Purdy's silliness surprised me. This was Vegas sideburn food, what the Apollo astronauts should have gotten in their shiny pouches along with freeze-dried banana splits. Maybe we'd still be on the moon if they had. We'd have time-shares on the moon, as so many otherwise visionary thinkers always assumed we would. I shared this timely thought about the time-shares with the table.

"But we went there already," said Ginny.

"One small step," said Lisa.

"I guess I'm just nostalgic for the future," I said.

"Funny you should say that," said Charles. "There's a bit about that in my new book."

"What's your book about?" said Ginny.

"Oh, a bunch of things really. I try to advance a new approach to transcendentalism in the face of technology and interconnectivity."

"Sounds amazing," said Lisa.

"Sure," I said. "But it's still the rulers and the ruled."

"Not sure how you mean that."

"I think you're very sure."

"Okay," said Charles. "Should we talk about the controlled demolition of the towers now?"

"That's not what I meant," I said.

Ginny and Lisa popped cockatoos into each other's mouth.

"Hummus!"

"Maybe. Saltier."

"Ladies," said Charles.

"Women," said Ginny.

"Dames," said Charles, and the women giggled. I knocked back my double.

"Think I need a refill," I said, steadied myself on the table.

The barman bowed at my approach, scooped some ice into a glass, reached for the bottle on the stool.

"No," I said.

"No ice?"

"Yes, ice. Just pour that into it."

I pointed to the swill, saw a new sad knowing in the barman's eyes.

I took my drink back to the table. Charles, abandoned, leaned over his plate with a butter knife, sliced the wings off a tiny magenta duck.

"They went to the bathroom," he said. "I'll refrain from some clichéd comment about how they always go in pairs."

"Thanks for refraining," I said.

"How you doing there, buddy?" said Charles. "Looks like you're partaking of a wee dram or two."

"You have any coke?" I said.

"Coca-cola?"

"No, the other kind."

"You must be kidding."

"Coke can be pretty transcendental. And interconnective. First couple bumps, anyway."

"I don't have any coke. I never had any coke. You know that."

"I don't know. I remember you were always trying to get laid and nobody would ever go to bed with you. And this was a time and place when being able to explain Horkheimer would get you action easy."

"I never really saw it that way."

"But you figured it out, because Emerson, Thoreau, that's where the real tail is, right? The dependable stuff. I'm just guessing."

"When did you get like this, Milo?"

"Seriously? About twenty years ago. And then about two

months ago. And then about ten minutes ago. Why should I want
to deck you? I'm wracking my brain. I can't think of why I should
deck you. I always pretty much liked you. I know you thought I
was a lightweight, but I didn't mind. I thought you were a bore,
and that my paintings would outlive your tedious summaries of
other people's books. But it looks like I was wrong."

"Man, you take self-pity to new and astonishing heights,
don't you?"

"Probably," I said.

"Constance thought so."

"Constance said that? When?"

"A long time ago."

"Oh."

"Look, this is weird. I didn't mean to get into it with you."

"You still haven't told me why I should deck you. Is this
about my knife?"

"Your knife?"

"My Spanish dueling knife."

"No. It's not anything, I guess."

"Do you see Constance?" I said.

"Sometimes. She's my ex-wife."

"Really?"

"Yeah, I thought you knew. I thought . . . we thought you
were angry, still angry ten years later when we sent out the invi-
tations. We invited you to the wedding. You never responded."

"I don't think I got it."

"Bullshit."

"I don't know what to say, Charles. I'm sorry. I've been an
asshole for years."

"Constance thought you were heartbroken."

"She did?"

"We always thought of maybe reaching out to you, but she
was afraid you were too angry."

"I would have been glad that she was happy."

"It's good to hear that. Constance would probably love to hear that."

"What happened to you guys, anyway?"

"What happens to people, Milo?"

Now Ginny and Lisa rejoined us, just as Purdy clambered up on his chair at a nearby table, clinked his glass with a spoon.

"Hi, everybody," he said. "Just wanted to thank you all for coming. I see so many people from different parts of my life. It makes me so happy. There really wasn't an occasion for this party. I was trying hard to come up with one. I looked into historical birthdays. There were some contenders, a medieval tsar, as I remember, and a noted National League southpaw from the seventies, but nobody seemed worth the big bash. Maybe, I thought, I'll just call it Melinda's Ovaries Day, a celebration of the little old egg that could. God knows how many couldn't."

"The ancient mariners in your ball sack were the problem!" called the guy with the pink polo shirt.

"Thanks, Kyle," said Purdy. "That's Kyle Northridge, a now *former* principal in Groupuscule Media."

"You can't afford to fire me!"

"Fire him from what? The whole thing's in the shitter!" called a man next to Kyle.

"True," said Purdy.

"Say it ain't so!"

"But really, folks, it's not about business. It's not. It's about people. And it is a bona fide delight to see you people types enjoying yourselves in my home. Our home, I mean. Soon to be the home of little Arnold Horshack Stuart."

"Don't do it!" somebody called.

"No? What do you guys think of Space Lab Stuart?"

"Sea Monkeys," somebody said.

"Too self-conscious!" somebody called.

"How about Red Dye Number Two Stuart?" called another.

"You're not getting it!"

"Carter Malaise Stuart!"

"Marzipan!"

"I hate marzipan!" said Purdy.

"Hey," called a new voice, high, strained. "How about Fallujah?"

There was a clatter near the kitchen door.

One of the caterers stood with a tray of cups and saucers. Other than his short white jacket he didn't look much like the others. He wore his hair up in a beige bandana. He'd rolled his sweatpants up past his knee. The sunlight spearing through the steep windows made his metal shins twinkle.

"Come again?" said Kyle Northridge.

Don's tray hit the floor with a clap. Cup shards skidded. Don strode toward us, his gait a near glide, smoother than I'd ever seen it. Purdy slid down into a crouch on the chair.

"I said, 'How about Fallujah?' " said Don. "Or Baghdad. Or fucking Anbar. Anbar Awakening Stuart. Or maybe just Surge. What do you think? Surge Stuart?"

"Hey," said Purdy. "Those are all good."

"Really."

"Hey, yeah," said Purdy, gentle, beseeching. "Yes. How are you?"

"How am I?"

"Yes."

"How am I?"

"It's good to see you."

"Oh," said Don. "Is it? Is it good to see me?"

"Of course," said Purdy. "You are like family. I mean, like, family."

"Thanks, Dad."

Purdy looked down on Don from his perch. They both appeared to quiver. It occurred to me that Purdy had never seen his son before. Don had only caught sight of his father in photographs, through motel windows.

"You've earned it, son."

Don's eyes softened, beamed, something boyish and quasi-sainted glowing in them.

Now came the slap of hard shoes, dark fabrics flashing, a glint of jewels. Giant men swooped in from the edge of the room. You could tell they were the bodyguards because they dressed better than the guests. The rangier one guided Purdy down from the chair. The other, his head the size and hue of a glazed ham, cupped Don's elbow with bling-sheathed fingers.

"What the hell?" said Don.

"You really have earned it, son," said Purdy, nodded at Don's legs. "For what happened to you. For what's happened to so many of you. We are all in your debt. And we should all take responsibility."

"Is that a fucking joke?" said Don.

He shook off the bodyguard, but the huge man snatched Don's hand, bent it behind his back.

"I was over there, too," said the bodyguard. "Don't be a fool."

"Blue falcon," said Don.

"I ain't no buddy fucker," said the bodyguard. "This is my job."

"You could have waited to move her until I got back," said Don, looked hard at Purdy.

"What difference would that have made?"

"You rotten shit. I should just—"

"Don."

"Don't even say my fucking name."

"Don, please . . ." said Purdy.

"I said don't say it."

Now Michael Florida crossed the oak floor in a pair of alligator boots, leaned forward to whisper in Purdy's ear.

"Right," said Purdy.

"What?" said Don.

Purdy nodded to Melinda, turned stiffly to the tables.

"What's going on?" said Don.

"I'm afraid we're going to have to cut this evening a little short," Purdy said. "I've just this moment received some awful news about a dear friend. Lee Moss has died. I suspect he did so with his loving family at his bedside, as he wanted and deserved. I feel I've lost another father. I think it's better if we grieve quietly tonight."

Purdy pinched his lips, made a short, grave bow, walked off toward the study.

"Where the fuck are you going now!" shouted Don. "Come back, Daddy!"

Michael Florida flicked his chin and the bodyguard let Don go. Don jogged a few steps toward his father, his boat shoes stabbing at the antique oak. His heel caught a scoop in the wood and he slid, twisted, pitched over in an violent braid of metal and meat. Somehow he got to his knees.

"She loved you more than anything!" called Don.

Purdy stopped for moment, seemed about to turn around.

"She did," Don sobbed.

Purdy ducked into the study and shut the door.

"She did," said Don again, softer, as though suddenly aware of the room, his audience, who had already begun to look away and whisper.

I walked over and knelt near Don, rubbed his arm.

"Hey," I said. "It's okay."

"Get the fuck off me," he said.

"Really, Don, it's okay. Let's just get out of here."

"I'll kill you," Don snarled.

I rose, backed away, watched Don sit with his head on his knees, rock. Michael Florida walked over and squatted beside him. He must have said something amusing because Don looked up with an odd half-smile. Michael Florida began to talk, very rapidly, it seemed, and Don cocked his head.

Now Michael Florida stood and hoisted Don up, looped the boy's arm across his neck like they were soldiers in some statue about blood and brotherhood. Together they stumbled out of the room.

I was about to follow them when Melinda stood to speak, worried the thin platinum chain at her throat.

"Please," she said. "Let me apologize for all of this."

"Don't even, Melinda," Ginny said. "It's okay."

"Really," said Charles Goldfarb.

"It's nobody's fault," said Kyle Northridge.

"No, I think I should explain. I doubt any of you knew, because he doesn't like to brag, but that boy, well, Purdy's been doing some work with an organization that helps young vets. A lot of them have severe problems. Don has been one of Purdy's projects. I'm afraid it's not going that well right now. But don't let that dissuade you from getting involved in this very important cause. With everything that's happened in this country, we are forgetting about these poor kids. Not even to mention what we've done to the men, women, and children of those other countries. It may not be fashionable anymore, but that's precisely why now is the time to revisit these issues and really give your support. I hope you'll excuse us this hasty end to the evening. We all love you very much and can't wait to see you in a more joyful context real soon."

Melinda palmed her belly, the context. Other women closed around for soothing squeezes.

"These fucking wars," said Charles Goldfarb, tilted back in his chair. "Only the historians will have a true sense of what they did to us."

"Fantastic," I said. "Blistering."

"Who's Lee Moss again?" said Lisa.

"He's the conveniently dead guy," I said.

I drained my Scotch, scooped a handful of chocolate stag beetles into my pocket. People began to gather their coats and bags.

"Milo, hold up, I'll walk out with you."

"No thanks, Charles. Think I want to be alone."

"Suit yourself."

"Say hello to Constance for me," I said.

"I will. I mean, I hardly see her but . . . yes, I will."

"Tell her I'm happy for her," I said. "And sad for her. And also happy-sad. Tell her to get a better haircut. She looks like the middle-aged head of a girl's prep school."

"That's what she is."

"It's the end of us, Charles."

"I'm doing fine, Milo."

"Didn't Adorno say that to write think pieces for mainstream magazines after Auschwitz is barbaric?"

"No, he didn't."

"What about Schopenhauer?"

"What about him?"

"Give me the capsule."

"The what?"

"The takeaway."

"Pardon?"

"You're not the enemy, Charles, but fuck you."

"You're incredibly drunk."

"To tell you the truth, I'm not even clear on whether I'm standing up or sitting down right now."

"Then maybe you should sit down."

"No," I said. "I think that would be a bad idea."

Twenty-seven

That sleeper fiend, my hangover, had given notice at the smelting plant, deposited his family under the floorboards of his garden shed. He stood over me now in Claudia and Francine's guest room, his eyes fish-dead behind the barrel of his skull-mulching gun.

"Please don't shoot," I moaned.

"It's nothing personal."

"But why?"

"Why what?"

"Why are you here?"

"You sent for me."

"I did?"

"You're an alcoholic."

"No," I said, "I'm just a heavy drinker."

"Maybe," said my assassin, "but who's got the gun?"

I stood dazed in the shower for forty minutes, half dozing, half soaped, loosed wet, scorching farts, muttered things like "Christ," and "swill," and "malaise." When I'd wasted enough water to hydrate an Eritrean village for a year, I remembered the climax of the previous evening, the appearance of Don, his truncated challenge, those stylish goons under stern Floridian command, Michael Florida himself hauling Don out, and to where, exactly? Worry got me onto the rose-embroidered bath mat and into my clothes. I called Don's cell and left a message. I called Purdy's cell and left a message. I texted Purdy to find out if he had gotten my message. Then I staggered over to Claudia's wicker lounger and collapsed.

Later, misery beaten back into temporary cover with a pot of coffee and some Valium from Francine's dresser, I made my way to Jackson Heights, stabbed Don's buzzer, sat on the stoop to wait. A basement door banged open and a young guy in a basketball jersey stepped out.

"Hey," I said.

The man waved.

"Nabeel?"

"Do I know you?"

"No. My friend lives here. Said your name once."

"Oh, yeah? Why did he say my name?"

"Just talking is all. Telling me about the crazy boiler."

"The boiler."

"Yeah," I said. "So, you like basketball?"

"Basketball?"

"Your shirt."

"Shit, man, it's a shirt. Not a statement."

"Sorry, just making conversation."

"Don't do that. And why are you smiling? You stick out. You see anybody smiling around here?"

Nearby an old lady in a calico dress knelt on the sidewalk, slid a dog turd into a Ziploc bag. Though maybe it was some other order of turd, as I saw no dog.

"No," I said. "I don't."

"I rest my case."

It was not clear to me what, for this kid, constituted a case.

"I'm waiting for a buddy of mine," I said. "Seen him?"

"How would I know if I'd seen him?"

"You'd know," I said. "He's got metal legs."

"Sure he's your friend?" said the man.

"What do you mean?"

"The guys here last night, they said they were his friends. Don's been pretty quiet. Suddenly he has a lot of friends."

"Who was here last night?"

"Like I said, some guys."

"Have you seen Don today?"

"No."

"Let me into the building, I need to see him. You can come with me. I need to see that he's okay."

"I can't do that. My uncle would be pissed."

"Please," I said.

"I can't do it."

"How much can you not do it for?" I said.

"I can't do it for between one and fifty-nine dollars."

I slid three twenties from my wallet.

"Here."

We climbed through the hot stink of the stairwell.

"Don," said Nabeel, knocked hard on the door. "Don!"

The way he called the name, the intimacy of tone, made me wonder if they'd talked some, if Don had told him anything about Purdy.

"You ever rap to Don about his life?"

"Rap? What kind of word is that? Are you a cop?"

"No."

"So why are you asking this stuff? It's weird."

"I just want to help Don," I said. "Did he tell you anything?"

"Don invited me up for beers a few times."

"Did you talk about anything?"

"We talked about pussy. Maybe he said something about the war a few times. But really we talked about pussy. We had good talks. We each had our insights, you know? So, what's the deal?"

"Pardon?"

We stood there for a moment, silent. A TV roared, a toilet flushed, somebody maybe dragged a child into a room.

"Open the door," I said.

"I don't have the key."

"Of course you do. He could be OD'd in there."

"If he's dead, he's dead."

"He could be alive. People hold on for hours. A day, even. But nobody comes. Open the fucking door."

"Okay," said Nabeel.

Then the door swung open and Don stood before us, his pants held up in his fist.

"Milo," he said. "Come on in. I'm just finishing up a shit. Make yourself at home. Nabeel, you're welcome, too."

"No, I should go," said Nabeel.

I followed Don into the apartment. He slipped back into the bathroom, shut the door. The room looked brighter and bigger than last time, the red drapes heaped on the floor, the apartment stripped. He had never owned much, but now he was down to the card table, one folding chair, a saucepan, some smudged water glasses, a spoon. Papers lay curled under the radiator. I picked one up, a pencil sketch, a fairly good one, of a World War One–era military officer with a bushy mustache, his legs sheathed in shiny black boots. Phone numbers and email addresses and odd bits of math sprouted in the spaces around and between the soldier's thighs. One number was circled, the same figure I'd seen on the cashier's check in Lee Moss's office.

I picked up the spoon, saw burn marks on it, heard Don's girls creak on the floor behind me.

"Could have used that spoon in the john just now. Colon needs a serious scooping."

"Thank you for not sharing," I said.

Don flopped on the bed.

"We're going to scoop shit and we're going to cook dope," he said. "The trick is to use different spoons."

"The teachings of Lee Moss," I said.

"That dude," said Don.

We sat in silence for a moment.

"So," said Don, "did you come here to tell me what a fool I was last night? Because I already know. Some others from your crew have already been by. It's all been explained."

"They're not my crew."

"Oh, no? Well, I don't care anymore. I'm leaving this goddamn city."

"To go where. Pangburn Falls?"

"That's right, Bangburn Balls, baby."

"Don, there could be more for you in life than that."

"Than what?"

Don stared at me, tapped his knuckles on the wall behind his head.

"I don't know," I said.

"No, you don't. Why would you even say that kind of thing? Did it ever occur to you that unless you have money, every place is equally shitty? You know, those guys, my father, they just wanted to pay me some money to shut me up. Like hell I'll take it, but at least it's understandable. It's scumbags of one breed dealing with a scumbag of another. But you, what are you about? What are you selling? Or are you buying?"

"I've never been clear on that."

"Don't work it out on me. And don't try to humanize me, you fuck. It's insulting. Why did you come here?"

"I wanted to make sure you were okay."

"I'm never going to be okay. Now leave, leech."

•

Back at the Mediocre suite, I slouched at my workstation and wondered how I'd gone so wrong. Where was my dignity? Also, where was my computer? I noticed now that my workstation lacked its primary instrument of work. The telephone looked forlorn by itself on the desk. I slid a pad and some pencils beside it, wrote: "Ask about your computer. And ask for more Post-Its. It's your time."

Horace walked by, hummed the theme song from a TV show canceled before his birth. I remembered the show, my devastation at its demise. It was maybe the first time I understood there were powerful people far away who could destroy your world without even knowing it.

"Milo, toosh dev warrior king, what's the fine word?"

"Hi, Horace," I said. "Where's my computer?"

"Repair guy took it to fix."

"Why couldn't he fix it here? And it wasn't broken. Who told him it was broken?"

"Calm down. Afraid he'll find the naughty stuff?"

"I wouldn't be dumb enough to use an office computer," I said.

"Me," said Horace, "I've got the whole system beat."

"How's that?"

"I'm back to actual magazines. Keep some in my desk, even. Who would ever bother to look? My hard drive is pristine. Not a dirty cookie in sight. I jerk it in the men's room with real glossy stock on my knees. Like my father, and his father before him."

"That's very clever," I said.

"If a vengeful theocracy took over this country tomorrow, they'd have nothing on me. Probably put me on the morals squad."

Horace walked off and I picked up my desk phone, dialed.

"Greetings. You have reached the voice mail of the Unknown Soldier. Please leave a massage. Happy endings preferred."

I'm not sure what I meant to say. I hung there in silence, waited for something unleechlike to arrive.

"Savitsky," I said. "The officer with the boots in the story your mother liked. His name was Savitsky. It's from a story by Isaac

Babel. I read it in a literature class in college. Maybe your mother read it there, too. Goodbye, Don. Take care."

And that was, somehow, officially, that.

Just as I hung up the phone it rang again.

"Don?"

"Milo?"

"Vargina."

"Do you have a minute?"

"Sure."

"Conference room."

It occurred to me that calling from the Mediocre line was probably not wise. I'd only just found out six months ago there were surveillance cameras in the suite, and only after Horace directed a *sieg heil* toward a drilled hole in the ceiling tiles, received an email reprimand a week later. Maybe they tapped our phones, too. I'd always scoffed at conspiracy hobbyists, paranoid stylists. The corporate complex wasn't organized enough for master plans, I'd argue. We're all just flawed people with our flawed systems. But things had seemed rather organized in recent years. You had to wonder. Maybe the leaders of the global elite did all have secret lizard heads. Maybe my mother had a secret lizard head.

A whole trove of cockamamie theories deserved another look. Perhaps, for example, Lena had told me I was only moderately talented because she felt compelled to speak the truth. Maybe Maura still desired me but for her own sanity could stay in our marriage only if I chose to confront my rage and resentment. There was even a chance happiness had something to do with acceptance, and something to do with love.

No, this was ridiculous. These notions were all part of the trick, the scam. The asks had me nailed from the get-go, ever since they installed the selfware, back in Milo Year Zero. That's how the whole long con got started.

•

The conference room felt smaller than it had on my coronation the day before. A berry spritzer tallboy sat half collapsed on the conference table.

Another dented can.

Somehow Vargina and I ended up seated beside each other, the way some couples arrange themselves in restaurants. I'd never understood the appeal, though now I wondered if Maura and I should have given it a whirl. Maybe it granted you a whole new perspective on coupledom, or at least served as a welcome breather from having to look each other in the eye, glimpse all that mutilated hope.

Vargina re-angled her chair.

"This is weird," she said.

"You mean how we're sitting?"

"No, what I need to tell you. Your computer isn't broken, Milo."

"That's what I was trying to tell Horace. I was just thinking that . . ."

The truth sank in as I spoke. I tried my best to resemble a man in whom the truth had just been sunk, to the hilt. I owed Vargina that much, if only for elevating this encounter with use of the conference room.

"I'm fired again," I said.

"This time there's severance."

"Why? Why now?"

"I don't know the full story, Milo. Call came in from Cooley about it. Your absence was necessary for certain things to go forward."

"That's a nice way of putting it."

"I'm a craftswoman. And don't feel too bad. Sometime next month there's going to be a big bloodletting. Our endowment is in worse shape than anybody will admit."

"So, I'd be fired in a month anyway?"

"Probably."

"I can't do this anymore," I said.

"That's what we're saying."

"Sleep tight, you world, you motherfucker."

"Are you finished?"

"Yes," I said.

"You'll be okay, Milo," said Vargina. "Here."

Vargina pushed an index card across the table. It was a recipe for egg salad.

"I watched my husband make it. He can never know. Nobody can ever know."

"Thank you, Vargina."

"No more turkey wraps, Milo. They're gross."

"I see that now," I said.

Twenty-eight

I still had the key to the life I'd been evicted from, and the next morning I took the train out to Astoria, let myself into the apartment. Life was doing fine without me. There was Maura, jabbing at her laptop, always this, the work before work. It wasn't her fault. It was how they had us. There was Bernie on the sofa, watching his favorite show, the one where children mutated into gooey robots, sneered. It was like a parable from a religion based entirely on sarcasm. I'd seen the program before, tried to ban it. But there was no banning it. This wasn't China. This was dead America. If Bernie lucked out, he'd only be as warped as Horace. I could live with that. Assuming I could live.

"Bernie," said Maura. "Put on your velcros. Daddy's taking you to school. I'll see you at pickup."

There were not too many school days left. It would be another summer on Christine's concrete apron: blood and corn dogs.

I gathered up Bernie's sandals, slipped them on his feet.

"I want to see this show," he said. "Daddy, are you crying?"

"I have something in my eye," I said.

"Both eyes?"

"Yes, Bernie."

I walked into the bedroom, threw a few things into a knapsack. I took the money Purdy had given me, peeled off some for my wallet, wadded up the rest with a rubber band.

I dropped the wad next to Maura's laptop.

"What's this?"

"I don't know," I said. "Child support?"

"Do you need to be so dramatic? This is still your home. We're still your family. We're in a rough patch. We're taking a break."

"Rough patch? That's kind of a worn image, isn't it? I'm not sure what it means. Is it a driving thing? We're driving over a patch that's rough? Or is it like a patch on your coat? A smooth coat except for this little rough flap you ironed over a rip in the elbow? Or maybe the elbow skin is rough. Remember that time you said my elbow skin was like an elephant's? Is that what this is about? Is that what it's always fucking been about?"

"Language," said Maura.

"Indoor voice," said Bernie.

"Let's just patch up this rough patch now," I said. "I can't take this anymore. I want us all together."

"You seem really strung out, Milo. You need some rest. Aren't you getting rest at your mother's house?"

"Yeah," I said. "Nothing but rest."

·

I walked Bernie down Ditmars toward his new school. His little hand slid around in my palm.

"Daddy, are you sick?"

"No, I'm fine. Why?"

"You look funny."

"I'm just tired."

We passed a souvlaki cart and just beyond it a man with a chapped face slept sitting up on a bus bench. A pint of gin stuck out of his sweatpants.

"That's Larry!" said Bernie. "He must be back from Elmira. I wonder if Aiden knows."

I pushed Bernie past the bench.

"Bernie," I said. "I want you to be a good boy."

"Why?"

"Why what?"

"Why do you want me to be a good boy?"

"Because that's the best thing to be."

"That's stupid."

I took a knee on the sidewalk, clasped Bernie by the shoulders. I'd seen fathers kneel like this in movies, standard posture for the rushed essentials, the Polonius rundown. A little too in love with itself, Don might judge this moment, but that didn't diminish its necessity. Bernie might not understand what I told him today, but he would carry the words with him forever, and with them, me.

"Listen," I said.

"Yes, Daddy?"

"Squander it. Always squander it. Give it all away."

"Give what away? My toys?"

"No, yes, sure, your toys, too. Whatever it is. Squander it. Do you understand?"

"Not really."

"Don't save a little part of you inside yourself. Not even a scrap. It gets tainted in there. It rots."

"What does?"

"I can't explain right now. Someday you'll know. But promise me you'll squander it."

"I promise. What's squander?"

"You don't need to know that yet. Here's what you need to know: The boy can walk away from the ogre's castle. He doesn't have to knock. Some people will tell you that it's better the boy get hurt or even die than never know whether he could have defeated the ogre and won the ogre's treasure. But those are the people who tell us stories to keep us slaves."

"Daddy?" said Bernie.

"Yes?"

"Can I have a stegosaurus cake for my birthday like Jeremy got?"

"Yes, of course. For your birthday."

I yanked him to me, buried my face against his strong, tiny neck.

"I love you, Bernie."

"Will I ever see you again?"

"Yes," I said. "Later today."

"Will you be dead?"

"No."

"Will I?"

"No."

"Can it be a brontosaurus cake instead?"

"Yes."

"With an asteroid flying into his face?"

"Sounds wonderful."

"Let's go to school."

"Good idea," I said, stood.

•

After I'd dropped off Bernie I walked down to the park under the Hell Gate Bridge. It was one of those beautiful Fridays when everybody decides to ditch work, trust sheer numbers will protect them from retribution. Hondurans roasted chickens near the river, kicked soccer balls at their toddlers' knees. Indian families spread out curry feasts on blankets. A magician did card tricks for a field trip of drooling tweens. Mothers puttered around the quarter-mile track in velour running slacks.

Beside a stone tower some youngish men played touch football with a battered Nerf. They were young me's by the look of them, their watch caps and lazy passing routes, their Clinton-era trash talk. They had marked the end zones with packs of organic cigarettes and film theory pamphlets.

I skirted their game, found a quiet spot in the grass under an elm, read Schopenhauer, or read a scholar's long introduction in the paperback I'd dug out of my closet. Some of the stuff I remembered from college. It was foolish to want. You would never get what you wanted. Even if you got what you wanted you would never get what you wanted. It was better to strip yourself of the wanting. But this was impossible. So you suffered. Your raw eyeballs suffered.

I fell asleep before I got to Professor Schopenhauer's tips on dating. The introduction noted that he once beat a woman sense-less on his doorstep. She sued for assault and he paid her off for twenty years. When she died, he wrote, "Obit anus, abit onus."

"The old woman is dead, the burden is lifted."

As I slept in Astoria Park, I dreamed of a park in 1820s Ber-lin. I squatted at the lip of a pond, tossed hunks of black bread to geese. A man with fierce side-whiskers and a greasy coat pushed an immaculate Maclaren stroller along the walkway. A cigarette bobbed in his lips. Two children hunched in the stroller, a boy and a girl. The boy sat on the girl's lap. They were laughing, but suddenly the boy punched the girl in the mouth.

"Anus," said the man, "don't hit your sister."

I tried to say something, couldn't get my tongue right.

The man smiled, spoke, his voice muddy and loud.

"Hey, you," he said.

Something pressed into my side and I opened my eyes.

Predrag stood over me. He tapped my ribs with his boot.

"You," he said.

"Predrag," I said.

"Hungry?" He dropped a doughnut on my chest.

"Thanks," I said, sat up, bit into a honey-glazed. "Thank you. Wow, I was having the weirdest dream."

Predrag held up his doughnut sack.

"I like to take some around, spread the wealth, you know? I usually give them out to homeless guys. But then I saw you."

"I might be homeless one of these days."

"Yeah?"

"It's tough to call."

"You come to the store, you need help."

"That's nice of you."

"We've got to stick together," said Predrag, lifted his face to the sun.

"Who exactly are we?" I asked.

"The American Dreamers. There aren't too many of us left."

"I don't know if I qualify."

"You an American? Or want to be an American?"

"I am an American."

"You said you were having a dream."

"It's true, I did."

"Was it the one where you're inside the girl and you are pumping her and pumping her and you are so happy but then it turns out it's not a girl, it's really one of those super poisonous box jellyfish, and it stings you and you are screaming and screaming and the sky rains the diarrhea of babies?"

"The . . . no, I don't think so."

"I get that sometimes. Anyway, see you around."

•

I went home to the home that Maura said was still my home and made myself some breakfast. It had been a while since I'd been alone in the apartment. I pulled books off shelves, dug into boxes of old junk, snooped through Maura's drawers. The pills were gone. I sat on the sofa and did nothing for a good hour but sit on the sofa. I could not remember the last time I had managed such a thing.

I tried to recall the words I'd hurled at McKenzie Rayfield, the outburst that started it all. I couldn't really summon them, or at least the proper sequence. A few individual utterances returned, like "shut," and "mouth," and "spoiled" and "dreck" and "sopressatta" and "daddysauce." But most of it was gone. I was glad of it. Those words had never made me proud.

Out the window I watched a deliveryman ride up on a bicycle, buzz the house across the street. He wore a sweatshirt that read "New York Yankees 2001 World Champions." The Yankees, however, had lost the series that year. Arizona, with no regard for the national narrative, or even story, beat them in game seven. The deliveryman must have gotten the shirt in a poor country in Asia or Africa or South America, wherever they sell the runner-up crap, the memorabilia of a parallel universe, maybe the one with the gesso-smeared assistant and my name on public radio. I wondered if Sasha had learned to tip these guys yet.

I still had her cell phone number and I called her now. When she answered, it took her a moment to place me.

"Right," she said. "That guy. The envelope man. Why are you calling?"

"Just . . . I don't know . . . checking in."

"You still on some kind of mission? For Purdy?"

"I don't work for Purdy. I don't work for anybody right now."

"Got downsized?"

"Right," I said. "Cut down to size."

"Okay," said Sasha.

"I wanted to say hello," I said. "Maybe I could even . . . I don't know. Come up and talk about things. About all that's happened."

"You think I might ask you to squeeze my tits again."

She spoke evenly, nothing coy in her tone.

"It hadn't occurred to me."

"Liar. Anyway, you know how high I was that last time? I had to get away from Don to get my head straight. Unlike you, I do have a job now. And a guy I love. And I'm going to school."

"Don told me. That's great. I didn't call for that. I really didn't. I just wanted to talk. To ask some questions."

"What, like a detective?"

"Not really. I'm just . . ."

"You're a little too obsessed, is what you are. A little too involved in a situation that's got nothing to do with you."

"You're probably right. Things have been pretty tough for me."

"Believe me, mister, I don't want to hear it."

"Sorry. Well, I guess Don's heading back your way."

"I know. He called me. Like I'm up here waiting for that bastard. I've moved on. My boyfriend, Bobby, is the best thing that ever happened to me. Besides, this is probably not the best place for Don these days."

"What do you mean?"

"Things got sort of bad up here for him before we went down to the city. He had a fight with some guys at Cudahy's. You know how it is. You can bitch about the government all you want, but don't talk shit about the troops. He shot his mouth off about something or other. They really started messing with him, kicking his girls and stuff—I can't believe I still call them girls. God, he was crazy! But those guys got out of hand. They were clubbing him with pool cues."

"Was it that guy Todd? The happy warrior?"

"Todd Wilkes? You've got a good memory. No. Some of them were Todd's friends, maybe. Todd really doesn't leave his house much anymore. People say he's got PTSD really bad. And his burns, they never really got better. He's a sad case. Anyway, after those guys messed with Don at Cudahy's, Don went and got a tire iron from his car. People busted it up before it could get too bad, but Don broke one guy's ribs. A rumor went around they were planning to go after Don. And the whole thing didn't help his reputation around here. Probably why he was itching to get out in the first place. Everybody treated him nice with what happened to his mom and the injury. But then they started to wonder about him. At least the ones drinking at Cudahy's. Look, I've got to go pick up my boyfriend."

"Okay."

"You have my number in your phone?"

"Yes."

"Do me a favor. Delete it."

"Delete it?"

"Just do me the favor. Just for peace of mind. My mind. I want to start over. I don't want people like you to know where I am."

"I'm not one of those people," I said.

"Right," said Sasha. "Bye."

I did not delete her number.

I studied our block in the sun's glitter, listened to the wind in the trees, thought vaguely of Jimmy Easter. Then I watched some television. There was a movie with the male lead's father from *Caller I Do*. He was much younger, on a chestnut stallion, waving, or maybe brandishing a saber for the Confederacy. He loved a lady but he had no cell phone and could not save her from the Union cannon.

Maura would be home soon. Then it would be time to get Bernie at Christine's. But this really wasn't my life right now. My life was across the river. My life was in the rough patch. My life was vaporing about. But I'd be back. I belonged here.

•

A man sat beside me on the bus out to Nearmont. He looked about my age, with black and gray stubble on his face, a flannel shirt. He tapped a packet of guitar strings in his hands.

"Do I know you?" he said. "You look familiar."

"I don't think so," I said.

"Pat?"

"No."

"No, that's me, Pat White. You look familiar. You play music? Did you ever play with Glave Wilkerson? Spacklefinger? Out of Eastern Valley?"

"No," I said.

"Sure?"

"Yes," I said. "I'm pretty sure."

I pointed to his packet.

"You play?"

"Hells, yeah," said Pat. "Used to have a band. Alternative. You like alternative?"

"I guess."

"What they play now, that's not really alternative. My generation, maybe our generation, looking at you, we were truly alternative. My band, we played all over. We dominated the area in terms of battle of the bands and whatnot. We even beat Spacklefinger one time."

"What was the name of your band?"

"Sontag."

"Really? That's an amazing name for a band."

"It means Sunday."

"Oh, right."

"That was the days of true alternative rock," said Pat. "Now it's just commercialized. But anyway, what was I saying?"

"I don't know," I said.

"That's 'cause I didn't say it yet." Pat laughed. "Oh yeah. We were good, is my point. But our drummer, he fucking signed up for the army, went to the Gulf War. Never came back. I mean never came back around here. Went to California. And that was the end of the band, because, I'll tell you, man, you can teach any human ejaculant to play bass or guitar or even front the frigging thing, but you can't turn somebody into a kickass drummer. People are born with that gift, and not many, bro, trust me. Look at what's his name, the British dude, who died of his own puke. Nobody's hit like that since, and that was forty years ago. Forty years is a lifetime. Forty years is my lifetime."

"Let's hope you have more than that," I said.

"Bro," said Pat, "I have no intention of outstaying my welcome. I came, I saw, I rocked, I made no money, I got Hep C. End of story."

Pat pulled a fifth of whiskey from the gym bag at his feet. He took some clandestine pulls, offered it up.

"No thanks," I said

"It's decent stuff."

"I'm trying to cut back."

"Dude who says that is never cutting back. He's either drinking or not drinking. I know all about it."

"All the same," I said.

Pat slipped the bottle back into his bag. We both put our seats back and stared out the window for a while. Night fell and I stared at the dark shapes of trees until they were just dark shapes.

There was city darkness and the dark outside the city, the Nearmont dark, the Eastern Valley dark, which, being only one town over, was pretty much the Nearmont dark. I pictured the Pangburn Falls dark as something else. Darker, maybe. Did Purdy ever stay the night in those upstate motels, cuddle with Nathalie under scratchy bleached-out sheets, kiss her shoulder to wake her before his dawn drive home? Or did Nathalie leave first, nervous about young Don, his dinner, his suspicions? Only Purdy knew. Only Purdy's version would ever stand for truth. Maybe that was what Don finally understood. There was no use fighting it. Especially when all you were really fighting for was the love of a man you hated.

Nobody was going to tell Nathalie's story. Stories were like people. We pretended they all counted, but almost none of them did.

"Hey," said Pat. "Want to rethink your decision?"

He was hunched over with the bottle near his knee.

"What the hell," I said, took a sip.

"That's the way," said Pat. "This country was built on the

backs of dudes who drank on buses. What we do honors them. Anyway, it's all highly dealable in the end."

"What's that?" I said, drank some more.

"Everything. As long you don't choke on your puke. That's my golden fucking rule."

Twenty-nine

We rolled into Nearmont late. I stepped off the bus and walked the berm of the county road. Big Jeeps and minivans roared by and a cold wind blew off Grandy Pond. It was hard to see inside the cars, but I could almost make out the mothers and fathers and children in them, the dirty cleats and grocery bags, the lulling glow of dashboard lights. Everybody wanted to get home. Home could be a ruined place, joyless, heaped with the ashes of scorched hearts, but come evening everybody hustled to get there.

Once I walked this road on early spring evenings, knapsack slung on one shoulder, the cars ripping along, headlights slashing the yard barrels and wet lawns, my hair wet, too, from the track team showers, my body sore and buzzy from the weight room, all those snatches and squats and curls.

I threw the javelin then, was no champion, not even a contender for regional ribbons, just good enough to know the happiness of making your body a part of that spear, to get a good trot up to the throwing line, to slip into a rabbity sideways hop and snap your hips, launch a steel-tipped proxy of yourself at the sky.

I would savor the long walk home, the sweet, achy daze of it, drift into the jagged excitements of my future, paintings, parties, people, women people, a ceaseless celebration of my greedy, spangled destiny. There was nothing noble about such want. But it was me, and maybe some of you, walking home from school in April drizzle, dreaming.

And maybe it was me and some of you who took a nap before dinner, lay back on the sofa with a book, the assigned reading, another novel with the old-fashioned folk, their stiff speeches and chafed hearts. Maybe some of you, like me, shut your eyes with the book open on your chest, tumbled into another world, near and impossible, homeroom skin beneath rain-damp denim.

Certain noises would sever the reverie, a cough, my mother in the kitchen, the local news flipped on the kitchen TV—arson and elevator assaults across the river, or Don Mattingly, Donnie Baseball, with his leopard swing and porn-star mustache, on another hitting streak for the Yankees—the sounds of dishes pulled from their shelves, the rubber smooch of the refrigerator door, the tepid click of salad tongs, the hiss of garlic, frying.

No, Claudia never cooked with garlic. Maura did.

But this house in Nearmont, with all its woes, a Jolly Roger here and also never here, and the poison sadness seeping from my mother, even then this house in Nearmont was always a home, heated, with food, and familiar noises, and I was lucky to have it, this home to trust and hate, to launch myself from like a javelin that tails and wobbles and does not drive into the turf but skids to a halt at a slightly less-than-average distance, a mediocre distance, from the lumped lime line.

This is what the blessed get. A heated box, a stocked pantry, a clumpy metaphor.

The blessed get legs. The unblessed get humps, titanium girls.

•

I turned onto Eisenhower. Lights blazed in the bay window. Francine opened the door before I could knock.

"Come in, honey," she said.

I stepped into the foyer, heard Purdy's voice.

He sat with my mother on the sofa, sacks of chocolate and licorice between them. Michael Florida tipped forward in the rocking chair, winked.

"Purdy," I said, took a seat on the hassock.

"How come you never invited me to your mother's house? She's a force!"

"I've been calling you," I said.

"Your friend is making me fat," said Claudia. "I'll never fit into my racing suit."

"Give me a break," said Purdy. "You're a knockout."

"I like this guy," said my mother.

"Did you get my messages?" I said.

"I'm sure I did."

"What the fuck does that mean?"

"Sweetie," said Claudia, "you seem a little wound up."

"Your mom was just telling us some funny stories about young Milo Burke."

"Hilarious stuff," shouted Francine from the kitchen. "Hey, guys, I've got stone-ground crackers and pony cans of pumpkin beer. Who's game?"

"Bring on the crackers!" called Michael Florida. "Heck, let me get in there and help."

Michael Florida trotted off to the kitchen.

"What kinds of stories?"

"Well, we just heard the one where you brought this nice Japanese girl home and then, just as you were about to kiss her, you shit your jeans," said Purdy. "That was pretty good."

"That never happened."

"Plausible deniability. Well done."

"I don't care. It just didn't happen. My mother is conflating."

"It's true," said Claudia. "I'm a notorious conflater. And we shouldn't tease Milo. He's always been thin-skinned. A very nervous boy. Anxious."

"I wonder why," I said.

"These things are chemical," said Claudia. "We all have different temperaments."

"So you think the nurture bit was top quality? Even the sociopathic cokehead dad part? And your perpetual war on flatware?"

Claudia smiled.

"Who knows what helps and what hurts, honey. Francine! Let me do something! Purdy, would you and your friend like to stay for dinner?"

"Love to," said Purdy. "But we've got to get back to the city. Melinda really appreciates me being around these days."

"Of course. It's so wonderful. A baby."

"Mom, you hate children."

"You know that's not true, Milo."

"Just mine."

"Don't be silly."

Claudia rose, joined Francine in the kitchen.

I leaned forward on my elbows toward Purdy.

"What the hell are you doing here?"

Purdy glanced over at the glass door that led out to the patio, the yard.

"Tetherball? Lordy. May we?"

We walked out to the rusted pole. A shrunken ball, just a hunk of desiccated leather, dangled from the cord. Years ago, during a rare moment of domestic tranquillity, Jolly Roger had dug the dirt and sunk the pole and poured the cement. We'd played a few spirited games after the cement dried, to "test the apparatus," then never again. Later, in my teens, I liked to stand out there alone, punch the ball, watch it whip and switch directions, duck as the thing looped back around, asteroidal, screaming.

All the creatures of planet Milo, extincted.

Purdy unwound the ball, slapped it into the air. The pole creaked. The ball sliced through the patio lights.

"What a crappy setup," he said.

"It's not so bad."

I whacked the hunk back. Purdy caught it.

"You know what?" he said.

"What?"

"I always regretted not convincing you to work for me back in the day. It really was the best thing you could have done. We both knew the art stuff wasn't going to happen."

"We did?"

"You didn't?"

"No, I didn't."

"Right, I guess you didn't. Or you wouldn't have kept trying."

Purdy tossed the ball up, smashed it into orbit.

"Why didn't you tell me?" I said.

"How could I? Besides, what did I know? I'm not in charge of everybody's destiny."

"You're not?" I said.

Purdy stared until he seemed to understand.

"No," he said. "I'm not."

"Oh."

"Don't be so down, buddy. I'm sorry about this job of yours. I know they pulled the rug out on you today. We all just thought it was best to uncomplicate things. To disentangle. But I'll make it up to you somehow."

"I'm sure you will."

"There's that negative tone again. You know, Milo, it was always pretty hard to be your friend. You have a lot to offer but you're so afraid to give up your best. It's like at the supermarket, when they put the old milk at the front of the shelf, so people will buy it. That's you."

"What's me? The milk? I'm the milk? Or am I the supermarket? Or am I buying the milk?"

"I'll get back to you on that."

"Get back to me on this: Why did you come here tonight?"

"I came by to say hello. To make sure we were cool."

"Cool?"

"That's right, Milo. Are we cool?"

"Sure, we're cool. I mean, you are definitely cool."

"Good."

"What could be cooler than all the stuff you've done? To your wife. To your girlfriend. To your son. That's cool shit. I could be cool, too. I could learn."

"See," said Purdy, caught the ball, cradled it. "You're confusing things. You think you're talking to me, but you're not. Because you have no right to talk to me that way. And because you're talking to somebody else."

"To somebody else? Whom would that be?"

"Fuck if I know," said Purdy.

"No, really," I said. "Tell me. I'm so curious."

"Are you?"

"Absolutely."

"Probably you are talking to yourself, Milo. You are probably talking to yourself. Or the deadbeat junkie that bought this ridiculously sad tetherball set for you."

I lunged, snatched Purdy by the collar, yanked him into my chest, wrapped the cord around his neck.

"Jesus!" he gasped.

"Sonofabitch," I said.

"Milo, cut this shit out right . . ."

I tugged hard on the rope. Purdy clawed at his neck.

"Where are the bodies?"

"Bodies?" gurgled Purdy.

"Where are the bodies, you motherfucking murderer!" I said.

"You're . . . insane," said Purdy. "Bodies? No bodies."

"I know," I said. "It's just fun to say. I'm making my own fun. I just really feel like choking you right now. Is that cool? Are we cool?"

"Stop . . . this shit. Can't breathe. Help!"

I heard the patio door swing open, a swish in the grass.

"Help!" said Purdy, choked, drooled.

I pulled Purdy to the ground, cinched the cord tight. Something heavy stabbed my head. A pointy hammer, I thought, right before thought stopped.

I woke a moment later in the wet grass, saw a blur of boots and black trousers, a flicker of metal, gone. Michael Florida stood over me.

"Man." Purdy coughed. "This is ridiculous. What the hell? You can't do that. Who does that? My fucking neck. My fucking *trachea*. What the . . . I mean, that's . . . what, were you going to kill me?"

Purdy coughed again, stood.

"Probably not," I said.

"Ridiculous. Unbelievable."

"I think it was a joke," I said. "I can't think."

"Get up," said Michael Florida, pulled me to my feet.

The patio door swung open again.

"What's going on?" said Claudia.

"Nothing," said Purdy, unspooled himself from the cord, coughed once more, hocked phlegm into the hedges. "Everything's fine."

"We heard these noises."

"Ladies," said Purdy, "it's been a beautiful evening. Let's do it again real soon."

Francine and Claudia nodded, frozen. Some sound, almost a growl, started up Claudia's throat, fell back.

"Milo," said Purdy. "Walk us to our car?"

Part of me considered resisting this little frog march across the street, but I was still dizzy and Michael Florida's grip on my arm was strong. He shoved me in the back of the sedan. He and Purdy slid in front. The door locks clicked. Purdy stared straight ahead. I rubbed the throb from my skull.

"Well," said Purdy. "We tried. You can't say we didn't try. But I really don't think we can be buddies anymore. It's so hard to keep up the old friendships, isn't it? People change. Priorities change. It's sad, but it's also natural, I guess. Let's remember the good times. The parties, the high blood-toxicity levels, the laughs. We had a lot of laughs. But those days are over, I think. Those days are definitely done. Let's just leave it back on Staley Street, shall we? Let's just never write or speak to each other ever again. That would be wonderful. Let me not ever see your face again and I will die, well, not a happy man, but maybe vaguely content on the subject of Milo Burke and how he tried to strangle me—with a fucking tetherball rope, mind you—because he happens to be a sick freak living in a pathetic hallucination of a life, though you wouldn't know that right away because he comes off as fairly normal at first so you might even befriend him, or re-befriend him, as the case may be, and then go so far as to trust him with some sensitive information until you realize, almost too late, that he is completely out of his fucking tree. Yes, I foresee vague contentment on my deathbed if we stick to this plan. Does that sound okay by you?"

"Sure," I said.

"I can't hear you, you piece of psychotic shit."

"Yes," I said.

"Good. Now, I know you're getting some severance from the university. But I also know how tough things are out there, and you with a kid, who nobody can blame for having a father like you. So, here's our severance to add to your other severance. Mix all that severance together. It's like a jambalaya of fucking severance. It's tasty and you can stuff your fat treacherous face with it. Michael?"

Michael Florida slid an envelope between the bucket seats.

Everything with Purdy had been these envelopes, these seats. It could really put you off envelopes.

"That, along with the other cash I've given you, it should hold you for a while, no?"

"Sure," I said.

"Sure, he says."

"This should be sufficient," I said, everything still blurred from the blow. I felt the tender bloom of the wound under my hand.

"Sufficient," said Purdy. "You're a fucking loser, Milo, and it's got nothing to do with the fact that you didn't win. Do you understand that?"

"Maybe," I said.

"All I ever did was give love, Milo. To everybody, I gave love. Even my old man, and that bastard . . ."

Purdy pinched his eyes shut, punched the glove box, lightly.

"I didn't wreck her car," he said. "I didn't put her in a coma. The doctors recommended she be moved. The state place was better suited. That was their phrase, better suited. It was their suggestion. I was still going to pay. I loved her. I still love her. I can't help it. And I am really tired of trying to help it when I truly cannot help it. You can all go to hell. None of you feel. You are feeling's assassins. Get out of my car."

The door locks clicked again.

"Wait," said Purdy. "Give it to him."

Michael Florida swiveled back. There was another glint in his hand.

"Jane heard you at the party," said Purdy.

"Pardon?"

Something dropped in my lap.

"And one more thing," said Purdy. "I never texted any drink order. That mojito? It was a mistake. They just made a mistake."

"What?" I said.

"Exit the fucking vehicle."

I got out of the car, watched it tear down Eisenhower, turn onto the county road.

I held my father's knife up to the moonless sky.

Thirty

Don called late in September. I was living in the kiddie-diddler's basement, his boiler room. It was the only place near Bernie I could afford. Maura and I still spoke, but we'd stopped going to the marriage counselor. Maura quit when the counselor suggested she take a break from having sex with Paul. There was talk of finding another counselor, one more amenable to Maura having sex with Paul, of inviting Paul to a session, even, but nothing happened. We were still, I believed, the loves of each other's life. But that life was maybe over now.

The kiddie-diddler was a kind and extremely unstable man named Harold. He had, as I suspected, once been in radio, voiced some very famous advertising campaigns. I no longer wondered why whenever he spoke I thought of a certain laundry detergent or strawberry-flavored milk.

Harold's brother Tommy slipped me extra cash to make sure Harold didn't wander the streets at night. Harold had dozens of stories he told over and over again, in the way of a man who has traveled the world, or never been anywhere at all. I listened to him talk less for the delight of his adventures than his timbre, his pitchman's pitch.

The shopping bag stuffed with shopping bags was never far from reach, but when I asked him its meaning or purpose he told me I didn't have the proper clearance. He let me look at his

notebooks, but I couldn't read his nanoscopic script. The drawings, far more maniacal than I'd imagined, depicted little girls
in snowpants. These bundled moppets rode a magic toboggan
through arctic skies. I figured my boy would be safe.

Every day I picked up Bernie at my old apartment, walked
him to school. Happy Salamander had reopened. They'd booted
Carl from the board. The creamery, apparently, was his new site
of revolutionary practice. Maddie had been sketchy about the
whole kerfuffle when she called Maura to offer Bernie a spot.
We made a joint decision, as separated but equally engaged parents, to give very inexpensive experimental preschool pedagogy
another go. Soon enough he'd be fresh meat for the wolf packs at
the local kindergarten.

I took Bernie in the afternoons, unless Nick needed me for a
job. When Nick heard about the governor's daughter's possible
interest in his project, or at least in him as a lesson in cultural
failure, he offered me work in gratitude. We did okay. For some
reason the deck bubble had not yet burst, and Nick and I had
evolved into a crackerjack team. I hauled the tools and the wood
and undertook a good deal of the construction. Nick snacked on
sausage subs and honed his broadcast vision. My body, it ached
all the time. The pain thrilled at first. Maybe it felt authentic.
Soon it was just pain.

I began to send out résumés. Late capitalism was a corpse, but
you could still get lucky, couldn't you? Besides, I was so unac-
complished, I could fit in anywhere. I'd never pose a threat to
colleagues. That would be my angle.

Most evenings I stayed in my basement room, reading or
watching television or painting. I had no illusions now. I did not
expect to jet down to Miami or over to Venice after the nearly
haphazard but ultimately inevitable discovery of my genius. I just
wanted to see what I could do with my cache of filched Mediocre paint. My current canvas was called *Raskovian/Replacable*. I

planned to give it to Harold for his birthday, thought he might get a kick out of the giraffe bukkake. One night as I touched up the rusted toboggan in the veldt grass, my phone rang.

"Hey," said a voice.

"Jesus, Don."

"No, just Don."

"Where are you?" I said.

"I'm here, bro. Home. Bangburn Balls. What a goddamn awesome feeling."

"It's good to hear from you," I said. "I've been wondering how you're doing."

"I have been to the mountain, my friend."

"The mountain?"

"Just screwing with you. I was in Texas. Visited Vasquez."

"Vasquez?"

"Yeah, you got a problem with that?"

"No. I just thought . . . you said Vasquez was dead."

"She is dead. I went to her grave. And to see her folks."

"That was good of you."

"It wasn't anything," said Don. "But I'm glad I went. You know, I'm calling because . . . well, I wanted to apologize."

"For what?"

"For whatever. I know I was a rat bastard. I don't have specifics."

"I understand."

"I still think you're a leech and a shithead."

"Thanks."

"But my sponsor says I have to make these calls."

"I get it," I said. "Good. You're taking care of yourself."

"I'm back with Sasha now. I'm living in her place in town."

"I'm glad to hear that."

"I'm in therapy. For the stress. I have money now."

"You signed the papers."

"They're just fucking papers."

"Right."

"I wasn't going to get love from that prick. Might as well take the money."

"I agree."

"I used to think if I took the money, he won. But now I see it's the opposite. If I don't take the money, he wins. And my anger wins. I'm talking about my anger a lot. I have a lot of anger."

"I'm sure that's true. You've earned it."

"Doesn't matter if I did. I can't keep it. It'll just kill me if keep it. I have to man up to my inner child. Do I sound like a fag? I bet both Nathalie and Purdy would laugh at me. But fuck them. Fuck you, too. And I mean that most sincerely. That's where I am now. You can all take the bad shit back and rot. I'm moving on."

"This is good, Don," I said.

"I don't need your goddamn approval, Milo."

"You called me," I said. "I know—your sponsor made you."

"Actually, I lied about that. I'm doing something a little different than making amends right now. What I'm doing tonight is getting high and calling up people to tell them what spineless twats they are."

Don chuckled, a tiny trace of Purdy's trace. We both hung wordless for a moment.

"You hear from Purdy?" I said.

"I signed some papers."

"No, I mean—"

"And I mean I signed some papers."

"Okay, I understand, Don. I should apologize to you, I guess. I'm sorry."

"Whatever."

"So, what's next? You guys going to stay up there?"

"Hell, no," said Don. "I'm trying to convince Sasha to vacate this hole with me. Like I said, I got some money. I want to travel. I want to go to Europe. Nathalie always talked about going to Europe. Maybe her dumbass son can."

"Of course he can."

"Yeah, I'll just tidy up some shit around here, and go."

"Why don't you just go now?"

"Not till I'm squared away."

"Okay, just so you go. It's too easy not to go."

"Don't talk to me about easy," said Don.

"Fair enough," I said.

My eyes fell on my father's knife. Bernie had found it in my desk last week, tried to cut his shoelaces with it. I snatched it away before he could hurt himself, but I could see its curve and heft had seduced him. He asked about its history, wondered if I would pass it down to him when he got old enough.

"Of course," I had told him. "That's a promise."

But it was not a promise. I knew I had to get the knife out of my family for good. Something very important depended upon it. But I also couldn't bring myself to throw it in the trash.

I could wrap it up in butcher's paper, walk to the post office, and stand in line. Or on line.

"Just give me your address, Don."

"My address?"

"I want to send you a gift."

"Why would I be stupid enough to give you my address?" said Don, but then he did.

"Thanks."

"It better be a good gift," said Don, and for a moment he sounded much younger, almost as young as Bernie.

"I promise," I said. "It will be a good gift."

"All right, then. I guess I can cross you off my hit list."

"Goodbye, Don," I said, but he'd already hung up.

I never did mail the knife. The parcel sat on the table for months. Sometimes I'd notice it, think of Don. I felt guilt for not posting it. Then I figured I was saving him from some kind of curse. Then I remembered I did not believe in curses. I believed in symbols and the wondrous ways they could wound.

After some books got piled on the parcel I did not notice it at all.

Mostly, if I ever thought of Don, I just hoped he was happy. Maybe he was in Europe with Sasha. Maybe he was dead in Bangburn Balls, but still, maybe he was in Europe with Sasha. Sometimes I'd picture them in the leafy, medieval quarter of some city, strolling through a park, sitting with a coffee, a beer, tired from walking all morning, tired in that contented way when you are moving through a land of alien pain, a land that expects nothing but your money in return for the privilege of strolling and drinking coffee and beer and being forever unaccountable for this city's particular and ancient agony.

Maybe Don would finally know that fallen joy, the empty liberation, of drinking an espresso or a crisp white ale and then strolling along some worn battlement where young men once lay in heaps, hacked and gored by halberds and axes and pikes, smashed by siege stones, and the women and children and old men lay nearby in other shit-streaked heaps, raped, dead of fever, all this slaughter just a little historical entertainment between café stops, the horror far in the past, bound up in modes of thought and styles of hosiery humankind would never abide again.

But maybe he wouldn't know that joy and liberation at all. Maybe he would read the plaques about the sieges and think of Vasquez's head exploding off her neck. Cr maybe he wouldn't be able to stroll much, his humps hot and itchy, the boat-shoed feet of his girls snagging in the cobbles of every rue or strasse or avenida. Perhaps I pictured this idyll just to avoid the truth, which was that Don was probably never going anywhere.

Then again, maybe I wasn't going anywhere, either.

Horace had been right about the parallel universe. I'd spent a long time living there. Purdy had been right about the bitterness. I had always been bitter, was still bitter, was bitter about the bitterness.

We were all of us just flushed with that feeling already fled.

But I had Bernie. I had my painting again, which could maybe deliver me some peace precisely because it would never deliver anything else. I even had a job lead. This local drug-and-alcohol rehab needed a part-time communications officer. Experience in fund-raising was a plus. Here was my chance to fail once more in an office environment. Worse came to worst, maybe I could get a discount on treatment. My hangover would hang up his gun.

No, I probably wasn't going anywhere.

I was digging in for the long night of here.

Sometimes I wondered if Don was doing the same, and a few months after I talked to him I sent him an email.

A week later Sasha replied from her own account, no message, just a link to the *Pangburn Falls Sentinel* website. I had to wade through some home-page reports about zoning disputes and a proposal for a new band shell before I scrolled down a sidebar of older articles. I guess she wanted me to wade, but after a while I saw the headline: POLICE CONTINUE SEARCH FOR SUSPECT IN LOCAL VETERAN'S DEATH.

I shuddered, almost clicked the window shut.

If I didn't read the story, if I turned my computer off right now, Don could still be okay. It was the thought of a child. It was the meaning of childhood.

According to the article, a young man had been murdered on an old logging road. An explosion heard for miles blew his truck into the trees. Pieces of the victim had scattered hundreds of feet down to the banks of a creek. Inspectors were disturbed to find evidence of an improvised explosive device, similar to those employed in recent conflicts overseas. The victim, Todd Wilkes, a native of Pangburn Falls and a decorated veteran of tours in Iraq and Afghanistan, was twenty-four. The police department's prime suspect, Don Charboneau, also of Pangburn Falls, had been missing from his last known residence since the day of the attack.

Authorities welcomed any information that could lead to his capture.